THE
VAMPIRE
AGENT

By Patricia Rosemoor and Marc Paoletti

THE LAST VAMPIRE
THE VAMPIRE AGENT

THE
VAMPIRE
AGENT

Book II of the Annals of Alchemy and Blood

PATRICIA ROSEMOOR & MARC PAOLETTI

BALLANTINE BOOKS • NEW YORK

A Del Rey Mass Market Original

Copyright © 2008 by Patricia Pinianski and Marc Paoletti

All rights reserved.

Published in the United States by Del Rey, an imprint of The Random House Publishing Group, a division of Random House, Inc., New York.

DEL REY is a registered trademark and the Del Rey colophon is a trademark of Random House, Inc.

ISBN 978-0-345-50105-9

Printed in the United States of America

www.delreybooks.com

OPM   9 8 7 6 5 4 3 2 1

To people who fill the world with light

Acknowledgments

Both Patricia and Marc would like to thank their agent, Jennifer Jackson, and their editor, Liz Scheier, for being so cool. They helped make the process of writing this book a true pleasure.

In addition, Marc sends love and thanks to his family and friends for enriching his life in countless ways. He sends special love to Tracy, who continues to give him more than he could ever hope for.

Prologue

"My name is Rachel Ackart," she whispered, rocking on the edge of her bed, furtively peering into the corners of her cell to make sure no one was there to eavesdrop.

But, as always, the corners were empty of anything human. She was alone, as she had been for most of the last year—eleven months, two weeks, four days, to be exact, if she could trust the scratches she'd made on the wall, one for each day she'd been incarcerated. Not that military personnel didn't spy on her via the camera installed high in one corner of the room. Why they needed to watch her 24/7 she didn't know. They already monitored her vital signs and brain waves through implanted chips. Medical personnel were in and out multiple times a day to inject her with meds or take her blood. She even had a daily visit from a so-called psychiatrist.

"Rachel Ackart . . . My name is Rachel Ackart. . . ."

She kept saying her name over and over so she would remember it. They'd pumped her up with so many damn drugs that she could hardly see straight.

Let alone think.

Let alone remember.

She gazed at her reflection in the piece of medical equipment that picked up her vitals and transmitted them to some unknown lab. Her blond hair appeared dull . . . her blue eyes unnaturally pale. . . . And weren't those tiny lines she saw forming in her heretofore flawless skin?

Heat flooded her, and she shoved the equipment away so hard that it bounced off the wall.

She'd gotten by all these years on accomplishments she'd been allowed because of her youthful beauty, and now, despite all she'd done to keep her looks, they were fading and the memories of her triumphs were disjointed and incomplete.

Forget remembering.

Forget using her powers. . . .

Rachel sprang off her bed and began pacing the perimeter of her cell. Undoubtedly her vital signs were bordering on explosive, alarming someone somewhere. They could descend on her at any moment and do whatever they wanted to her.

For her own good, of course.

She deserved better than this. After all she'd done for her country, for the military, for the government cabal running the Black Ops scientific experiments meant to strengthen the armed forces, she deserved to be treated with the respect she'd earned. She'd given up her life in service to that science, and look how she'd been rewarded.

Betrayed by her own blood. Locked in an eight-by-ten cell. No windows. No mirrors. No fresh air.

She clawed at her throat and gasped. If she didn't get some air, she was going to suffocate. . . .

They even buried their dead aboveground in this part of Louisiana, but not their scientific rejects. Where there was a will there was a way, and the military always found it. She was sequestered in an underground labyrinth that should have been impossible to build on land that was below sea level. Only the army had managed it somehow, and if the brass had their way, she would never breathe that fresh air, never see daylight again.

Escape was the only solution. Her thoughts whirled. Escape and then revenge.

Realizing her head was actually clearer than it had been in a long while, Rachel thought she must have built up some immunity to the drugs. A little gene splicing had turned her mind into a powerful weapon, the reason they'd been pumping chemicals into her. They wanted to control her. To further use her as a guinea pig. Her pulse threaded unevenly as she realized she had an opportunity to test her mental boundaries, maybe find some way of getting out of this damn hole.

She closed her eyes and allowed her mind to touch every inch of the room. But after several minutes of searching, she found nothing she would consider a real weakness.

Concentrating, she cast her net wider. She might not be able to leave the room physically, but that didn't mean she couldn't use her mind to search for a way out. If she found someone susceptible to suggestion, perhaps she could convince the person to open her door. Using frequencies the damn lab machines couldn't detect, she sent tentacles of mental energy in concentric circles that swept through the underground complex and beyond.

Suddenly, a male voice saying *"Rachel, I can help you . . ."* made her jam her back to the wall.

She looked around wildly, but, as always, she was alone in the room. The voice had filled her head before, but why now? Why when the drugs were wearing off?

Because she really was insane as they claimed?

She rushed to the door, to the small opening, to see who might be playing tricks on her. But the hallway outside her cell was empty.

The doctors said she'd had a breakdown and needed help. That was how they'd talked her into this damn cell in the first place. A temporary setback, they'd assured her. Now this. A bolt of terror rushed through her as she considered she might be losing what she had left of her mind.

Hot anger replaced fear. Rachel began searching her cell. The voice wasn't coming through the speaker next to the camera overhead, but that didn't mean there weren't others hidden in the room.

First she tore the medical equipment away from the wall. Then the small dresser. Then her bed. Nothing. She ripped away the mattress and threw it in a corner, then searched the bed frame, and when she still found nothing, picked up the thing as if it weighed no more than a child's toy and threw it against a wall.

"Where is the damn speaker?" she yelled, backing into a corner.

"If you close your eyes and concentrate, Rachel, you can find me."

Who the hell was screwing with her? The voice sounded familiar . . . someone she knew once long ago.

Almost against her will, she closed her eyes. A brilliant flash and a thunderous noise like the blast of an explosion filled her mind. She caught the sound of aircraft overhead . . . then the wail of a siren. . . .

Heart thumping, she opened her eyes, pushing away the splinters of memory that she recognized as World War II. Time and drugs had suppressed the past for so long, so how was she remembering now? What was this horrible dark sensation spreading through her, paralyzing her?

"I know all about you, Rachel. And you know me. All you have to do is open your mind. . . ."

The voice plunged her to new depths, to a place that made her stomach knot and the breath catch hot in her throat. Having faced evil many times in nine decades, she recognized the depths of darkness the voice promised. She was drowning in it.

With a gasp, Rachel fought back, more determined than ever to escape.

Needing to get out of there and now, she opened her mind again, though not in the way the voice had suggested. Without moving from her corner, she mentally felt her way around the room once more to the most vulnerable spot—the door, of course—and focused her mental energy on that. The rest of the room disappeared until the only thing she could see was the door itself, then only the hardware. The energy built in her mind until the metal lever began to vibrate. And then she let loose what she'd heard BB, the head scientist, call a psychic blast. The door vibrated so hard that it shook in its frame.

Still, it didn't open.

"If you ever want to get out of there, you need my help," came the voice, as if to taunt her.

Terror warring with her need to be free, Rachel got to her feet again and paced the small space like a caged animal, one ready to attack.

There had to be a way to get out of this damn place. She would do anything to breathe fresh air again. Anything to walk unfettered. To regain her power. To get revenge.

There had to be a way.

There was, of course. Darkness beckoned. She recognized it. Sensed how dangerous it could be. To her. To others.

Others had betrayed her. Others had kept her locked up like an animal, had taken her mind away from her for months. What did she owe anyone but herself?

Enough.

Rachel thought how she had given everything and everything had been taken from her in return. She had been betrayed. No matter the cost, it was time to think of herself. She could survive any evil.

All she had to do was hurl herself into the darkness of the voice to find the way out. . . .

Chapter 1

Thank God I'm locked up, Captain Scott Boulder thought. He'd jerked from a deep sleep and inadvertently bashed in the side of the metal bunk as easily as if it had been tinfoil. Fluorescent bulbs, triggered by the movement, cast a sickly green glow over the walls of the military cell. *I could have fucking killed somebody.*

He sat up, T-shirt and shorts soaked in sweat. He swung his legs over the edge of the paper-thin mattress and planted bare feet on cold cement as he glanced at the cell door.

It was locked tight, per his command.

Truth was, he didn't know how much of a danger he posed. Nobody did. The scientists on base talked out of their asses, unable to give him a straight answer about the extent of his supernatural powers.

Scott knew that his body had been contaminated. Knew that his humanity had been sabotaged. What he wanted to know—and what nobody could goddamn tell him—was if the bizarre powers would fade away. He wanted to know if the powers would mess with his bodily functions, and why he'd inherited certain powers and not others. Most important, Scott wanted to know if he would ever lose control of them. The very idea turned his stomach to ice. Next time, it could be more than just a damaged metal bunk. He could be trying to use his powers to protect someone and inadvertently hurt them instead. If that happened, he wouldn't be able to live with himself.

He had to be careful. So goddamn careful.

Pushing aside the disturbing thoughts, Scott focused on what had awakened him. He'd been sleeping dreamlessly when he'd heard a woman cry out.

Hadn't he?

Try as he might, he couldn't remember whether he'd recognized the voice. Or how distant or close it had been. But he was sure the voice had been more than a dream, although it seemed to echo strangely in his head—sure enough, anyway, to want to take a quick look outside the cell.

Scott stood and walked to the cell door, taking care not to touch it. Laced with gold alloy, the two-foot-thick door and walls harbored light-based energy that would counteract—painfully—the dark energy that hummed in his veins. If he ever did lose control, the cell would keep him at bay until backup arrived. That was the theory, anyway.

Scott peered through the cell door's tiny window and didn't see anything out of the ordinary; the long, stark hallway was empty. If a woman had been out there earlier, she wasn't now.

He was about to return to his bunk when a figure appeared at the far end of the corridor. A woman with short red hair, pale skin, and beautiful green eyes.

Leah. Smiling, Scott nearly pressed his hands against the cell door, which would have earned him a jolt.

Leah hadn't been the one who'd disturbed his sleep. He knew that for sure. He would have recognized the soft lilt of her voice immediately. The way she lingered briefly on the last word of each sentence she spoke.

He frowned. A couple of days ago, he'd sent her to his place to get some rest and then subsequently refused to see her. For her own safety. But deep down, he knew she'd find a way to check on him. He'd looked forward to it, in fact.

And now here she was.

Joy rushed through him, chasing away the reality of where he was, what he'd become, and any concern for the strange feminine voice that had awakened him.

All he could see—wanted to see—was Leah Maguire.

She wore a formfitting white blouse that hugged the contours of her slim body, and a brown, loose-fitting skirt that swayed with her hips as she approached. Even at this distance, her green eyes shone with intelligence and compassion.

Scott wondered if Leah could sense what he was thinking. She might blush if she did. The woman was an empath and had an uncanny way of knowing how he felt about everything, including her, which was a little awkward since he'd vowed to keep her at arm's length. He simply couldn't let emotion cloud or slow his judgment until his situation improved.

But when she spotted him looking at her and smiled, he felt his smile widen in reply.

Couldn't help it. What a sap he was.

And then another figure rounded the corner behind

her. Looming. Muscled. With sallow flesh, long black hair, and red, cruel eyes.

Andre Espinoza! Scott realized with horror. He couldn't believe it. Couldn't fucking believe it. He'd seen the vampire die. . . . He and Leah had torn the Philosopher's Stone from his chest and then decapitated him, sending his murderous soul back to hell. . . .

"Leah!" Scott yelled. "Behind you!" But the thick cell door swallowed his cries. Leah continued to walk toward him, smiling. Unaware of the threat behind her. "Leah!"

Scott felt his muscles surge with supernatural strength as his adrenaline redlined. He waved frantically at the video cameras monitoring his cell but knew he couldn't afford to wait for backup that might take several minutes to arrive.

Crouching, he charged the door like a linebacker. When his shoulder struck the reinforced steel, there was a thundering *boom,* accompanied by a blinding blue flash and bacon-fat hiss as his dark energy collided with the gold alloy's light-based energy.

But the door didn't budge. Despite the burning pain that lanced his shoulder, Scott backed up and charged the door again. And again. Booms and flashes ricocheted across the cell as the flesh on his shoulder began to char, then smoke.

Fear clawed Scott as he imagined what Andre might do to Leah—he couldn't lose her, not after all they'd been through—until the door finally bowed under his repeated assault. Not much, only enough to allow in a sliver of outside light.

All he needed.

Scott closed his eyes, calmed his mind as best he could. *My body is nothing. . . . My body is nothing. . . .*

No sooner had he issued the command than he felt his corporeal bulk become lighter and lighter until he transformed into white mist. He willed himself to flow through the crack in a dense river that spilled into the hallway and then towered like a cumulus cloud to create a hazy outline of his body before solidifying into the real thing.

Before him, Andre hoisted Leah by the throat as she gagged and struggled.

Scott didn't dare use his lightning to attack Andre since the deadly charge could travel through the vampire's body and injure Leah as well. Instead, he aimed a crippling blow at Andre's kidneys and felt his fist pass through absolutely nothing.

And then the entire scene—Andre and Leah both—crackled with static before blinking away completely. *What the fuck?*

"Holograms," came a voice from behind him. "Animated from images captured by security cameras and projected through hidden lenses in the ceiling."

Scott turned as Colonel James Harriman approached, personal bodyguard at his side.

Harriman was dressed in formal army greens with silver eagle pins that denoted his rank gleaming on his lapels. The man had to be late fifties or early sixties by now, Scott thought. And even though his hair had grayed at the temples, his blue eyes were clear as ever, and he moved strongly, confidently, with no hint that age had taken a toll.

Scott had been pleased to see Harriman for the first

time a few days ago after so many years, but that did nothing to improve his mood at the moment. "Neat trick," he said coldly, stepping forward to meet them. "And way out of line."

The bodyguard immediately crossed in front of Harriman, planted a hand on Scott's chest, and shoved him back a step. Scott grabbed the man's wrist and met his baleful gaze. Bald and narrow-faced, the bodyguard held an M4 assault rifle and wore a black assault vest over a khaki jumpsuit, which bore a gray silk screen of a cobra midstrike on each shoulder. Insignia of a private contractor. Scott had always disapproved of private contractors since they tended to attract men who wanted to fight for the wrong reasons. Never mind honor or patriotism, these mercenaries craved the chaos of battle and were often more than happy to take the first shot. Some considered these qualities essential for security forces—no doubt why the man had been assigned to Harriman by upper brass—but Scott believed the trade-off was rarely worth it.

"Stand down," Harriman told the man, and then to Scott, "Please excuse Mr. White. He can be overzealous about my safety at times."

White paused a moment before finally stepping back.

"No hard feelings, then," Scott said, but White simply glared. A private contractor who was trained to act, not speak, apparently.

"We had to make sure you could maintain control under extreme duress, Scott," Harriman continued, weathered features creased with purpose. "You passed with flying colors."

"Due respect, Colonel, but your impromptu test doesn't prove anything. You know as well as I do that my powers are unpredictable. The more I use them, the greater the chance somebody will get hurt. Things could have spiraled out of control."

"You don't give yourself enough credit, son. You have more control over yourself than you think. Something of a rarity with our other test subjects, believe me."

Scott looked evenly at Harriman, still furious that his feelings for Leah had been used in some test, and even more furious at himself for having provided the opportunity.

However, despite himself, he felt his anger at Harriman begin to subside. The man had been like a father to him years ago during his training at Fort Bragg. He'd taught him about honor, loyalty, and love of country while his real father—his biological father—had taught him only about betrayal and abandonment.

"I assume your exercise had another purpose besides testing my sanity," Scott said.

"Another mission, yes," Harriman replied. "Critical to national security. I'll have someone give Leah a call and then brief you both after she arrives."

As disgusted as Scott was with the notion of another mission—particularly one that required his powers—he was willing to hear Harriman out. Tactic with the hologram aside, the Colonel had always proved to be an honorable man. But he wanted to spare Leah if he could. "Leah's been through too much as it is, Colonel. Leave her out of it."

"She has abilities that are critical to the mission's success."

"Is this about the guy who took the Philosopher's Stone?"

Fear darkened Harriman's eyes. "It's imperative that we find him, Scott. Before he learns how to use it."

Chapter 2

"We need to find Danton," said a worried Scott, pacing the length of the war room.

Leah Maguire sat frozen in her chair, unable to tear her gaze from him. She drank in the rugged face she'd grown to love—high cheekbones and a straight Roman nose softened by wavy brown hair and amber eyes—then dropped to the military-fit body clad in black fatigues.

Her chest tightened as she thought about how she'd been kept from Scott for days and how she'd gone crazy wondering why. No one—not Harriman, not BB—would tell her anything other than that Scott didn't want to see her. All kinds of notions had gone through her mind, specifically that Scott's blood thirst had gotten the best of him.

At last they'd come face-to-face, and the first thing out of his mouth was about Danton.

"Scott, what's wrong?"

"We have a newly made vampire on the loose with a weapon that can make him immortal if he figures out how to use it." He didn't look at her. "That's plenty wrong in my book."

Finally, he met her gaze and faltered for a moment. Weakened. She could feel the shift in his energy to something softer than the dread and determination she'd walked in on.

Leah asked, "Didn't Harriman send anyone after Danton?"

"Of course he sent a Black Ops team, but they don't have your special skill at finding people. New Orleans seems to have swallowed Danton whole. If he's even there anymore."

Just then, the door opened and in walked Darryl Adams, affectionately known as BB, short for "Big Brain." The MIT-educated head researcher on Project 24 was a slight man, ordinary but for his explosive red hair and beard and arms covered with Celtic tattoos.

"Leah, I heard you were here. Good to see you again."

"What's up, BB?" Scott asked.

"That inhaler I told you about—pick it up before you leave. It'll help with the blood thirst."

"So you *are* having problems," Leah said.

"We've run Scott through every test we could think of," BB told her. "He passed them all with flying colors. So far, it seems Scott's stable." His face darkened. "But there's no way to be sure. At least not yet."

And if he'd failed one? What would they have done to him then? Lock Scott away like they had their mistakes? Cold sliced through Leah and tightened her chest.

She turned to Scott. "So that's what's been going on the last few days?"

Scott nodded. "It's for the best. If Harriman hadn't ordered the tests, I would have insisted."

Leah believed him. Scott was the most honorable

ian she'd ever met. He would never knowingly put
nyone at risk, and he'd been having difficulty dealing
vith the vampiric powers he'd gotten from Andre. Not
› mention the blood thirst. She wondered exactly how
ad that had become.

BB's expression was remorseful. "Some early vol-
nteers suffered terrible side effects . . . sick . . .
eformed . . . insane."

Remembering the corridor that held dozens of con-
ained soldiers, she felt her pulse rush.

"I'm going to go see what's taking Harriman so
ong," Scott said. "And I'll get that inhaler while I'm
t it."

Leah nodded. Only when the door closed behind
im did she face the scientist. "Is Scott really as good
s you indicated?"

"Better. Keep the faith, Leah. The inhaler will help
vith the blood thirst, and I'm this close to an anti-
ote." He held out his forefingers, tips nearly touch-
1g. "I just need to test it on a control group of
atients."

"Thank God." Leah took a deep breath meant to
uell her building anxiety. "Scott didn't ask for any of
1is."

"That's an understatement. He was relieved to be
1e ghost on Team Ultra, the only one without any of
1e powers. He doesn't like letting go of control."

Which the vampire had taken away when he'd at-
1cked Scott, Leah thought. "The loss of control over
imself is the worst damage a man like Scott could
1ffer."

"Leah, I brought you something to put a smile

back on that pretty face." BB removed an object from his lab coat pocket and held it out.

Leah's heart beat a little faster as she took the digital recorder from him. "Thank you for taking care of this for me." Though she smiled slightly, tears sprang to her eyes as well. She curled her fingers tightly around the recorder as if she could reintegrate the memories it held. "You have no idea how much this means to me."

"I didn't listen to it, so you don't have to worry about me blackmailing you or anything."

Leah laughed and realized it had been too long since her sense of humor had been engaged. "Blackmail away." She slipped the recorder into her soft case that held candles and packets of herbs and small vials of oils—the tools of her trade. "I have nothing of value to give you as payment, though."

"Don't sell yourself short." BB winked and headed for the door. "I have to get back to the lab, get on that antidote."

Even as BB left, Colonel Harriman arrived.

"Ms. Maguire. I'm assuming Captain Boulder brought you up to speed on the hostile situation."

"We don't know that Danton Dumas is a hostile yet."

"You're right that we have no idea how the vampire's blood affected him," Harriman said, "but better to be prepared for the worst. Who knows how many others he's turned. Any which way, he has the potential to be a real danger, made even more so by his possession of the Philosopher's Stone."

Leah frowned. "He didn't try to hurt me, and he could have."

"But he's had time to grow into his new powers. And into his blood thirst."

"I haven't heard about any unusual deaths, none like there were when Andre was on the loose. You haven't done any more cover-up, have you, Colonel?"

After they'd destroyed Andre, Harriman's cleaning team had done a thorough cover-up. The media had reported on thwarted terrorists rather than a vampire on the loose.

"This Danton could simply be more circumspect," Harriman said. "He might feed quietly in hidden corners of the city. Give it time. . . ."

"I don't think you should make any assumptions," Leah argued.

"Do you want to see more needless deaths?"

"No, of course not. That's my point." The violence she'd had to endure to stop Andre made her sick inside. "If I help to bring in Danton, you have to promise me that you'll treat him with respect until you're certain he *is* a danger."

Harriman's visage darkened. "I don't have to promise you a thing, Ms. Maguire, other than a cell if you don't cooperate. I'm concerned for the people of this city, of this country. Danton Dumas could start a plague of death and destruction, could create more of his kind."

Knowing that she really had no choice, Leah only hoped that once she and Scott found Danton, Harriman would be more reasonable than he sounded. "Perhaps someone in the military should have thought of that before experimenting with vampire DNA to enhance soldiers."

Harriman had no retort for that.

Chapter 3

"Wow, you're in some hurry!"

Danton heard the voice call to him from across the restaurant's busy kitchen as he passed through on his way to the back alley door. He took a few more steps, adjusting the messenger bag hanging from his shoulder and pretending he hadn't heard, when the voice came again, louder this time. "Danton! It's me! Over here!"

"Hi, Lilly," Danton said, turning. Normally, he might enjoy the opportunity for small talk, but not now. God, not now. As she approached, yet another pain raked through his stomach, and it took everything he had to remain standing.

"Hi, yourself!" Lilly said. "Where are you off to in such a rush?"

"You know . . . places. . . ." Danton replied through clenched teeth. Sweat rolled down his temple, and he wiped it away. "Errands."

"Yeah, errands. They can be so annoying." She nodded to emphasize the point and then flashed a grin that once again reminded him of how little Lilly Fry had changed since they'd become friends at Tulane University four years ago. Lilly was always smiling, her bright white teeth framed by thin, merry lips. Picture-perfect, the same smile every time. She was till slender as ever, too, with long black hair and shy, kind eyes behind her thickly framed glasses. Lilly had been studying culinary arts while he'd been earning a PhD in linguistics. She was putting her degree to good use here as a sous chef at White Fish Grill, one of the finest seafood restaurants on Bourbon Street.

"Can you do that thing you used to do?" she asked. "You know, your Song of Salutations?"

"What?"

"Back in school, you said wishing a person good day was a commonality found in every language. One of the few that connected everyone to the human family, remember? You used to recite thirty ways to say hello to the tune of 'The Girl from Ipanema.'"

Danton played dumb but knew exactly what she meant. He hadn't thought about linguistics or the sonata in years and doubted if he could remember it. "Lilly—"

"Please!"

Suspecting Lilly wouldn't let him leave until she heard it, Danton took a deep breath, trying his best to ignore the pain in his stomach, and recited haltingly, off-key, "Hello, Guten Tag, Hola, Shwmai, Barev . . . Salut, Ciao, Hafa Adai . . . Konnichi wa, Hej, Na-naste. . . ."

When he finished the litany, Lilly flashed him another perfectly gleeful smile. Prolonged this time. "Um, anyway, I just wanted to see how you were doing, Danton," she said, nervously smoothing her chef's whites with both hands. "We didn't really get to talk after you moved in."

"Yeah, well, I'm sorry about that," Danton said, wincing as another pain tore through his stomach.

Fortunately, Lilly had been looking at her shoes, too
shy to sustain steady eye contact to notice. He
gripped the messenger bag more tightly to his body,
feeling the solid, curved swell of the object inside. He
had to get out of here and get rid of it. Hide it before
it was too late. "I've sort of had a lot on my mind,
Lilly. Now if you'll excuse—"

"Oh, there's no need to apologize, Danton!" Lilly
interjected quickly. "You've been through so much,
you poor, poor thing." Her eyeglasses crept down the
bridge of her nose, and she pushed them back up with
her thumb. "I just wanted to tell you to make yourself
at home here, okay? If there's anything you need,
anything at all, feel free to ask."

"I will."

"Anything at all," Lilly repeated, self-consciously
smoothing her apron. "I can get you leftovers from
the kitchen, throw your laundry in with the restaurant's. We have a great deal with the Laundromat on
the corner, only a dollar a pound, but I can sneak
yours in for free. Whatever you like!"

Danton edged closer to the alley door, using the
wall for support as subtly as he could, but Lilly followed him step for step, finally crossing in front of
him to block his way. Such a bold move must have
been difficult for her, Danton knew. But she'd done it
just the same and was now staring at him intently.
Earnestly. "Lilly, I have to get go—"

"If you ever need to talk . . ." She blushed, steadied
herself. Smoothed her apron. "You know . . . about
what's happened. I'm here most of the time, Danton,
working right downstairs from you. I'd be happy to
listen."

Danton looked at Lilly as she continued but could barely concentrate on what she was saying. The cloying odor of fried food and shellfish was making his head swim, nearly making him gag, as sawblade pains rippled through his stomach in waves.

He was suffering from hunger. Severe hunger. But not for ordinary food.

So Lilly wanted to talk, he thought grimly, wiping another sticky thread of sweat from his temple. But how could she possibly understand what had happened to him? The terrible choices he now had to make?

He felt a flash of sizzling anger so intense that it momentarily blocked out the pain. *Damn you, Rebecca!* He knew his sister had only been trying to help, but she should have thought things through before bringing *him* into their house.

The vampire. Andre Espinoza.

The name sent a chill up Danton's spine. Rebecca had convinced the creature to transfuse him with blood to save him from leukemia—an act that had carried a terrible price.

". . . What was the name of the bar your sister owned?" Lilly asked.

"Magic Nights," Danton managed, swallowing thickly. Doing his best to respond as kindly as he could because she had been so kind to him. "It was a gentlemen's club."

"A gentlemen's club, right." Lilly blushed. "Well, if you need help going through the debris . . . I mean, finding what's left . . . I mean . . . Oh God, I'm being so insensitive. . . . What I mean to say is, I can help you try to get back what you lost, if you want."

"I can handle it, thanks."

As Lilly went on nervously, Danton felt his strength ebb as the searing pain in his stomach grew. How could Lilly possibly help him reclaim what he'd lost? Both his beloved sister and his humanity to the same foul beast. Grief smothered Danton like a mudslide. He struggled to choke back tears as Lilly continued, oblivious to his pain. He was completely alone now. Rebecca was gone, and he was trapped in some nightmare state between life and death, between living and dying.

Lilly stopped talking abruptly and canted her head like a curious, bespectacled puppy. "If you don't mind me saying so, Danton, you look a little pale."

Danton, too, had noticed that his once caramel-colored skin had faded with the vampiric transformation. "I *feel* pale," he rasped, stepping past her.

"Oh my God, I didn't mean that in a bad way!" Lilly said quickly. "You look good, Danton! Really, really good! I was just wondering if you're getting enough to eat!"

Danton's vision pinwheeled. He propped his hand against a metal fridge to keep from falling. "I don't want to put you through any trouble, Lilly."

"No trouble at all!" she exclaimed, and bustled off. Thank God. . . .

But when Danton took another step toward the alley door, his legs turned to rubber. He pitched forward, slamming into a dish cart. The clattering impact popped the Philosopher's Stone free from the messenger bag, and he could only watch helplessly as the beaming-red, baseball-sized rock rolled loudly along a countertop, then plunged off the far edge into a large glass tank teeming with lobsters.

Danton crumpled to the ground near the doorway. Luckily, it was off-peak hours, and the cooking staff had moved to the other side of the massive kitchen to take a break. But he couldn't let Lilly find him like this and call an ambulance. The police would get involved, and that might mean the military, too.

Seeing a flicker of movement in the alley, Danton lashed out and grabbed the rat before it could escape down a storm drain. Careful to avoid the tiny snapping teeth, he broke the rat's neck with a sharp twist and then, with a groan of resignation, bit deeply into the flesh of its stomach. Danton nearly gagged as a flood of bitter, red-black blood poured down his throat. But as horrible as the blood tasted, it eased the hunger that raked his stomach. He forced himself to swallow, swallow, swallow as the pain in his stomach diminished to a dull ache.

He had been reduced to feeding on vermin to sate his blood hunger, but that was far better than the alternative. He would rather die than take a human life and become even more disconnected from the human family than he already was. A tragedy his knowledge of language could never remedy. He refused to become like Andre, who had been a savage, murderous parasite who'd taken others' lives only to prolong his own.

Regaining enough strength to clamber to his feet, Danton glanced at the lobster tank. The water glowed brightly with red light from the Stone, which lay on the bottom. The lobsters had scurried away from the Stone when it first splashed into the tank, but now, realizing it didn't pose a threat, they converged and covered it with their bodies.

A decent enough hiding place, Danton thought wearily. There were ten huge lobster tanks here, so chances were good the Stone would stay hidden for a couple of days at least. More than enough time to retrieve a few of Rebecca's voodoo books from Magic Nights and figure out how he could use the Stone to get back what he'd lost.

Before Lilly could return and delay him further, Danton slipped out the alley door, thinking again about how magic had turned his sister into a dark soul consumed with anger and violence. He could only pray that the Stone wouldn't have the same effect on him.

Chapter 4

Magic had its price.

Waiting for Scott in a Humvee outside the entrance to the labs, Leah pulled a tattered three-by-five photograph of her father and brother from her case and thought about how using magic had already cost her so much.

She tried in vain to connect with any memories of Dad and Gabe. It wasn't simply a matter of time, of seventeen years passing since Andre Espinoza had slaughtered them. It had been a matter of using magic to stop the vampire once and for all. And now she was going to use magic again to locate Danton Dumas.

Magic always had its price, and the price inevitably was the thing most precious to the conjurer.

Nothing was more precious to Leah than memories of her loved ones . . . and the memories grew fainter with each act of magic she executed. That's why she'd recorded as many as she could, and before she and Scott had gone after Andre, she'd given the recorder to BB for safekeeping.

Wondering what was taking Scott so long—the Louisiana afternoon was unusually hot and humid, salted with the stench of a nearby underground marsh fire—Leah grew uncomfortable. She didn't have the vehicle's keys, or she would have started the engine and turned on the air-conditioning. As it was, her peacock blue cotton blouse and long skirt clung to her flesh uncomfortably, and sweat rolled down her neck and between her breasts. Scott had gone to fetch something belonging to Danton they could use to help find the man. The military had taken jurisdiction of Magic Nights, the gentlemen's club owned by Danton's deceased sister. They'd also confiscated some of his belongings from the premises.

Impatience growing, Leah fanned herself with a section of the *Times-Picayune* she found on the floor, leaned back into the passenger seat, and started the first recording.

"Dad made sure my eleventh birthday was really special. He planned a family trip to San Diego because he knew how much I loved animals. The zoo was great, the wild animal park better. On a VIP tour, we were allowed to pet a couple of baby rhinos. I remember Gabe getting rhino spit all over his hands. . . ."

The fact that she didn't really remember brought tears to her eyes.

Listening to the recording was like looking at her photo, flat and two-dimensional. Her chest tightened. She couldn't *feel* Gabe's laugh or appreciate Dad's expression when he took photographs that day or smirk at the way Mom must have been trying to herd them around. No, not really a memory. The recording and photos were all she had unless she found a way to reverse the loss.

Loss . . . a way of life for her. It seemed she'd been alone forever. First Dad and Gabe had been taken. Then her mother had withdrawn into herself. Leah had spent seventeen years alone in her own mind and heart, seventeen years protecting herself. And then she had met Scott. Despite their obvious differences, they had been drawn to each other, and she had opened to him more emotionally than to anyone since the attack. And now it seemed he wanted to keep her at a distance, leaving her alone once again.

The driver's door opened, startling her out of her search for the past. Dressed in khakis and a loose shirt that hid the pistol holstered at his waist, Scott slid in behind the wheel. "Sorry. Didn't mean to keep you waiting."

Leah said, "Not a problem. I kept myself occupied."

He glanced over at her, and she knew he saw the recorder and photo before she slipped them into her bag.

"So I see. You look upset."

"I still miss them."

The humidity was making her miserable. She began searching her bag for a pack of tissues.

"Lose something?"

"I'm soaking wet from this damn humidity. I'm just looking for something to dry off with." But the tissues eluded her.

"Here." Scott held out a bandana.

Leah reached for it and their hands touched, and for a moment both sat frozen to the spot by the connection. Not that Leah was cold. If possible, she grew even hotter. Her breath caught in her throat, and her pulse sped up so that she could hear the blood rushing through her.

And from the glint in Scott's eyes, so could he. . . .

Swearing softly, he tore his hand away and looked out the window, and she sensed the difficulty with which he kept himself under control. So he wouldn't be tempted to kiss her? Or taste her blood?

He wouldn't do that, she thought, wiping away the rivulets of sweat making her so uncomfortable. Scott would never hurt her.

Even so, the thought that he was tempted uppermost in her mind, she sank into silence until they were on the interstate, headed for New Orleans, before trying once more to engage him.

"So what did you find of Danton's that I can use?" she asked.

He handed her a book. "This came right from his nightstand. Apparently he likes nonfiction."

She turned it over and opened the cover. "Linguistics. It's a textbook."

"Apparently he was in a PhD program at Tulane before he got so sick."

Which meant he would have been in the anthropology department, Leah knew, so they had something in common. Their specialties might be different—hers being Apotropaic Magic, the knowledge to turn away evil—but they came from similar educational backgrounds. She knew linguists relied on their skills to understand the intentions of a wide range of speakers and writers, and she hoped that would apply to her appeal to Danton as well. She'd had enough of death and violence and hoped Danton would prefer logic over combat.

She would soon find out.

In the meantime, Leah couldn't stop herself from trying to connect with Scott on a more personal level.

"These last few days . . . I was worried about you. No one would tell me anything."

She noted he stiffened when he said, "There was nothing to tell until the tests were run."

"They treated you like a hostile."

"How do we know I'm not?"

"You have a soul, Scott." She'd made sure of that and had gladly sacrificed what she'd needed to. "And a moral code no one could question."

"I also have an unnatural thirst."

"BB will fix it."

"He'll try."

"Sometimes we make our own reality. Think that you will heal and you'll be on the right road. Negativity can be damaging."

Scott didn't answer, merely tightened his grip on the steering wheel. Leah sighed and tried not to take his reticence personally. He'd been through so much in the last ten days. As had she. Danger had brought them together, had made them depend on each other. The lull since apparently had made Scott think twice about things.

About them.

Again, she sank into silence.

The silence grew and gutted her all the way into New Orleans. The stink of the marsh fire intensified the closer they got to the city. Despite the vehicle's air-conditioning, she could still smell the burning peat. Early on, a portion of the fire had been aboveground, but it had died down without jumping the canals and continued to smolder underground.

Hidden . . . like her life.

She, too, lived underground, both literally and figuratively. Other than the people she worked with in the underground military complex, no one could know of her true capabilities. No one could know what had been let loose on the city of New Orleans in the name of military development lest there be widespread panic.

She wanted to believe she could make her own positive reality as she'd encouraged Scott to do. Wanted to . . . but really didn't.

Scott exited east of the Superdome and pulled over to a near-empty parking lot. Danton could be anywhere, but she was certain he was still in New Orleans, where he'd lived his whole life. He had to be adjusting to the changes that had happened to him, and she couldn't imagine him leaving the only place he knew. They'd pulled over in a non-neighborhood in the center of the city, in the midst of the spaghetti strands of highway and the business and warehouse districts. Wherever Danton was, she would be able to locate him using a finding spell.

They stepped out of the vehicle. While Scott looked around to make sure they had no witnesses, Leah took her tools from her case: four white candles, a green candle, and a green stone.

"Are we all right?" she asked.

"Do it."

She arranged the four white candles on the pavement in the four directions, then set Danton's linguistics text on a stone in the center. She motioned to Scott to join her. Unlike the first time they'd done this—he'd resisted believing in anything but science—he swiftly moved to her side. Her purpose was to triangulate a location, and she needed two things onnected to Danton from different directions, the ook being one, Scott the other. Like Danton's, cott's blood mingled with Andre's.

"Ready," she said, lighting the white candles and in er mind's eye seeing a magic circle form around hem. When she lit the green candle, she concentrated n Danton's visage as it had been the only time she'd een him—thin and pale and heartbroken and furious—and murmured, "Danton Dumas, you will not e able to hide from us." She allowed a bit of wax o drip on the text. "Link what is connected to the man. . . ."

She'd barely finished the command when a hazy urple line that only she and Scott could see joined im and the book, and two additional purple lines retched forth and converged in the distance to the est.

"It looks like he might be in the Garden District omewhere," she said.

"Let's find out."

Quickly gathering her tools, Leah climbed back to the Humvee and they were off. She wondered if anton even noticed anything unusual. If he did, ould he understand what she'd done?

As Scott drove, Leah held the book in her hands nd, using the purple haze and a street map of New Orleans, navigated. Soon they were headed west on t. Charles Avenue, and the triangle was shortening ster and faster. They hadn't even reached the Garden District yet, and their target was almost upon hem.

"He's on the move . . ." Leah noted, ". . . like he's oving toward us."

"He must be in a car."

She nodded, then froze as she saw a red-trimmed olive green streetcar—a trolley attaching it to an electric power line overhead—moving in their direction. "Or a streetcar." The apex of the triangulation hit the front of the car. "Danton has to be a passenger."

By the time the words were out of her mouth, the streetcar was passing the Humvee. The electric line split St. Charles Avenue, traffic flowing in opposite directions on each side of the island of grass and trees and rails and power poles.

"Damn it!" Scott yelled. "I have to go to the next crossing."

Leah wrenched around in her seat. The apex of the triangulation now touched the rear of the car.

Scott took the double turn so fast and hard, she swore the vehicle went up on two wheels. Her heart pounded as they chased the streetcar for several minutes while it headed toward the edge of the French Quarter.

Scott gunned the accelerator, and they shot past the streetcar. "Look for a stop and be ready to get out fast."

They were about a block ahead of the streetcar when she saw the oval yellow sign announcing Car Stop.

"There."

Scott pulled over, and they left the Humvee for the stop. The streetcar slowed, and a woman got out.

"Get on and try to talk to Danton," Scott said, guiding her into the car. "I'll take care of the driver."

As Leah complied, Scott was saying something to the man, but her entire focus was on the dark-haired guy sitting on one of the wooden seats near the back, his eyes closed, his head wedged against the half-open window. Only a handful of people were scattered between her and him. Waves of torment from Danton—grief and anger and despair—filled her. Not wanting to scare him into running, she passed him and stood between him and the rear doors. He was trapped between her and Scott with no way out.

"Danton?" she called softly. "We need to talk."

His head whipped up and around, and the little color in his face seemed to drain away. "I know you. You're the one responsible for Rebecca's death." Fury crowded out everything else as he lunged to his feet.

"I didn't kill her, Danton. You know that. Your sister was sick—"

"*I* was the one who was sick, and *she* was the one who was trying to heal me."

"Your sister was soul sick from using black magic," Leah said, trying to engage his logic. She noted Scott stopped a few seats on the other side of Danton, waiting to back her up. She didn't want that to be necessary. She didn't want anyone else hurt. "I tried to help her, to give her back the humanity she lost. In those last moments, Rebecca *was* whole again, Danton. And sorry for what she'd done. Her death was a terrible accident."

"What do you want now? To kill *me*?"

His voice rose and with it the interest of the other passengers. Leah felt their shock and anxiety roil and pummel her.

"No one wants to hurt you, Danton. You have nothing to fear from me."

"I'll bet you said that to Rebecca right before you _healed_ her to death."

"The terrible things your sister did caught up to her, but not because of me."

"Rebecca gave up everything for me, and she would still be alive if you'd just let her alone. _She_ should be alive . . . not you."

Leah gasped, but before she could gather her wits to calm the man, Scott went after Danton.

"Listen, you punk . . ."

Danton's eyes widened as he realized he was trapped between them.

"Hey, _cher_, these people are messing with me!" Danton yelled to the driver.

"Settle down," Scott ordered, reaching for him.

At which Danton ducked his shoulder and, with a wild look, walked straight through the wall of the car.

Chapter 5

Scott blinked, momentarily stunned by what he'd just witnessed, and then bolted to the other end of the streetcar, keeping pace with Danton, who was suddenly sprinting down the sidewalk. *How the fuck did he do that?!*

Seeing Danton pass though the side panel of the streetcar triggered a series of familiar, deep-seated fears in Scott. Was his own body still changing? Would he manifest strange powers like Danton? Powers he couldn't handle?

Leaping out the streetcar door, Scott tried to cut Danton off, but the guy made a hard left across Canal Street, quick as a jackrabbit, and then headed northeast past a strip club on Bourbon Street.

Danton was no dummy. He obviously planned to lose himself among the tourists in the French Quarter. Not that it mattered. The beam of purple light affixed to his back assured that he wouldn't be able to hide. Catching him was another matter.

Scott charged after Danton. Weaving through groups of pedestrians, he pressed a hand to his ear jack to dim ambient noise and then called into the throat mike attached to his collar. "Leah, I'll handle this one. Fall back to the Humvee."

"Harriman sent us both to retrieve Danton," came

her crackling reply, "and that's what we're going to try to do."

Scott gritted his teeth. Yes, she'd been sent along to help with the capture, but the situation had changed. If Danton could walk through walls, God knew what else he could do. Scott refused to expose her to that kind of risk. "The matter isn't open for discussion, Leah. Fall back. That's an order."

"We're a team, Scott. Here to back each other up. Besides, you wouldn't say that if I were an Army Ranger under your command."

She was right about that, but his feelings made things far more complicated, which was why he'd been trying to distance himself from her. It also didn't help that her presence—hell, the mere sound of her voice—was a goddamn distraction.

It was nearly all he could do not to think about pushing her into a corner like he'd done at his apartment a few days ago . . . far, far too long ago. He ached to feel the soft weight of her breasts in his hands, taste the languid heat of her tongue as her body tensed and the sound of her breathless orgasms filled his ears. . . .

Shit! Scott snapped back to reality as he clipped a trash barrel with his knee, toppling it over with a crash. *Case in point,* he thought grimly. The connection between them created unanticipated vulnerabilities that he could not afford to have exploited here—or anywhere—for both their sakes. "Leah—"

"I can see the beam from where I'm standing," she continued as though the matter were settled. "Judging from its trajectory, Danton is heading northeast.

I'll cut up to Dauphine in the Humvee and try to get ahead of him."

Scott glanced down the street, and, sure enough, Danton had just scampered across Conti on a direct course for Jackson Square. The purple beam kept pace, pointing him out in the crowd like an accusatory finger. "Roger that," he replied, knowing it was useless to argue. Leah's unwavering resolve was a quality he found incredibly attractive, but it drove him crazy sometimes, too.

Little bugger's fast, Scott thought, forcing his legs to pump faster. Danton was a block ahead and still going strong. Now that they were in the heart of the French Quarter, the gray cityscape gave way to an explosion of colorful storefronts that shone brightly in the afternoon sun. The quality of the air itself changed, too. From a lingering smell of polluted exhaust to an intermingling of spices, alcohol, tobacco, seafood, and ripening fruit. The transition never failed to affect Scott. Sometimes he became so consumed with the military that he forgot the expressions of life that existed in such close proximity to the lab. As Scott continued to chase Danton past a dizzying array of hole-in-the-wall shops that hawked everything from jazz to voodoo to gumbo, he noticed people's faces as they took in the sights—the expressions of wonder, relaxation, and joy.

When was the last time you felt contentment like that? he asked himself, and the answer was fast in coming. *The last time you were alone with Leah.*

Despite their differences, Leah had awakened long-dead feelings in him. Unfortunately, thanks to Andre

Espinoza, something malignant and inhuman had rustled to life inside him, too. Leah deserved much more than that. She deserved everything he wasn't. Everything he couldn't give her.

Leah's voice crackled in his ear. "I'm turning right on Ursulines. Where's Danton now?"

Scott cut through a gaggle of foreign tourists taking photographs of Saint Louis Cathedral and the nearby statue of Andrew Jackson. "He just crossed Jackson Square at St. Ann."

"Keep flushing him in that direction and I'll be able to cut him off!"

For a fleeting moment, Scott considered firing a lightning bolt at the back of Danton's knees to take him down but quickly dismissed the idea. What if he missed? What if the lightning had become stronger since he'd used it against Andre, and he killed Danton by mistake?

Pushing himself, Scott closed to within half a block of Danton, but then his progress slowed as the street became thick with street performers at the eastern end of the French Market.

An old woman wearing an orange shawl and holding a tarot deck stepped into his path. "Tell your fortune, young man?"

"Thank you, but I know too much already," Scott said, dodging around her. Whenever he lost sight of Danton in the crowd, the purple beam brought him back on target.

Scott noticed the crowd didn't seem to slow Danton at all. On the contrary, Danton pulled away steadily, as though he were running down an empty street. And then Scott saw why.

Danton was running *through* people. His slender
form disappeared into body after body—theirs seeming to swallow his whole—before he emerged fullspeed
on the other side. A few yelped in confused surprise,
others lost their footing and fell, but for the most
part, they all seemed fine.

Scott knew he'd lose the guy despite the purple
beam if he didn't act fast. "Danton Dumas!" he
yelled. "I know you can hear me! Stop, or your sister
will have died in vain!"

It was the only thing Scott could think of to say.
Play to the guy's emotions, see what happened. To his
surprise, it worked.

Danton stopped dead in his tracks. Whirled.

Still running, Scott was about to tell Leah that
Danton had given up when Danton rushed him on a
clear collision course.

Scott was so stunned that he didn't think to move
as Danton quickly closed the distance between them,
and then—

Scott sucked a breath as a terrible heaviness in-
vaded his body. For a seemingly endless moment, it
felt as though he were under the effect of a much
stronger gravitational pull. The bizarre oscillation of
weight threw off his balance, and he nose-dived into
the cobblestone street.

Cursing and holding his nose, Scott rolled over in
time to see Danton disappear through the white canvas wall of a booth selling papier-mâché masks and
colorful strings of Mardi Gras beads.

Leah's voice crackled in his ear. "Scott, I'm at
Royal now—"

"Stay back!"

"I thought we covered this already."

Scott stood, his body still buzzing from the encounter with Danton. The guy was unpredictable. Too willing to use his power. He couldn't let Leah get anywhere close to him. "Dammit, Leah, why can't you just trust me on this?"

There was a pause before she said quietly, "I do trust you, Scott. God knows I do. Even if you don't trust yourself sometimes."

Trust himself? What the hell did that have to do with anything? He was about to reply when she said, "I see him, Scott. On this side of the French Market."

"Try to back him into an alley, then," he said, leaping to his feet. When was he going to learn to keep his emotions out of the equation? "I'll be right there."

Scott cut down a long row of French Market booths before exiting on Royal. He then turned hard down a nearby alley to see Danton at the other end, backing away from the Humvee as it drove slowly past.

Danton was so focused on the Humvee that Scott was able to get the drop on him easily. "I'll take that," he said, plucking the messenger bag from Danton's shoulder.

Danton darted toward the alley wall, clearly intending to go through it, but before he could escape Scott flattened him with a glancing blow to the jaw.

Leah arrived a moment later and knelt by the unconscious man. "Is he okay?"

"I pulled the punch," Scott said, opening the messenger bag. Inside were only books and papers. "I don't know if we should be worried or relieved that he doesn't have the Stone."

From the way Leah met his gaze, Scott knew that she sensed his uncertainty about his powers. His fear. But despite their disagreement, she didn't mention it. Instead, she stepped close and touched his arm. Her touch felt good, as it always did.

"I just got off the radio with Harriman," she said. "He wants us to return to base. There's something he wants to show us, and it isn't good."

Chapter 6

Leah was happy to let Scott take over behind the wheel. She was worried about Danton and kept looking to the rear of the Humvee, where he lay unconscious across the seat. Scott had fastened Danton's hands behind his back and attached them to his secured ankles with BB-prepared flexicuffs. Halfway to the base, however, Danton came to with a moan and began struggling with his bonds. He was extremely pale. Leah realized he needed to feed and therefore was in a weakened state. She also wondered if using his powers had drained him.

Despite the fact that he had the blood thirst, there was hope for Danton because he still had his soul—she could sense its presence through the emotions that seemed to be awakening along with the man.

"What the hell?"

Relieved that he seemed to be all right despite the fear and anxiety emanating from him, Leah said, "Don't fight, please. You might hurt yourself."

"What do you care?" Danton struggled harder. "You chased me down like an animal."

"Then you shouldn't have run," Scott said. "You took possession of something that's too dangerous to be out on the streets—"

Leah stopped Scott from going on by placing her hand on his thigh and squeezing. Hard.

When Scott took his eyes off the road to glance at her, she gave him a look, silently asking him to stay out of this. Now his irritation battered her as well. She didn't break the gaze. Better that he leave Danton to her. Better for everyone if she could talk Danton into doing what they wanted. Finally, she felt him step down.

In the backseat, their prisoner was exhausting himself trying to get free. "Why can't I get out of these damn things?"

"Relax, please. You can't fight gold—the cuffs are lined with a gold alloy." Leah ignored Scott's fierce, disapproving glare. If she wanted Danton's cooperation, she had to be truthful with him. "We know what happened to you, Danton. What Rebecca did—"

"Leave my sister out of this."

"All right. Then let's talk about you. That's what we want to do is talk. To find out exactly what changes you've gone through."

He slumped against the backseat, saying, "I'm not telling you anything."

"Then you'll rot in a jail cell until you do."

"Scott, please," Leah said, irritated. "Let me handle this."

Danton asked, "What makes you think you can handle me?"

"What I meant is that I don't like violence. Or threats. I prefer a more reasonable path. And I don't think you've done anything wrong, Danton. I think you're Andre's victim, one of many, and I want to help you if I can."

"There are more like me?"

"There are. We want to help them, too. We'll do our best to work with you . . . but you have to cooperate with us."

She only hoped that Harriman would back her and treat Danton with respect.

Danton didn't respond, but he calmed down a bit. Leah felt his anger and anxiety levels lower, though she was left feeling a throbbing fear. Who could blame him? His whole life had turned upside down, something he hadn't asked for, and now he was trussed up like a criminal.

"I understand how you feel," she said.

"The hell you do."

"Fearful . . . angry . . . hopeless. You don't know why this happened to you or what you can do to change it. I understand because I was Andre's victim as well."

His face narrowed in suspicion. "I would know if you were like me."

"I survived his attack with only this to show for it." She let him see the scar on her palm where Andre's ring had branded her. "My father and brother weren't so lucky—Andre slaughtered them. So I understand your feelings of loss and grief." Thinking about how she'd lost even her memories of her loved ones, Leah felt a catch in her voice. "You never get over it, Danton. You think you will, but you don't. You just learn to live with it somehow."

Leah sensed Danton's fear and anger fade as a softer emotion added to the mix. Sorrow for her loss? Or his own? Fearing his reaction if she brought up Rebecca again, she waited to see if he would do so.

But it seemed she'd given him a lot to think about. He settled back as best he could and lapsed into silence.

She checked on him a few times—each time he seemed paler, weaker. He definitely needed to feed.

When they arrived at the base, medics were waiting—Scott having called ahead. Without releasing Danton from his bonds, they lifted him onto a stretcher.

A medic immediately checked him over. "His vitals are okay. We'll bring him to the infirmary to check him out further."

Leah gave Danton a worried look and touched his shoulder. His energy was faint, and she was barely getting a read on his emotions. "He's very weak, maybe ill. Give him blood right away," she told the medic. Catching Danton's gaze, she held it. "It's going to be all right."

The medics wheeled Danton away.

Scott didn't say anything. His jaw tightened, and he got that distant look in his eyes again, intensified when a uniformed soldier stopped in front of them and saluted.

"Captain Boulder . . . Ms. Maguire . . . this way, please."

The young soldier—no more than a boy, really—escorted them down several levels to the control room where they'd first connected with Colonel Harriman when he took over Major Ackart's command. The monitors were on, but the room was empty.

Scott said, "I thought Colonel Harriman wanted to see us right away."

"He does, sir. He had to check on a situation, but

he said he wouldn't be long and to wait for him here."

The soldier saluted Scott, then left the room.

"I wonder what kind of situation," Leah murmured.

"Considering the things they've been doing in this place, who the hell knows?"

Scott's expression darkened as he studied the various monitors, each showing a different cell in the complex, each home to another experiment gone wrong. His horror transferred to Leah, and she drew physically closer, took his hand, and turned his attention away from the tragedies locked up underground and pulled his focus to her. She gazed into his amber eyes, and though he tried to close himself off from her, she wouldn't let him look away.

Now that Scott had come down from the chase after Danton, under her close scrutiny his layers of self-protection peeled away like an onion skin. Leah sensed a panoply of emotions warring with one another, most strongly his mental weariness with the burden he carried. Though Scott had talked about wanting to walk away from the military—he'd had enough of death and destruction for a lifetime—his sense of responsibility was too ingrained, too great for him to do anything but stay on and continue the fight.

But wasn't the fight over with Danton's capture?

"Maybe now is the time," she said softly.

"For what?"

"For you to walk away. We have Danton. The threat is contained."

"How did you know what I was thinking?"

"Because we have a connection that goes deep," Leah said, pressing his hand over her heart.

He scowled and tried to remove his hand, but she refused to let go. "But you aren't like me," he said, his jaw clenched. "I wouldn't want you to be with Andre's blood running through me."

She felt that blood running through his hand, transferring through her breast to the rest of her. That blood poisoned everything it touched, but she wasn't going to let it poison her relationship with Scott.

"Don't lock me out."

"I just want to keep you safe, Leah."

"As I do you," she said. "You're part of me, and no matter what happens, that will never change." Swallowing with difficulty, she did her best to keep her voice even. "Everyone needs someone, Scott, even you. Don't push me away when we're stronger together."

His expression softened, and he pulled her hard into him, trapping their hands together between their bodies. Leah ached for more, to get even closer, flesh whispering against flesh.

"I only want what's best for you," he said softly.

His pulse beat fiercely against her heart, and Leah murmured, "*You're* what's best for me."

With a groan, Scott lost his fight for control and kissed her. The touch of his lips, the exploration of his tongue, brought back a flood of memories . . . a flood of desire. His hand shifted, cupped her breast, and the tip pebbled with need. Every inch of her burned for him, and if they weren't on base . . .

But they were.

Tearing herself from the connection, Leah pulled

back with a frustrated gasp. Pulse pounding so hard that its rush filled her head with sweet sound, she didn't say anything. Neither did Scott. Raw desire cut through him, evident in his expression. In his aggressive stance. She knew he wanted her as much as she did him, no matter what he said. They *would* be together again, Leah thought. Soon. She would simply have to be patient.

The control room door opened and Colonel Harriman walked in, and Scott stood at attention.

"Good job, both of you," Harriman said. "You make quite a team." He directed the next at Scott. "The hostile has been secured in your old cell. I had the door fixed while you were gone."

"He did get blood, right?" Leah asked anxiously.

"We are civilized, Ms. Maguire. Of course his needs were met, disgusting as they are."

Leah felt Scott tense as she asked, "What are you going to do with Danton?"

"Keep him locked up, at least until BB perfects that cure. The gold alloy should keep him in the cell."

Heat rose to Leah's cheeks, and she kept her voice even with difficulty. "Danton didn't do anything wrong to be locked up like a criminal. You could try treating him like a decent human being, ask him to cooperate."

"He isn't human anymore. He has Andre's powers. At least some of them." Harriman faced the monitors. "We won't know to what extent until he's been tested."

Scott related to Danton in a way that Harriman couldn't understand, both being recipients of powers they hadn't asked for. Leah locked gazes with him . . .

could practically hear his thoughts . . . his worry about his being inhuman and therefore a danger to everyone he was close to . . . a danger to her.

Furtively, she touched the side of his hand and mentally willed him to believe in himself, to believe in them.

It took a moment, but finally he relaxed and said, "Colonel, Danton may indeed be dangerous, but we don't know that he chose what happened to him. I ask that you treat him like a human being."

"We can't take any chances," Harriman said.

Leah spoke up. "Danton hates me for what happened to his sister. He could easily have killed me, hurt or killed Scott, but he didn't do either."

"He went straight through me," Scott said.

"In trying to get away from you—"

"Whoa, back up." Harriman aimed a piercing gaze at Scott. "What do you mean he went *through* you?"

"Danton has a new power that I've never seen before. We had him trapped on a streetcar, and he got away by walking through a wall . . . and then, in the chase, he ran right through *me*."

A fact that Scott hadn't shared with her, Leah realized as the colonel picked up a phone and punched in a code. She and Scott were partners. Why hadn't he told her what Danton had done to him? Undoubtedly his idea of keeping her safe.

On the phone, Harriman said, "Station a guard outside the new hostile's cell immediately. Make sure the guard is armed with gold bullets. And should there be any disturbance, alert me immediately."

"Don't do this, Colonel," Leah said the second he

set down the phone. "Don't treat Danton as though he's a criminal. Give me a chance to talk to him—"

"That can wait," Harriman said. "We may have a more pressing problem, the reason I called the two of you back."

"Which would be?" Scott asked.

"One of the early volunteers—who unfortunately went insane—is exhibiting unusual behavior, even for her. We need to know what it means."

Harriman turned back to the bank of monitors and pressed a couple of buttons that brought up a digital video recording of a woman with curly blond hair who paced her cell like an animal in a cage.

"*Of course I want to be free,*" she said, as if she were talking directly to someone.

She seemed to be listening for a moment. Then she made a sharp sound of protest and wrapped her arms around her head even as she turned toward the camera.

Even so, Leah made out something of what she was saying.

"*I want more than anything to leave this place behind.*" She muttered something indistinguishable, then lowered her arms and smiled. "*Your touch is so familiar. . . . Have we met before, Josef Neumann?*"

Harriman turned down the sound. "She's been talking like this for hours, like she's not alone. With everything else that's been going on, she might not be. Maybe there's an invisible hostile in the room with her."

But fixated on the sight before her, Leah barely heard him as she gasped, "It's Major Wallas Ackart!"

Next to her, Scott jerked and protested, "Ackart is

fucking dead." He turned to Harriman. "You took over her command."

"Her name *is* Ackart," Harriman agreed. "*Rachel* Ackart."

"Major Ackart's twin?" Leah asked.

Harriman hesitated only a second before saying, "Try her grandmother."

"But that's impossible." Leah couldn't take her eyes off the monitor. "This woman is in her thirties. What you're suggesting . . . that would make her nearly a hundred years old."

"Ninety-three, to be exact. She's been part of our clandestine scientific unit since she was hired." Harriman picked up a thick accordion-pleated folder and handed it to Scott. "Her history with the military."

But Leah was still staring at the image on the monitor, at the woman who looked fit as an athlete. A young athlete without wrinkles.

"Can I see her? In person, I mean." Where she could read this Rachel's emotions.

"No way. Not until we figure out what's going on. It could be too dangerous. Rachel was always a sociopath—you'll find early evaluations in her records—but that played to her role in working for the military. And she was in control. Rachel's mind was further impaired during the experiment."

"Impaired how?" Leah asked.

"Not only does Rachel have this psychic blast power—telekinesis, I guess you call it—but she lost all normal control. Probably most people have gotten so angry at one time or other that they want to kill someone. But a moral compass—or fear of reprisal— stops them. Not her, not anymore. She had a heated argument with one of the techs trying to hook her up to a test, and the next thing we knew, the tech was dead. And Rachel felt she was justified. So she's been given heavy meds ever since to keep her under control. Now I've increased security, stationed a guard outside her door 24/7. You go through her files, watch the recording. All the recordings, if you need to."

"To what end?" Leah asked. "I can get nothing of her emotions through an electronic recording." No more than she could get memories from the recordings she herself had made mere days ago.

"See what you can get," Harriman said curtly. "I'll give you time to research the woman, come up with a plan of action should it be necessary to deal with her."

Leah gaped at the colonel as he left the control room.

And then she and Scott got to work on an impossible task. She reviewed the recorded footage while he went through the dossier.

"Born in Columbus, Ohio, . . . raised in the German Village neighborhood . . . went to school at Georgetown in D.C. . . . graduated at twenty, top of her class in human science—"

"Human science?" Leah interrupted. "That sounds like she might have been a medical researcher, which makes sense considering where she ended up."

"Looks like," Scott agreed. "There's a stack of top secret docs labeled Fountain of Youth, but most of the pages have been blacked out."

"Hmm . . . a ninety-three-year-old woman who looks sixty years younger . . ."

Scott went back to reading in silence, and Leah listened to Rachel's recorded, one-sided conversation. She grew more certain Rachel really was talking to someone they couldn't hear. Not a ghost. Not in the common sense. Not here.

"Rachel worked as a biology research assistant in Virginia," Scott suddenly said. "Then, in 1942, Senator Wynn Merrill, head of the Committee on Military Affairs, recommended her for a position working on medical research for the Army, for what looks like a Black Ops unit that did advanced research to enhance the capabilities of the troops in the European theater. Some more blacked-out information here, but it looks like her work wasn't restricted to research."

"What then?"

"She was a spy and had a new identity as Gretchen Volker."

"Is there anything about her alias?"

"They wouldn't reveal sensitive information like that here."

"A spy . . . and she's been talking to someone named Josef Neumann. What if the conversation isn't one-sided?"

"What do you mean? A ghost?"

Leah shook her head. "What if Rachel Ackart can penetrate the Astral Plane?"

"What are you talking about?"

"This is only one plane of existence, Scott. Because our bodies die—"

"So you think someone's talking to her from heaven? Or is it hell?"

"Maybe neither. A different reality . . . one I took you to in the mansion."

Scott grew silent, but his resistance to the idea was strong. Leah felt waves of his discomfort. She knew that he wanted to disbelieve, but that he couldn't.

"Open your mind, Scott. You're connected to her through Andre's DNA. You may be the only one who can do it."

"Do what? What exactly are you suggesting, Leah?"

"That there might be a way to find out who she's talking to and why . . . what he wants her to do."

"How?"

"If you're willing, we can use a spell that will allow you to peer around in Rachel's subconscious. And I know exactly the object we need to do it. Major Ackart told me her grandmother gave her the caduceus she always wore. I assume she meant Rachel." Leah also remembered the major indicating her grandmother had loved foolishly. "The question is, was the caduceus retrieved from the mansion before the place was blown up?"

Chapter 7

After reviewing the dossier, Scott watched Leah move a metal chair away from the control panel and then surround it with several white candles from her bag. "Is this the only way?"

"Not the only way," Leah replied. "But a good way."

Searching through Rachel Ackart's past consciousness would mean seeing what Rachel had seen through *her* eyes, and feeling what she'd felt.

Leah's spell was powerful and would give them the information they were looking for—or at least give them a better idea about what was going on. But, man, the experience was creepy. Diving into Andre's consciousness three times before had been weird enough. But a woman?

Leah pulled the caduceus from Rachel Ackart's dossier, its metal chain scraping the cardboard of the accordion folder. Scott had expected to see blood on the chain where Andre had used it to sever Major Ackart's neck. Someone must have cleaned it.

Leah indicated the chair with a nod. "Ready?"

Scott sat. "Not really, but go ahead."

Leah took his hands in hers. Somehow her hands always seemed warm. "Remember, you'll feel some disorientation before you reach the host consciousness. And if things get too intense, your mind will automatically kick you out."

"Do we know what we're looking for?"

"Anything out of the ordinary."

"What about Josef Neumann?"

"He might play a role. Then again, he might not."

"Clear as mud." Scott smiled, and thought about pulling Leah onto his lap to take true advantage of the mood lighting. "Okay, let's do this."

Leah lit the candles and then whispered a string of words he couldn't quite hear. She finished with, "Link the memories that are now connected."

Scott reached out for the caduceus pendant swaying in her fingers. The second he made contact, he jerked, as though his body were connected to a parachute rip cord that had been pulled.

A moment later, he no longer felt the cold metal chair beneath him. He was tumbling through deep red space, like a rag doll that had been tossed carelessly across a room. His stomach flipped. This was the fourth time he'd gone through the process, and he still hadn't gotten used to the bizarre disorientation.

Leah's words faded to an echoing whisper as he continued to plummet, when suddenly it felt like he was standing on a lightly vibrating platform. He also smelled the sweet fragrance of jasmine—perfume?—as amorphous streaks of color and shadow sharpened slowly to reveal that Rachel was standing alone in a small elevator lined with polished brass and rounded, floor-to-ceiling mirrors.

Scott looked through Rachel's eyes as she examined herself in the mirrors. She looked stunning in a black silk evening gown with her full figure, pale skin,

and curled blond hair that fell around her slender
shoulders. She pursed red lips and then turned to regard the deep V in the back of the dress that revealed
the sultry curve of her spine.

It usually took a few minutes to pick up thoughts
from the host consciousness, but Scott could nevertheless sense potent vanity in Rachel as she relished
her pinup-girl looks. He searched her consciousness
for information about what her mission might be but
found nothing of value—only fragmented thoughts
that precisely validated the information in her dossier.
In fact, the validation was almost *too* precise. And
then Scott realized why.

Rachel was repressing her own experiences in favor
of the role she was about to play—a suspicion confirmed when the doors opened to reveal a wood-
paneled dining room crowded with SS officers clad in
black uniforms with red swastika armbands. They
stood with their wives—or mistresses—and grazed
on rich-smelling hors d'oeuvres while sipping cham-
pagne from crystal glasses. Now fully immersed in
her persona, Rachel strode past the officers into an
octagonal room furnished with overstuffed jade green
chairs.

Her gaze landed on a man speaking with an SS officer near a black marble fireplace. The man, who had
a hawkish face and slicked blond hair, wasn't dressed
in a military uniform but in a black tuxedo. Scott felt
Rachel's stomach flutter as she approached. "Herr
Doktor?"

The man glanced at Rachel, clearly annoyed by the
interruption, but his manner changed when he saw
that a beautiful woman had caused the infraction. He

waved away the SS officer. "May I help you, Fräulein?" Scott didn't speak German but understood every word through Rachel.

"Please excuse the interruption. Are you Dr. Josef Neumann?"

"I am."

"Pardon my impudence," Rachel said, "but I had to meet you."

Scott saw an expression cross Neumann's face similar to the one that must have crossed his own face when Leah kissed him for the first time: a blend of pleasure and disbelief that he was interacting with such a beautiful creature. "You have me at a disadvantage, my dear. You are?"

"Gretchen Volker."

Neumann took her hand and kissed it. His eyes never left hers as he did so, and Scott was surprised to feel a layer of Rachel's operational training peel away as hot emotion blossomed in her chest. The swell was one of passion coupled with surprise that Neumann would affect her in this way.

"You are an appreciator of science?" he asked.

"I'm receiving my degree in developmental biology from the University of Freiburg," she said. "I would like to devote my final year of study to the advancements you have made."

He smiled again, clearly surprised by her education and flattered by her knowledge of his work. "And you come to us how, Gretchen?"

Scott felt Rachel blush. "I-I must admit," she stammered, "that I should not be here."

"Is that so?" A large Alsatian appeared, and Neumann unconsciously let his long fingers trace through

the dog's thick coat as it passed. Scott could feel that
Rachel found the gesture intensely sexual by the sudden tingling heat between her legs.

Scott couldn't help but focus on the sensation. Liquid . . . languid . . . indirect but at the same time very
direct, like a roiling core of molten rock. Was this the
way Leah felt when they—? He stopped, angry that
he'd become distracted. *Hey, jerk, concentrate on the
matter at hand. . . .*

Rachel looked out a picture window at a sweeping
mountain view. The move was meant to be coy, but it
held an undercurrent of truth. Scott could sense that
Rachel felt giddy and taken with the man's professional acumen.

"My academic adviser received the invitation to
this party," Rachel said. "But when I heard that you
would be here, I changed his name to mine. Please
forgive me. It was wrong, I know."

"And very clever, my dear. A quality every research
assistant should have if they are to excel in our field."
Neumann glanced at the officers around him. "One
that is as much about science as it is about politics."

Just then, there was a commotion from the dining
room. As Rachel turned, Scott saw the officers snap
to attention as a man, not quite visible, made his way
through the crowd. Many of the officers cried out
"Heil" while extending their right arms in salute.

Suddenly, it all made sense to Scott . . . the SS officers, the Alsatians, the mountain view. Rachel was in
the Eagle's Nest, the Bavarian mountain home of—

"Heil Hitler!" Neumann exclaimed as a tiny man
with a flop of black hair and small, square mustache
appeared.

"Dr. Neumann," Hitler said. "I trust that your experiment is continuing apace?"

"Of course, Mein Führer."

"See to it that you do not fail me."

Neumann nodded as the man disappeared again into the crowd.

Jesus, Scott thought. He'd just seen Adolf Hitler. *The* Adolf Hitler. What the hell was going on?

"I must go," Neumann told Rachel. "But I would like you to meet me in my lab in a few days. Will you do that?" He pulled a caduceus pin from his inside jacket pocket, gently pressed it into her palm, and closed her fingers around it. "Show the guards this. They will know you received it from me."

When Neumann pressed the pin in her hand, Rachel experienced an attraction so strong it nearly distracted her from her purpose. "The Führer," she whispered. "What experiment was he talking about?"

Scott hung on the answer. . . . It could break this mystery wide open. But when Neumann moved to reply, he glared at Rachel suddenly with venom.

Not at Rachel, Scott realized. At *him.*

And then Scott felt Andre's essence lash out from Rachel's memory of Neumann. It struck him like an icy wave of poison, casting him back into the crimson abyss, where he tumbled end-over-end until he felt the control room chair slam up against him. He leaped to his feet, soaked with sweat.

"Scott? What is it?" Leah asked, taking his hands in hers.

"Worse than we thought," he said. "A hell of a lot worse."

Chapter 8

Andre Espinoza de Madrid laughed.

He would have thrown back his head while doing so if he had a head, would have clenched his fists in triumph if he had hands or, for that matter, a body. He existed only as consciousness now—the essence of his former corporeal self—and laughed as much as pure consciousness could laugh as the scene from Rachel Ackart's memory disappeared around him, dissolving into a realm of boundless white.

The realm was not quite heaven, not quite limbo, not quite hell. It was a realm that his father had described as the *Space Between*. A realm that consisted of boundless, unseen energy that connected all inert and living things, a realm that existed in conjunction with the corporeal plane yet entirely separate and distinct from it.

Andre continued to laugh, causing the gelid, gossamer tendrils of his essence to shimmer with iridescent color, streaking the pure, colorless space like oil in a mountain stream. It had felt good to strike fear in the heart of Scott Boulder—the bastard who, along with Leah Maguire, had helped instigate his death.

Andre could almost still feel the blinding agony of having the Philosopher's Stone torn from his chest. The pain had been so terrible that it had nearly crippled his ability to garner the will to escape into the Space Between. Had that happened, he would have been trapped forever by the eternal bonds of hell.

That Scott Boulder had been in the Space Between at all meant that Leah Maguire was with him. Casting the man out had been about more than petty retribution, of course. It had been imperative to keep them from uncovering his intentions. Nonetheless, Andre allowed himself the momentary satisfaction of besting them before giving thought to his next course of action. One that needed to be carefully considered since the very nature of his existence depended on it.

Andre concentrated, and a different scene began to take shape around him.

One from *his* memory this time.

Fragments of color and pattern and texture began to slowly materialize like debris from a sunken ship rising out of a white sea. And then those fragments began to flow and stitch together, the filaments reaching out for one another like strands of cobweb floating on the wind, blending and braiding to create reality, but not quite reality.

A manifestation of his desire.

The fragments flowed and connected around him, slowly at first, to create a stone floor, and then they arced overhead like soaring fireworks to create a ceiling and walls buttressed by thick wooden beams. And then the room became filled with dervishes of swirling, colored light as detail after detail was added to finally create his father's alchemical lab. At its center was a large oaken table crowded with glass retorts filled with bubbling, colored liquids and connected by spiral copper tubing. The room looked exactly as he

emembered it before fleeing Spain more than four
hundred years ago to escape agents of the Catholic
Church.

Andre's body materialized next. His pale, lean
musculature draped in brown robes, his long black
hair falling around his shoulders, and his blazing red
eyes, which beamed in the flickering, torchlit shadows. Just as he had looked at his death.

Striding alongside the table, Andre relished the
sound of his boots striking stone, the rough feel of the
oak beneath his fingertips, and the pungent, earthy
aroma of the potions boiling around him—even though
he knew the sensations were figments of his memory
as well.

Using the Space Between to create his father's lab
brought him comfort. It was also a sign of respect.
Andre was deeply thankful for the gifts his father had
given him. Papi had taught him how to become one
with the Earth so that he could harness magnetism
and lightning—natural powers that he had wielded in
lethal concert with powers granted to him by Vlad
Tepes. A vampire.

Papi had also taught him how to enter and manifest his desires within the Space Between, so that he
could use it as a staging area to reenter the corporeal
plane.

Andre could still feel the remnants of Rachel
Ackart's consciousness around him. Her essence reverberated through the walls of the lab like a desperate, wanting moan. How she wanted to escape her
earthly torments. It was this wanting that had made
his blood connection to her a powerful conduit for
manipulation.

Although Andre shared a blood connection with Scott Boulder and Danton Dumas as well, only Rachel Ackart's mind was malleable enough to be of service to him. He could look deep into her mind to see her past and know her thoughts, as confused as they might be.

Andre smiled. Manipulating her memories and love for Josef Neumann had been the right choice. Rachel was confused enough to believe that her lover could come back from the dead with her help. Perfect. He would continue to speak to her as Neumann, then, and convince her that Danton was vital both to freeing her from her prison and to bringing Josef Neumann back from the dead.

But it would not be Neumann that she helped resurrect, of course.

It would be *him*.

Because as compliant as the Space Between could be, Andre knew it was ultimately a cold place, where desires held no true meaning or depth. His rightful place was on the corporeal plane, where he could draw power from the Philosopher's Stone and continue to wage war against the Catholic Church.

Andre stopped beside a wooden stand that held his father's alchemical tome, a thick text of aged yellowed parchment, elegantly bound in worn leather. He had spent much time as a young man mastering its elemental secrets. He traced the fingers of one hand along its cracked spine as he held out his other and concentrated.

The air above his open palm shimmered as the Space Between responded to his mental request. It glistened, became opaque, and then hardened into the shape of a tiny winged staff wrapped by twin snakes.

The caduceus pin.

Rachel's conscious and subconscious had truly come alive with passion when Neumann had given it to her. Andre knew that passion would make her all the more malleable to his will—as long as he reconnected with her in a future memory using the caduceus as a guide.

Andre regarded the pin as its polished surface glinted in the torchlight. The next time he made contact with Rachel, he would manipulate her emotions and cause her to act with decisive brutality. It was time to put his plan into action.

Chapter 9

"No-o-o!"

Rachel's shout reverberated through her cell, bounced off the walls, and returned to pummel her with a sense of panic greater than her anger at being abandoned. Prisoner once more, she was alone again, surrounded only by cement block and electronic monitoring equipment.

What had happened?

She had escaped all this, but only for a while. For a short while, she'd experienced a miracle, had been reunited with the only man she'd ever loved.

Love—had it been?—had she found love in the darkness promised by the voice that had been echoing through her head for days now?

Or had it been *despite* the darkness?

Her thoughts scattered and she had trouble concentrating, trouble trying to decipher what exactly had happened to her. She remembered accepting the voice's invitation—anything to get out of here—and once more knowing the deep intrinsic pleasure of being an intelligent, beautiful woman desired by an equally worthy man.

"Josef? Where did you go?"

Closing her eyes, she grasped at bits and pieces of the past, but she couldn't hold on to them.

Time passed slowly. She didn't know how long she sat on the edge of her bunk—minutes? hours?—willing herself back to that night at the Eagle's Nest without result. Her memories still eluded her like flotsam and jetsam.

"Please . . . please, Josef . . . don't leave me alone in here."

A tingling sensation spread through her, and her mind seemed to clear a bit. She yearned for memories to take her away from the horrible reality of her existence. Concentrating, she finally—finally—managed to dispel the cold bleakness of her cell. . . .

Deep green conifers towered skyward, casting a darkish glow along the path on their late afternoon hike through the Black Forest. Josef had taken them away from the war for a few days, and her spirit felt light even in the darkest reaches of the woods. The density of pine trees and the nearby mountains cast their shadows over the valleys so that the area looked black even from a distance.

An owl hooted, making Rachel start.

"You're not afraid, are you?" Josef asked, squeezing her hand.

Her heart was pounding, but she laughed. "These woods are said to be haunted by werewolves, sorcerers, witches, and even the Devil himself." The sun had already set, their surroundings getting darker, sparking her imagination. "Where are they?"

"Your fascination with the occult will get you into trouble one day."

Josef led her up a steep, rock-strewn path, where he pulled her to him for a fast kiss before pressing on. He might be her enemy and they might be in the middle of a horrific war, but there were many ways to accomplish a mission.

Still, Josef got to her like no man ever had.

How had this happened? She who used men to get what she wanted normally did so without emotion. What had happened to the calculating undercover agent who had approached SS Storm Command Leader Josef Neumann to learn the scientific discoveries he kept secret?

Josef had let her into his confidence, had even allowed her to work on the experiment. Not that she'd gotten a look at the actual formula. Yet. She would, of course, complete her mission by making Josef her sexual slave this weekend.

Suddenly, the quiet was broken by the drone of warplanes overhead. Looking up, Rachel could see their silhouettes dance along the treetops. The sky had already grown dark.

"Messerschmitts," Josef said. "The Luftwaffe is sending out the night fighters. We should get back to the hotel, where we'll be safe. . . ."

His voice faded off as did his image, and no matter how hard she tried, Rachel couldn't hold on to them. She stared once more at the gray of her cell walls, the rest of the memory eluding her. She couldn't resurrect it.

Her pulse sped up, and anger took hold of her. She'd lost herself to the military, and they'd taken away everything. Her freedom. Even her memories by means of the drugs used to control her.

Fury made the blood rush through her veins, through her head, clearing away some of the fog. Wanting to banish the confusion from her thoughts—

the drugs didn't seem to be working with the same ef-
ficiency as they once had—she turned her attention to
the electronic monitors that helped keep her prisoner.
They began to rattle and dance along the floor, and
when she narrowed her focus even more, tried to
make them fly across the cell, they merely tipped over
and crashed to the floor in response.

Maybe if she kept practicing—maybe if she could
conjure more memories—she could find a way to
fight herself out of this hole.

Her mind settled and, working at it for a while, she
was finally able to go back to that romantic trip in the
middle of the war, to hang on to a wavering image of
Josef's face once more. . . .

His smile was seductive, the glint in his eyes knowing as he stood waiting for her to join him at the entrance to what looked like a temple, a dome with
elaborate frescoes above a central bathing pool.
Friedrichsbad was a spa in Baden-Baden, a town with
thermal springs. The warm water would soothe their
aching muscles from the earlier hike.

At the edge of the Black Forest, Baden-Baden had
so far survived the war, but even now Rachel could
hear the constant pummel of bombing in the distance
and wondered what strategic points were being eradicated and whether or not the Luftwaffe night fighters
would take down more American planes.

She was getting closer to her target, making him
more susceptible to her. More trusting of her. She'd
never had any difficulty using her body to get what
she wanted. She began shedding her clothing, gently
touched the caduceus pinned to her blouse and felt

her stomach roll and her chest tighten before she let the garment slip from her fingers.

Already nude, as was required by the spa, Josef backed toward the water. "Come join me."

He was ready for her, his penis turgid. Men were so easy. Heat shimmered along her flesh as she took the first step toward him . . .

. . . only to have the image before her disappear.

And to have cold flash through her mind and limbs alike at his loss.

"Come back, Josef!"

"It is you who must come to me."

The voice again . . . familiar but edged with a darkness that knifed through her. What did that mean? Was it Josef or not?

Her head was clearer now, as though the memory burned away some of the fog, so Rachel tried concentrating again. Although she got flashes of marble-smooth flesh, she couldn't see the whole as she had for those few seconds. Frustration accelerated through her, and she tried putting a fist through the wall, leaving another pockmark to taunt her.

"Let me back in," she demanded, on some level knowing she couldn't do this alone.

But she *was* alone . . . had been for eleven months, two weeks, four days . . . or was it five now? She swept her gaze over the marks she'd cut into the wall to keep track, but she didn't have the heart to count them.

"If you want to be with me, then you must escape."

"I've tried."

"Someone in the prison complex can help you,"

came the chillingly seductive voice that she would swear belonged to Josef. *"Danton Dumas."*

"I don't know any Danton, but if he can do it, then tell him to get me out of here."

"You must find him and tell him yourself. You and he are connected through blood and therefore linked psychically. He can take you through these walls to the outside. You can use the power of your mind to prevent anyone from getting in your way."

Rachel shook her head. She didn't trust the voice. Its darkness pierced her once more. She didn't trust her own abilities either.

"It won't work," she muttered as she paced, the circular pattern growing smaller and tighter with each round. "Nothing works. Nothing."

Certainly not her attempts to bring Josef back. No matter how hard she tried, she simply couldn't do it. Little blips of memory would tease and then evade her. Eagle's Nest . . . the laboratory where they worked together . . . Friedrichsbad . . . a bunker being bombed . . . She couldn't make any memory take full shape in her seething mind.

Insane . . . She didn't want to believe it . . . but she was hearing things . . . imagining things that weren't real. . . .

What would it hurt to give over to the voice again . . . maybe rediscover a few moments of happiness . . . ?

At least she wouldn't be alone.

Frustrated and angry and at her wits' end—yes, perhaps she was insane—Rachel gave over to the voice. To the darkness that dwelled inside her being

as well as inside her head. She would do anything . . .
be anything . . . to be free and with Josef again.

"Tell me what to do."

*"Think your way through the physical barriers and
appeal to Danton Dumas. Convince him you are a
woman unjustly jailed and in need of his help."*

At least she wouldn't have to pretend. Being jailed
for sacrificing herself for her country *was* unjust, and
she desperately needed help to get free. She'd always
been able to manipulate men to do her bidding.

But before she could do as the voice demanded, her
cell door opened. A white-coated medic backed by an
armed guard entered.

"What did you do to this equipment?" he asked,
picking up a shattered monitor.

Not one to hesitate at an opportunity, Rachel
began concentrating. "The same thing I'm going to
do to you to get out of here."

The anger she needed was already primed. She narrowed her focus, and a second later, the equipment
flew up into the medic's head. Bits of flesh and brain
splattered the cell walls and the guard behind him.

The soldier squawked and aimed his rifle at her, but
he fumbled with the trigger.

Rachel narrowed her gaze on him. "Your turn."

Chapter 10

Andre Espinoza de Madrid was back to haunt them, Leah realized, an icy coldness enveloping her as Scott told her what he had experienced via her spell.

They might have destroyed the vampire's body, but apparently Andre's consciousness had been strong enough to survive. For all intents and purposes, the Astral Plane was now his home. But not for long, she was certain—not if he could help it. The knowledge that they weren't done with Andre shuddered through her, and she fisted the caduceus that had been their link to the vampire via Rachel Ackart.

"Andre's trying to find a way back," she told Scott, her voice as stiff as her limbs.

"How?"

"I'm not sure. But he's obviously trying to manipulate Rachel somehow."

"You think he wants to take over her body?"

"He wants to use her, that's for certain." She white-knuckled the metal in her hand.

"Hey, are you okay?"

Scott gently pried open her fist and took the caduceus from her. Originally, the medical symbol had been a pin owned by Josef Neumann. Apparently, Rachel Ackart had added a chain so she could wear it as a necklace. The pin had opened and had nicked

Leah's flesh. Droplets of blood bubbled up from her palm and became the sudden focus of Scott's attention.

She could feel his heart speed up, as did the waves of hunger and pain that swept from him through her. It took all her strength not to double up when her intestines suddenly felt as if they were being ripped by shards of glass. Moments like this made her wish she could better control her empathic ability, which was especially strong with Scott.

She fell victim to every dark, terrible emotion roiling through him.

He wanted to feed . . . on her.

Though Leah's instincts told her to pull her hand from his—to break the painful, seductive connection—her love for Scott was greater than her fear of what he could become, and she wouldn't let him think she didn't trust him. So instead of pulling free and turning away from him, she stepped in closer, ran her fingers along his cheek, and trapped his amber gaze with her own.

"It's all right, Scott. You can fight it. This will pass."

Confusion danced in his eyes and through his essence. She could sense him failing to deny the blood hunger. She had to give him something equally powerful to use.

"Stay with me, Scott." She brushed her lips over his mouth, flicked her tongue against his, nipped his lip—all in hopes that the remembrance of his intimate connection to her would serve him as an effective weapon. Something good to combat evil. "You're strong. You're in command."

A choked sound escaped Scott, and he pulled her against him. He was aroused, his muscles trembling with twin needs. She could see the fight altering his expression and flickering in his eyes so they seemed bright with fever.

Her heart raced with fear.

Or was it desire?

The two warred within her even as desire and addiction warred within him. She was playing a dangerous game, and she knew it. Scott could choose to sate both hungers—feed on her while taking her—and then who would save *her* soul?

Unwilling to believe Scott would hurt her that way, Leah kissed him again, this time clinging to him, wrapping herself around him, wanting with all her heart to be the strength he needed to overcome the bloodlust. She sensed the fight in him subsiding a little, and then a little more even before he pushed her away.

Relief that it had worked washed through Leah.

When Scott didn't say anything, she collected the candles she'd set out for the spell after blowing out the flames. He brushed her face with a soft, deep look, but only for a moment. Then he narrowed his gaze and turned away from her, and she knew he was trying to keep his distance to protect her.

"Sometimes you just have to believe that things will work out for the good, Scott. Believe in yourself. And in us."

His expression tightened. "Other than working together, there is no us."

Not unexpected but still difficult to hear, his words tore another hole in her heart. Leah knew Scott was being ridiculously noble to protect her, but she didn't have the energy to argue with him. Her bigger worry was that if BB didn't come up with a cure, Scott might never change his mind, shattering any hope she might have of a future for them.

Sucking in a deep breath, Leah fought the chill that overtook her and replaced the candles in her bag. Her hands shook slightly, and she hid them so he wouldn't know how badly his rejection had hurt her. She wished Scott could accept his life changes. Until he did, she could talk herself silly and not get through to him.

Scott cleared his throat. "So how do we handle this? Andre's influence over Rachel, that is?"

A quick turnabout. And though he was speaking to her, he was steadfastly refusing to meet her gaze. Instead, he focused his attention on the equipment console, started fooling with the computer, going through the files.

"Obviously, we can't reason with Rachel. We have to keep Andre away from Rachel so he can't influence her."

"A cell lined with gold alloy?"

Leah shook her head. "He's not corporeal. Gold won't stop him from getting inside her mind. Maybe the only thing that can is magic."

"Can you do it?" He finally looked at her. Discomfort now radiated from him. "Create a spell to keep him out or negate his influence over her?"

Unsure, Leah shrugged. "I can try."

"Good. Maybe you can add something to keep her from escaping if anything goes wrong." Tapping a computer link, he brought up a prison schematic on one of the monitors. "We're here." He pointed, then shifted his finger down the corridor. "Rachel's here now." Then went to the corridor on the next level down. "And we'll move her to this available cell near Danton's. You can find it yourself, right? Or maybe I should have a guard go with you."

But not him. Leah shook her head. "Not necessary. It shouldn't take me long."

"I'll leave you to it, then." Scott opened the control room door and indicated she should precede him. "I need to check on BB's progress with the cure and update Harriman on what we've learned. When you're done, why don't you go back to the motel, get some rest. Nothing else for you to do here anyway," he added, indicating she would be in the way.

"Got it," she muttered, picking up her bag of tricks and hurrying out the door.

Scott wanted her out of the way, wanted to remove temptation from his path.

Was he really going to leave it like this between them—so impersonal and awkward?

Apparently so, Leah realized, as without another word, Scott strode off in the opposite direction. He didn't so much as look back at her. Determination or guilt? she wondered, staring after him until he turned the corner. Sighing, she headed for the stairwell.

About to take the staircase down a level, she stopped. Before casting a spell to keep Andre out of Rachel's mind, it would be helpful to talk to the woman, to feel the energy radiating from her, see how aware she was of what was happening to her. Harriman should have let her do that earlier at her request rather than confining her to viewing recorded tapes.

Leah figured her empathic ability might help her hook onto something in Rachel she could use in casting her spell. Harriman might not like it, but he didn't have to know until after the fact. Nor Scott.

Still, Leah wouldn't be foolish. She wouldn't go in alone. But as she headed down the corridor, she didn't see that guard Harriman had told them about outside Rachel Ackart's door. So what was going on?

Getting closer, Leah saw a booted foot sticking out from the room into the corridor. Her breath caught in her throat as she realized the door was open. Was Rachel in her cell? Quietly, Leah crossed to the other side of the hall and crept just close enough to see through the doorway.

Nothing moving. No Rachel. The insane woman had escaped.

Only then, only when she was certain there was no immediate danger for her, did she take a better look at what Rachel had left behind.

"Dear God . . . ," she breathed.

What was left of the guard lay sprawled face forward . . . or would have been if he still had a face. Or a head, for that matter.

The guard's torso crossed that of a body wearing a white lab coat. He hadn't fared much better. Bits and pieces of viscous matter and blood were sprayed around the room. It seemed as if the equipment had attacked them, Leah thought, remembering Rachel supposedly had some kind of psychic blast at her command. . . .

Leah's stomach tightened and churned, and her head went unbearably light. She'd seen horror like this before, compliments of Andre, but the familiarity

dn't make the sight easier to bear. Her stomach
emptied—she barely had time to bend over first.

Afterward, wiping her arm across her mouth, Leah
looked for the nearest alarm station to call for help
and spotted one at the end of the hallway.

A raucous din stopped her from moving—raised
voices . . . glass breaking . . . a horrific scream. . . .

Realizing the sounds were coming closer, Leah
acted on pure instinct, headed for the nearest door
that wasn't the one to Rachel's cell and opened it. Another stairwell. When a body came flying down the
corridor, she didn't hesitate but stepped through the
doorway and viewed the unfolding scene through
the small rectangular window set into the steel panel.

A woman coming down the hall oozed blood from
every orifice. Following, a man had eyes that were
pure white. And yet another's muscles—the body
parts she could see—were ruptured, leaving the man
covered with seeping wounds.

Her heart raced and she tried to calm it, to make
it—and her—less of a target for bloodthirsty vampires. No one had to tell her that these were the initial
volunteers—the experimental rejects—escaped from
their cells.

"Guards!" one of the escapees yelled. "Let's eat!"

The screaming horde raced forward to do battle.

Throat closing, barely breathing, Leah hunkered
back against the wall, making herself as small as she
could lest one of the monsters glance through the
window into the stairwell and find her.

Chapter 11

After changing into black fatigues, Scott walked down the hallway leading to Danton's cell, pausing only to slide the inhaler between his lips. He sucked in as he triggered the device, feeling the thick, acrid spray slide down his throat and penetrate his lungs. After a few moments, he felt the wailing need to feast on human blood subside to a low, churning hum.

He shook his head disgustedly as he swapped out the cartridge and then dropped the inhaler back into his pocket. *I'm a danger to everyone around me,* he thought. *Once this mission is over, I'm going to lock myself in solitary and throw away the key until BB can find a cure.*

Sometimes it felt like Leah had some sort of magical influence over him. Her kiss had minimized the blood thirst more quickly and completely than the inhaler ever had. Hell, BB should try to bottle Leah's essence, make a cure out of that. It'd be a lot more pleasant than the skunk spray he had to suck down every few hours.

But Leah wouldn't be there every time he fell prey to the terrible urge. Nor could he always rely on the inhaler. Under fire, there was little chance he could consistently administer the dose necessary to keep from becoming a threat to friend as well as foe. Th

nly option would be to take himself out of the fight
s soon as he could.

Scott turned a corner to find Colonel Harriman in
ront of Danton's cell. White stood nearby and looked
t Scott impassively.

Harriman nodded in greeting, but Scott knew the
nan well enough to know he would have something
) say about the day's assignment.

"How's our prisoner?" Scott asked.

"Still down for the count," Harriman said. "BB
hought it best to dose him with anesthetic gas until
ve learned the true extent of his powers."

Scott nodded and peered through the cell door's
hick window. Danton was curled in a fetal position
n a bunk against the far wall. His chest rose and
ipped in his sleep. Scott knew the feeling of being
rapped all too well. As a prisoner of war in the past,
nd now as a prisoner to what his body had become—
nd was still becoming.

"What did you learn about Rachel Ackart?" Harri-
nan asked.

"She could be under an outside influence."

"From whom?"

Scott faced him. "Andre Espinoza. He might be
rying to manipulate her from beyond the grave. I
now that may sound incredible, but Leah believes
's true. So do I."

Harriman frowned. "No more incredible than
vhat we've seen so far. Come this way."

Harriman ushered Scott down a short hallway into
control room while White stood post outside. The
oom held computer equipment and monitors that
ictured the different cells and their inhabitants, pre-

sumably those on this particular wing. One patient
pounded on his door while another huddled on the
floor and another lay on his bunk with IV tubes
connected to points on his arms, legs, and throat. The
uppermost screen held the image of Danton, who
continued to sleep.

Harriman excused the three techs within the control room and closed the door after they left. "Do you
have any idea what Andre might be after?"

"Possibly the Philosopher's Stone. He might be
able to use it to come back from the dead."

"We should move Rachel to a more secure location."

"My thinking exactly. In the meantime, we can
hold her in a cell that Leah is now preparing to resist
Andre's magic." Scott paused. "It's also a compelling
reason to destroy the Stone once we find it."

"Nice try, son." Harriman smirked. "But we'll do
no such thing."

"I've seen the power of the Stone firsthand, Colonel. In the wrong hands, it's a terrible weapon."

"Think about how it could be used in the right
hands, then." Harriman went to a file cabinet and
pulled out several thick manila folders, which he
dropped with a thud onto a table.

"What are these?" Scott asked.

"I wanted to show you the lengths to which we've
already gone to find the Stone. We've been searching
for a long time, Scott. In countries all over the world.
We can't stop now that we're so close."

"We're better off letting the Stone stay lost. No one
should have power over it."

Harriman looked at him with incredulity, and Scott was surprised at how much the disapproval stung. It harkened back to the shame he'd felt as a child in the presence of his dictatorial father.

"Our duty isn't to judge," Harriman said. "It's to protect our country the best way we know how. Think about it, Scott. The Stone could be used to develop extraordinary capabilities for our military and civilian populations. Imagine soldiers who can't die, portals to other dimensions, contact with alien life-forms and advanced technology."

"How can you be sure the Philosopher's Stone is the key to all that? It might offer nothing more than giving Andre renewed life."

"You said yourself that Andre Espinoza is trying to manipulate Rachel Ackart from a different plane of existence. If the Stone can access one plane, why not two or three? Or hundreds? The possibilities could be more wondrous than we think, perhaps even more wondrous than we're capable of thinking."

"Or more horrible than we can imagine."

"Can we really afford to let one prisoner keep us from exploring the opportunity?"

Scott followed Harriman's gaze to Danton and then looked at the men on the other monitors. These were soldiers he'd once trained or served with—all reduced to wretched, deformed creatures. Was that what he had to look forward to as well? "The opportunities you've explored so far don't seem to be paying off very well for some."

"Is that what your hesitation is about?" Harriman asked. "Risk?"

"Unacceptable risk," Scott corrected.

"I see," Harriman said, and reorganized the scattered folders into a stack. "Let's take your missio
today. It took you and Ms. Maguire more than thre
hours to capture the suspect."

Scott was thrown by the apparent non sequitu
"What does that have to do with anything?"

"It would have taken far less time if you'd use
your powers," Harriman replied. "If you'd disre
garded your notion about 'unnecessary risk.' "

Scott felt ambushed by Harriman for the secon
time that day. "That may be, Colonel, but you can
deny what I've become. Or what might happen if I'r
not careful."

"I know you've been thrown for a loop by wha
Andre did to you," Harriman said, gathering up th
folders and returning them to the file cabinet. "But
want you to use that fear to your advantage. Not hi:
Remember, it's not the weapon that matters. It's th
man who wields the weapon."

"It's a little different when the man *is* the weapon.

Harriman put his hand on Scott's shoulder in a ges
ture of peace as he led him from the control room
The staff filed back in as White fell into step behin
them.

"Our differences aside, Scott, I still have faith i
you. Always have. That's why I'm granting you fu
autonomy during these operations. You may cor
tinue to act as field conditions dictate, and as you se
fit. I refuse to handicap you by playing armchair gen
eral. Or colonel, as the case may be."

Scott nodded but knew the gesture was not entirel
altruistic. Autonomy would afford him a better chanc
of success, but it would also insulate Harriman fror

fallout if things went bad. In addition, there was no such thing as true autonomy in the military. Everyone answered to someone. The only variable was the length of the leash.

As they headed back to Danton's cell, Scott wondered if Harriman planned to pursue the Stone no matter what the cost. Scott wanted to believe that Harriman was the same man he'd always known, the father figure who'd helped him surpass physical and psychological limits during training at Fort Bragg that went far beyond what he would have defined for himself.

"What now?" Scott asked.

"We wake Danton and interrogate him as to the whereabouts of—"

Harriman was interrupted by a cry from behind. They whirled to see a woman from the control room rushing toward them, her long white coat flapping behind like a cape.

"They're out. . . . They're all out . . ." the woman panted, and then slumped forward.

Scott caught her by the shoulders and gently guided her to the floor. Her pupils were dilated, and her skin was clammy. Shock.

"Stay with her," Scott told White, and then ran for the control room with Harriman close behind. When they burst through the door, the other staff members were gone.

Scott saw why when he looked up at the monitors. All the cells were empty, including Danton's.

Chapter 12

Danton crept quickly down the hallway.

Flat-screen monitors set into the steel walls around him flashed LOCKDOWN in red letters while a klaxon sounded, plangent and harsh. There was another noise, too. Distant, barely discernible. Something that sounded like . . . growls? Screams?

He fought growing panic as he headed away from the terrible noises.

Just two hours earlier, he'd been at the mercy of grim-faced soldiers who had transfused him with blood. And now . . . he had no idea how or why his cell door had opened. And frankly, he didn't care. All that mattered was getting out of this place.

He fully expected to run into guards, staff, or other patients, but the hallways were deserted. He passed several rooms, also with open doors. All were empty.

Danton continued forward, not knowing where he was or where to go, stomach in knots. As he traveled, he slid a palm along the cold wall, unconsciously allowing his fingertips to sink through the smooth surface as if it were water instead of steel.

Sure, he could pass through the prison walls, then try to climb up through the earth to reach the surface. But he would be taking a huge risk. He was at least fifty feet underground, judging from the time he'd spent in the elevator to reach this level. Passing through solid matter was like scuba diving in a pitch-black ocean. It was easy enough to make progress, but one wrong turn could spell disaster. Despite the blood transfusion, he still felt weak, and God forbid he lose focus while passing through a vein of bedrock. No, he'd have to get closer to the surface before trying to walk his way out.

He also felt like he couldn't leave before he found Leah Maguire. If there was anyone who could help him figure out his role in this mess and, more important, become human again, it was probably her. She'd been kind to him in the Humvee—unlike the soldier who'd chased him down—and seemed sincere in her desire to make things right. Maybe he was going on instinct, but he believed Leah when she'd explained that her role in Rebecca's death had been an accident.

He felt a swell of grief as Rebecca's face shimmered through his memory—her café-au-lait skin, long braids, and piercing dark eyes, which had held contempt for most people but compassion and love for him.

Danton shook his head as tears flowed down his cheeks, then froze suddenly.

In front of him lay a woman's severed arm in a pool of blood. He'd been so lost in his thoughts that he'd almost stumbled over it. Worse, the limb looked as though it had been chewed through.

Danton stared in disbelief. And then panic blossomed. He had no idea what was going on, but he was right in the middle of it, right in the terrible, bloody thick of it. And then he remembered three little words—words that Lilly Fry had said to him after he'd contracted leukemia. *Panic never helps.*

He'd almost lost his mind in front of Lilly after

learning his diagnosis, but she'd gently taken his hands and urged him to breathe while smiling her everlasting smile and promising him they'd deal with it together. *Panic never helps.*

He took a deep breath, let it out slowly. *Breeeeathe. You can do this. You can get out of here.* Danton forced himself to walk around the severed arm when a rush of anger edged out his fear.

He was being held against his will when he'd done nothing wrong. He didn't even want the Philosopher's Stone; he only thought it might make him human again. But he didn't dare tell the military where it was. God only knew what they would do with him once they had it.

Danton continued on through a series of winding corridors, finding more streaks of blood but no more body parts, thank God. The klaxon finally stopped, but the growls and screams that he'd heard earlier seemed to echo all around him. He quickened his pace.

"Danton . . . Can you hear me?"

Danton nearly leaped from his skin. He whirled, searching for the woman who'd just called his name.

"Please answer me! I need your help!"

Danton looked around feverishly but saw nothing. Maybe the voice was a symptom of insanity, he thought with dread. Another side effect of consuming Andre Espinoza's blood.

And then another possibility occurred to him. Maybe it was Leah. He knew that she was a practitioner of magic as Rebecca had been. This could be telepathy—the only way to contact him during the lockdown.

The idea thrilled him, momentarily eclipsing his

fear. He could be experiencing a novel form of communication. A language all its own. Certainly the idea was no more incredible than what had already happened. He wondered what his linguistics adviser in grad school might have said if he'd proposed studying the voices he heard in his head.

"Leah?" he asked. "Is that you?"

"My name is Rachel."

Fear slammed down again. And suspicion. "I don't know any Rachel," he said, feeling like an idiot for talking to a woman he couldn't see.

"I'm a prisoner in this complex, too. I know you have the power to help me escape, Danton. Please try to find me. I'm begging you."

Danton frowned. Instead of providing answers, the woman's response only raised questions. How did she know who he was? And did she really know about his powers?

He continued down the hallway, almost jumping out of his skin when someone—some*thing*—howled in the distance. He still wanted to find Leah, but could he really leave this Rachel woman to the mercy of the military? She'd probably been detained for reasons she didn't fully understand either. Could he really leave without finding out for sure?

"Danton, are you there?"

"I'm here."

"Are you coming?"

"I . . . I don't know."

"Please, Danton."

Danton marveled again at the method of communication. He didn't hear Rachel's words as much as feel them—a series of husky syllables that vibrated against his eardrum. His face flushed. Other parts of him responded, too.

Despite his fear, he found himself wondering what she looked like. Long brown hair. Or maybe blond. Piercing blue or hazel eyes with long lashes. Full lips. Definitely full lips with a sultry voice like that . . .

He shoved the thoughts from his mind. He had to concentrate. Learning where the hell he was inside the complex would definitely help.

Danton stopped in front of a flashing monitor, took a breath, and then slid his hand through the screen. His body tingled as it always did when he passed through an object, as though he could feel the surrounding molecules brushing against his own.

When he'd pushed in his arm to the elbow, he willed his fingertips to become solid so he could manipulate the circuitry. As a kid, he'd taken apart and reassembled his mother's kitchen appliances. It was a skill that would come in useful now.

"Please don't be angry with me, Danton."

"I'm not angry. I just don't know what to do."

"You have no idea what they've done to me. Terrible things. With your help, they'll never hurt me again."

Rachel's soft voice took on a hard, wounded edge. But even as Danton felt sorry for her, he felt a nagging sense of danger that was similar to the sensation he'd felt around Andre Espinoza days ago. One that he couldn't ignore.

Using his sense of touch only, Danton located the monitor's central processor and twisted a few wires. The LOCKDOWN screen switched to an empty cell. He twisted the wires again, cycling through different images, until a schematic of the complex appeared.

Pulling his arm free, he stood back and examined the map.

The sprawling, rectangular complex was divided in two: Hospital rooms and supporting facilities such as locker rooms occupied the left half, while control rooms and research labs occupied the right. Every door on the left side of the schematic pulsed green. Open, he assumed. So there *had* to have been a breakout of some kind—and he was smack in the middle of it.

The screams and howls he'd heard . . . God only knew what the patients had done to the hospital staff. Or vice versa.

He examined the map again and saw that every hallway leading from the left side to the right side of the map ended in a pulsing red bar. Locked down.

But that made no difference to someone with his powers. Beyond the sealed doors was an elevator bank that led to the surface, and adjacent to that was a large room that looked like barracks. If Leah were still on this level, she would likely be there.

"Danton."

"I'm here, Rachel. I'm trying to find someone who can help us."

"I need you, Danton. Only you. You're the only one who can get us out of here. If you help me escape from this horrible place, I'll do anything you want. Be anything you want."

Danton's face flushed as prurient images danced through his head. He couldn't deny that he was interested. Still, he didn't know who this woman was or what she really wanted. He had to keep things in perspective.

As he moved away from the monitor, the howls behind him grew louder. He looked over his shoulder and saw shadows playing against a distant wall.

He broke into a run. Could he really leave Rachel to the mercy of these people? He could always abort the attempt if things got really bad. "Can you describe where you are?"

"Follow my voice."

"How?" he asked incredulously. "I'm hearing you inside my head."

"Follow my voice, Danton. You can do it if you try. Please hurry. They might come back any minute."

And then Danton realized he *could* follow her voice. When she spoke, there was a subtle imbalance in the way the words vibrated through him. The humming was slightly more pronounced in his right tympanic membrane.

". . . Follow my voice, Danton. . . . Follow my voice. . . ."

Almost involuntarily, he began to move east toward her and away from where the schematic had shown the barracks and elevator to be. He found himself wishing there was some way to meet this sensual mystery woman alone, free and far away from the underground complex and anyone associated with it.

And then he stopped himself, the nagging sense of danger stronger than ever. He shook his head to clear it, then started heading west. Too many things were happening at once.

He had to slow down and sort things out, or he might make an irreversible mistake.

Chapter 13

The corridor went eerily silent after the raucous battle ended.

A cautious Leah peered through the small rectangular window and made sure all was clear before leaving the stairwell. Trying to think of herself as being invisible, she slid along the wall, both hands clinging to the strap of her soft case as if it were a weapon, backtracking toward the door that would lead to the labs and offices.

Concentrating on her goal, she tried to ignore the remnants of chaos—several bodies strewn along the way and blood splashed everywhere—but her eyes filled with tears and she wanted to weep for the victims, whether they be guards or escapees. She settled for a quick prayer for their souls.

The sound of bedlam was distant now, but Leah knew the escaped patients—vampires—could return at any time.

How had they gotten loose?

Because of Rachel?

Had she used her psychic blast to escape and then freed the other scientific mistakes from their cells?

At last, Leah reached the door that separated the detainment area from the rest of the complex—laboratories and offices and sleeping quarters and control rooms. Heaving a relieved breath, she tried the latch, but the door wouldn't open. Locked. Her pulse kicked as Leah realized she was locked inside with man-made monsters. Seeing a guard she knew come through a doorway, she flat-handed the window, slapping it over and over until she got the man's attention. At first, he seemed shocked to see her, then his expression darkened, and he shook his head and indicated one of the LCD monitors set high in the hall.

Leah looked up.

On the screen, big red block letters pulsed: LOCK-DOWN. Her gaze flashed to another screen and another, all with the same message.

Lockdown? Meaning he *couldn't* open the door to her?

"No!" Leah cried, slamming her hand against the glass. Panic welled in her so strong that she feared her heart would give out. "Let me in. You know me. Let me in!"

Surely he would realize she was no danger to anyone.

But the guard shrugged and lifted his hands as if in regret and backed away.

"Please, don't leave me here."

Though he seemed torn, as if he wanted to let her in, he nevertheless shook his head, turned his back on her, and walked away.

"Noooo . . ." She pressed her forehead against the glass and waited for her cramped stomach to ease and her pulse to slow so she could think.

Scott . . . He didn't know she was still here. A

hone or an intercom . . . But where? Maybe near the
larm.

Hoping against hope that Scott was safe in the
ight part of the complex, Leah started down the cor-
idor once more only to pick up voices coming from
round the corner.

". . . don't hear nothin'."

"Let's check."

Not waiting for the response, Leah ducked into the
tairwell once more, this time tiptoeing up a level.
Maybe she could find her way out on another floor.
Or at least locate a phone or an intercom to get a
nessage to Scott. He would surely figure out a way to
get her out of there. She couldn't do this alone.

But she *was* alone.

The corridor looked clear. A scream froze her to
he spot, though she realized it could have come from
anywhere—another floor, even—so she made her way
o the opposite side of the hall, passing empty cells
and stepping over more bodies along the way. Light-
headed, she reached the end of the hallway.

No phone. And the intercom had been ripped from
he wall.

Now what?

Peering around the corner down another corridor,
she saw a set of doors standing open. The complex
was a huge maze, one she hadn't explored, so she
prayed this would afford her a way out. Cautiously
moving to the opening, she glanced inside and found
a sitting area with a couple of more doors on the
other side. A half dozen chairs were interspersed with
tables holding magazines and cans and plastic wrap-
pers.

A lounge for the guards. What about the other doors? Only one way to find out. The first opened to a small kitchen, the second to what looked like a locker room. Leah suddenly was alerted by the surge in noise that seemed to be advancing on her.

Raised voices . . .

. . . the crash of wood . . .

. . . a spine-tingling scream.

"Let's see what's in there," came a gravelly voice.

"Maybe some more blood-donor guards."

"Yeah. *Volunteers* for the greater good. Let's see how they like it."

Leah flew into the locker room, hoping for a way out on the other side. No door. The voices were coming closer. The tramp of several sets of feet told her they were entering the lounge—she could hear furniture being overturned. Another few seconds and she would be discovered.

Hide!

The toilet stalls were too obvious. Only one other place. A full-length locker in the middle of a long bank stood half open. Luckily it was empty. Luckily she was small enough to fit inside. She slid into the locker and somehow—sucking in her breath and standing as tall as she could—managed to close it. Never having been claustrophobic didn't make the waiting any easier. She felt as if she were in a coffin as the now-muffled voices came closer.

". . . want food . . . ," she heard from her hiding place. And then the sound of a fist slamming against metal. ". . . every guard who made me feel like a monster . . ."

Another slam and another—each one getting closer.

Sweat slicked Leah's back and made her slide gainst the metal locker wall. Luckily she caught herelf before banging her shoulder into one of the sides nd alerting the hunter to her position. As she did vhen meditating, she slowed her pulse, let her breath all shallow, hoping that would help hide her from the ampire.

"This fucker's locked!" came a growl followed by he earsplitting screech of metal being sheared. "Shit, othing but clothes."

"What did you expect to find in here?" a woman sked. "You think some juicy guard is hiding in one f those lockers? C'mon, let's get back to the others."

More blows against metal, right next to her now. Leah tried to let her mind go blank so she wouldn't eact. She didn't know what powers this vampire-xperiment-gone-wrong had been given—acute hearng would mean the death of her.

The metal in front of her banged so hard, the ocker trembled and Leah with it. The door twisted pen a crack so that she could see daylight and the esapee who was feeding on his own flesh. He'd opened vein in his arm and was greedily licking his blood, mearing it around his mouth.

Stomach roiling, fearing he would see her, Leah aid a quick prayer, certain she would finally be reinited with Dad and Gabe. The locker-coffin analogy eemed appropriate. As she had when she'd been witless to her family's slaughter, Leah resigned herself hat she was next and waited to die.

Only she hadn't been next then. . . .

"C'mon!" the woman insisted more loudly, and the

hunter turned away from the lockers and followed her out of the room.

And she wasn't next now.

Leah gasped and tried to breathe normally, but every part of her shook, even her breath. The space around her seemed to narrow further, but she was too terrified to move.

She didn't know how long she stayed like that. Waiting. Listening to the sounds of mayhem receding once more as the escapees sought fresh ground. Claustrophobia now held a new meaning for her, and she could think of nothing but getting someplace where she could take a normal breath.

When she finally tried to get out, however, the locker door wouldn't open. Mangled as the metal was, the catch stuck. Leah cleared her mind to quell her building anxiety. She felt around the catch. Luckily her fingers were small, and she was able to insert her forefinger into the mechanism and jiggle until the catch gave and the door popped open.

Falling out of her confinement with a sharp sob, still shaking, Leah looked down at herself and saw blood on her skin and clothes, the way she had after surviving Andre's slaughter. Her stomach cramped, and a wail built in her throat. She swallowed the sound before it could escape . . . willed her stomach to relax . . . and the blood faded and disappeared, nothing more than an illusion built on memory.

No matter what she did, she couldn't hold on to the good memories of her father and brother, but the horrific memory of seeing them slaughtered—of knowing that she was the one responsible—*that* she couldn't forget.

Standing amid destruction with potential death on the other side of the door, Leah had never felt so alone.

She was a healer, not a warrior. How was she going to get herself to safety? She'd lucked out this time, but what were the chances she could do it again?

Her heart pounded against her ribs, more screams welled up in her throat. But panic was not an option, not now, she told herself. Panic would surely get her killed.

Deep, welcome breaths of unconfined air helped Leah compose herself once more. She needed a clear mind if she wanted to get out of the detention area. And she would get out somehow. She would check another corridor, and if that led nowhere, another door. As always, she would use her intelligence to get herself through this. She would hide or use trickery or whatever else she could think of that didn't include violence to stay alive.

Hesitating at the doorway, she listened for any out-of-place sound, but the corridor seemed unnaturally quiet. A quick look assured her there was no other movement, so she ventured out, careful to make no noise.

When she turned the corner, she had to brace herself. More bodies. More deaths. Throat tight, she stared straight ahead as she made her way to the next corridor. She tried not to think about how these people died, but she knew. Her internal vision went as red as the blood splattered over the floors and walls.

And then it hit her that she was seeing red empathically—someone here was still alive.

Even as she thought it, a steel vise clamping down around her ankle made her jump.

"Aaah!"

Zapped with electric current that went from the hand around her ankle all the way up to the hair on her head, Leah struggled to free herself, to no avail.

Chapter 14

Scott ran down the corridor alongside Harriman to the complex's underground lab. The facility was nowhere near as expansive and well equipped as the main lab on the surface, but it had everything needed to test and monitor patients who had been injected with Andre's DNA. Distant howls and screams penetrated the walls around them.

"BB, what the hell is going on?" Harriman asked.

BB turned away from a table filled with instruments to face them, his shock of red hair in even greater disarray than usual. Down here, the man was ranking science officer and would be privy to any sitreps that had come in. Worry creased his usually lighthearted features. "I've got some bad news, and then I've got some news that's going to make the bad news seem downright peachy."

"Go ahead," Scott told him. BB wasn't the type to worry without cause, so if he said the situation was bad, it was probably catastrophic.

BB cleared his throat. "There's been a security breach."

"That much we know," Harriman said. "The subject we collected today has escaped."

"He's not the only one." BB walked to a computer console and tapped a few keys. The opposite wall, which was covered with thirty-six dark monitors, slowly flickered to life. "We couldn't bear to watch after a while, so we shut everything down," he said apologetically. "But as you can see, the breach is complexwide. All the patients are out, and, um, most of them aren't pleased with their extreme genetic makeovers."

When Scott saw what unfolded on the monitors, he realized that BB's off-color remark had actually been a desperate attempt to stave off panic. Each screen displayed its own episode of carnage as members of the hospital and security staffs were attacked by patients.

Scott couldn't believe his eyes. He'd had no idea there were so many failed test subjects of Project 24, no idea of the extent of the horror.

The patients were a mutated army—a hideous confluence of melted features, vestigial limbs, and abscessed, unidentifiable growths that writhed beneath the skin. Some had been lucky enough to retain a basic human shape, while others were nothing more than withered hulks that dragged themselves across the floor. Dozens were covered by what looked like a translucent veil of mucus that adhered to everything it touched. A few were literally covered by weeping sores, their faces masks of agony as they stumbled forward on spindly legs.

A tear slid down Scott's cheek. These were soldiers who had volunteered to serve their country. Now they were little more than hideous examples of redigested DNA. A true biochemical nightmare.

And then Scott realized that a few patients displayed actual powers—but these were powers that had spun desperately, tragically, out of control. On one monitor, a raving male patient turned from mist to flesh in rapid, looping succession, unable to stop. On another monitor, a female patient bolted from view, screaming as her skin bubbled and blackened from the electrical energy that crackled inside her core.

Whether the patients had been driven mad by the state of their bodies or the arcane pharmaceuticals dispensed to treat them seemed to make little difference. They attacked the hospital staff with primal savagery, disemboweling some with fire axes, tearing others limb from limb. Some patients took the violence to another level, pressing their mouths to the gushing wounds they inflicted or devouring the gutted remains.

Vampires, Scott realized. How long would it be before his blood thirst turned him into something like that? As if to punctuate his dread, a female patient came into view, whimpering about a terrible hunger. She then picked up a jagged triangle of glass from a shattered window and sliced deeply into her forearm to feast on her own blood.

Scott tore himself away from the hideous spectacle, wishing like hell he could do something to help the patients and hospital staff, while flushing the contagion from his own veins.

"How could this have happened?" he whispered to BB.

"Believe me, I've been asking that very same question," the scientist replied.

Scott knew BB wasn't at fault. Far from it. BB was an ethical man who only took part in experiments that had the promise of benefiting mankind. He'd been recruited to Project 24 late in the game and had perfected the gene-splicing technique to get Team Ultra up and running. No doubt the deformities were revealed to him after the fact, since now he was working feverishly to reverse the horror he'd inherited.

"How many patients are housed here?" Scott asked Harriman, forcing himself to focus on the matter at hand. There was nothing he could do to improve his own situation. All he could do was learn as much as possible about the complex and its inhabitants. He noticed that White had entered the room; the man seemed devoid of empathy as he watched the monitors.

"Two hundred patients," Harriman replied. "Plus forty staff."

Scott went pale. Thank God Leah had gotten out when she did. "You mentioned other news, BB."

"Again, it's easier just to show you," BB said, stress clearly taking its toll.

BB tapped a few computer keys. The screen at the far upper right went black and then resolved into another picture with a time code that indicated the recording had been captured an hour ago. A female patient paced frantically in her cell. Rachel Ackart. It wasn't long before a guard and medic rushed into her room—only to be killed by flying pieces of medical equipment. A new power? Scott wondered as Rachel slipped the key ring from the guard's belt and walked from the room.

"It's unlikely, almost impossible, for a person to

have the computer know-how to hack into every cell from a single control panel," BB said.

"But Rachel did," Scott said.

BB nodded. "Taxpayers got their money's worth with her."

"Rachel appears to be extremely lucid," Harriman told BB. "Much more lucid than we've seen her in months. That will make her even more dangerous."

"The power Rachel brought to bear against these men isn't one we're familiar with," Scott said.

"We hoped Rachel would be an isolated case," Harriman replied. "But then Danton Dumas proved otherwise."

Scott glanced at BB. "Isolated case?"

"Divergence," the scientist explained. "Rachel is displaying a psychic power most likely based on Andre's power of suggestion but ultimately diverged from it. Radically, as you saw."

"What about Danton?" Scott asked. "His power doesn't seem to stem from anything that Andre can do."

"Exactly the point," Harriman said. "The powers seem to be taking on a life of their own."

"Danton had leukemia, which may have had something to do with his divergence," BB continued. "But who knows what preexisting condition the next person will have, and how their power will be affected? Heck, someone could turn invisible, burst into flame, even become radioactive. We just don't know." He indicated the monitors. "The same is true for patients who were turned into vampires. No doubt they've passed the contagion to other patients, but who knows how the tainted blood will affect any one person?"

"Some might suffer from blood thirst," Scott said ruefully.

BB nodded. "And some might be unable to withstand sunlight, while others might not have that problem." He frowned. "The idea of vampires and mutants running around with divergent powers scares me, man. Like albums by William Shatner scare me, you know?"

"I hear you," Scott said absently. How powers manifested seemed to be a roll of the dice. You either dodged a bullet or got very, very unlucky. Another monitor caught his eye: a male and female patient, eyes cue-ball white, flailing at imagined enemies. He turned away. "I assume you have countermeasures for a situation like this, Colonel?"

"Only one," Harriman said. "Napalm."

Scott couldn't believe what he'd just heard. "These men and women are soldiers serving our country. We can't just burn them."

"We may not have a choice, son. If the situation doesn't improve within the next few hours, the detention area will be purged."

"Jesus, we can send in a riot team—"

"And risk contagion?" Harriman shook his head. "Unacceptable."

Scott turned to BB. "What about the antidote? You said you were close."

"I am," BB said. "But it's untested. Plus, I'll need to turn it into aerosol form so we can send it through the ventilation system and affect a wide area."

"You can test the antidote on me."

"Like hell," Harriman said.

"I plan to help these men and women in any way I can, Colonel," Scott said. "If that means acting as a guinea pig on their behalf as they've already done for us, then so be it."

His tone caused White to take a step forward, but Harriman waved him back. "You'll do more harm than good, son. If the antidote doesn't work, it could put you out of commission. If it does work, your powers will be gone when we may need them most." He shook his head. "I won't allow it—and that's an order, Captain."

Scott felt a surge of anger. It seemed Harriman was doing his best to undermine any effort to save the patients from certain death. But finally Scott conceded the point. Still, there was no way he would accept condemning the patients to a fiery death. Was this how Harriman would treat him if his powers took a turn for the worse? "Fine, but we continue developing the antidote in lieu of your countermeasure. How much more time do you need, BB?"

"No way to be sure."

"Then we'll try to push off the countermeasure until you are."

Again, Harriman objected. "With each passing minute, there's a greater chance the patients will escape. We can't expose the city of New Orleans to that kind of risk, especially when someone like Danton Dumas is among them. The guy can walk through walls, for Chrissake. We trigger the countermeasure as scheduled."

"Since Dumas is in the complex, the situation falls under my command, Colonel," Scott replied, this time refusing to give in. "Total autonomy, remember? We give the antidote a chance. If it doesn't work, and the situation spins out of control, then we'll use the countermeasure. But only if we have no other choice."

Harriman glared, but Scott could feel an underlying respect from the man. Harriman knew he'd made his own bed. Made a promise that perhaps he shouldn't have—or at least didn't think would come into play so soon. And now Scott was prepared to take full advantage.

"If you guys will excuse me," BB said, "I've got an antidote to perfect in record time."

Scott watched BB return to his instruments as Harriman moved back to the monitors for another videoconference.

Scott knew there was a part of Harriman that considered napalm a last resort. But he was also starting to realize that Harriman would do whatever needed to be done to keep the patients contained.

Harriman—and Major Wallas Ackart before him—had much in common. All bad. Yet another reason why Scott felt relieved that Leah was miles away, hopefully relaxing in some smoky Bourbon Street bar with a Hurricane in her hand, safe and sound.

Chapter 15

Andre extricated himself from the sleeping Caribbean woman who gently clung to him on the bearskin rug and then stood and walked across the alchemical lab to a sunken stone fire pit.

Like an amputee trying to scratch a phantom limb, Andre engaged in sex even though he could no longer experience physical pleasure as a vampire. He missed the sensation of orgasm, of course, but more important, he missed the human response the act could elicit. A woman's sigh, the toss of her hair, her clawing fingers on his back. Pleasures like these made sex a powerful catalyst to emotional connection—and the promise of these pleasures was exactly what he would use to further manipulate Rachel.

Andre glanced back at the caramel-skinned woman, who sat up and graced him with a sultry stare. He waved his hand dismissively, and her voluptuous form dissolved back into the infinite nothingness of the Space Between like sand dispersed by wind.

Refreshed by the diversion, Andre sat before the stone pit, feeling no heat from the phantasmal fire. He used the metrical rhythm of the flames and pluming smoke to help focus his thoughts and reach out for Rachel's mind.

So far, he'd been successful in pretending to be the

ghost of Rachel's lost love to make her act. At this point, he was fairly certain that she believed Josef Neumann was really speaking to her and that she would do anything to bring him back to life so she could be with him again.

As before, Andre found Rachel's mind to be a confused morass of pain. But still, there were memories that beamed from the darkness like intermittent stars in an overcast sky. He allowed Rachel's love for Neumann to act as a guide as images from her memories flashed before him above the flames. . . .

. . . she and Josef making love in a canopy-covered bed . . . the two of them working late in an underground lab . . . Rachel pulling a small radio from underneath a floorboard to communicate with her Allied handlers . . .

So Rachel was accomplished in duplicity, Andre mused. A woman after his own heart.

And then a memory appeared in the underground lab that piqued Andre's interest: Rachel swimming in a huge aquarium as Neumann pounded on the side, demanding she get out. Andre noted a large chalkboard nearby, its surface covered by a complicated discourse of runes written in yellow chalk.

Nude, Rachel's body was flawless. Andre marveled at her lithe beauty as she kicked lazily underwater, sliding from one side of the tank to the other as her blond hair floated gently around her head like a gossamer halo. The caduceus hung around her neck on a silver chain.

Neumann pounded again on the thick glass of the aquarium with his fist. "Gretchen! What in God's name are you doing? Get out of there this instant!"

Smiling, Rachel swam to a ladder attached to the opposite side of the tank and emerged dripping from the scarlet water. "It works, my love," she exclaimed, rushing toward him. "My body feels like it never has before."

A deft maneuver, Andre thought. Clearly, Rachel had been stealing scientific secrets but distracted Neumann by focusing him on her body.

"The bath has not been tested on human subjects," Neumann said as he turned her around, searching for signs of side effects. "How could you take such a risk?"

"How could I *not* take the risk? It would have taken months to begin human trials. But now . . ." She ran her hands across her breasts and stomach. "I can feel the heat across my body, Josef. My cells are transforming . . . growing younger. . . ." She continued to caress her body, purposely seductive, yet also clearly amazed at the sensations rushing through her.

Neumann cleared his throat, lust palpable. "This is highly irregular, Gretchen. I'm afraid I have no choice but to place you under arrest—"

Rachel took Neumann's hand and pressed it over her left breast. "Do you feel my heart?"

The man struggled to concentrate past the soft, heavy sensation. "Yes. Of course."

"Go into the tank, my love. We can be together forever without fear of getting sick or growing old. Imagine!" Her voice grew thick with genuine emotion. "We can flee Germany and work on whatever strikes our fancy!"

"I cannot just leave," Neumann said, but he was struggling, his willpower weakening.

"Do you not love me?" she asked.

Andre felt Rachel's intense anger: at Neumann for making her love him and at her Allied handlers for impelling her to lie to him. But if she won Neumann's defection, then she would win him, plus the secrets of the tank. The end would justify the means.

Neumann looked at her. Perhaps he could have resisted the promise of sex alone, but the promise of love was more difficult to refuse. The scientist might capitulate, and that was something Andre could not allow—not if he wanted to maintain control over Rachel. He had to intervene.

"Gretchen," Andre said through Josef. "Listen to me."

"Josef . . . ?"

Andre could feel Rachel struggle, feel her need to take back control of the memory. "I can come back to you, and not just in memory," Andre continued, working to turn her into a slave by the promise of her lover's return. "But you must do something first."

"But the water, Josef . . . We can be happy. . . . We can be together forever. . . ."

"Don't you want me to be more than a memory, Gretchen? We can be together again in the flesh, but first, you must escape from the underground complex."

He could sense her confusion as she tried to sort the present from the past. Her emotions engaged—fear, anger, despair.

"The underground complex . . ."

"You need to find Danton," Andre said in Neumann's voice. "He is the key to your escape. He also holds the key to bringing me back to you . . . forever."

"Danton is stubborn. He didn't come when I called." As she spoke, her mind continued to whirl as she tried to concentrate.

"I will tell you a few things to say about his sister. He will come," Andre/Josef said. "You will have me and much more, Gretchen. Everlasting life, power beyond imagination, and eternal youth."

Rachel shook her head. "People will try to stop me. They always do."

"Do what you must, Gretchen, but do not fail."

"I won't fail you, Josef." Her voice suddenly grew hard. "Not again."

Even as Andre wondered what Rachel meant by the last comment, he was satisfied that she would obey.

Retreating from her mind, he thought about the mystical equation on the blackboard. Apparently, it could transform water into a sort of fountain of youth. A grin cut his face. Earlier, he had hoped to be reborn into a homunculus—an alchemical, humanoid shell that would house his consciousness on the material plane. Now he could hope for much more.

Chapter 16

Where the hell was Danton Dumas?

That's what Rachel wanted to know as she set off down yet another corridor of the detention area littered with bodies, the walls splattered with blood. Every time she saw a downed guard or medic, she took satisfaction in knowing that punishment had been dispensed with a suitably heavy hand.

If Danton wouldn't come to her, then she would find *him*. Her powers of seduction were limited by the separation. Certain if only she could approach him in the flesh, she would get him to cooperate, Rachel grew impatient.

"Danton, where are you?" she asked, Josef's promise of everlasting life, power beyond imagination, and eternal youth driving her. "What level are you on?"

"I'm on six," came his reluctant reply in her mind.

Now that her mind was clearing of the drugs, her memory was sharpening. That included the layout of the whole complex. She knew where everything was, including the armory on the third level. Indeed, Danton might be able to get her out of this prison as Josef had suggested, but she wouldn't miss any opportunity. No doubt explosives were stored in the armory, and if necessary, she would find someone who knew how to use them.

"Start making your way up to three." Rachel looked for a stairwell so she could ascend two levels herself. Spotting a sign, she followed the path around a corner and saw the doorway halfway down the corridor. "I'll meet you there. Simply follow my voice to find me." When he didn't agree—or respond at all— she thought about what Andre had told her. "I *need* you, Danton, but you need me, too. I know you're all alone in the world like I am." She paused a second before coloring her words with counterfeit emotion. "Your *sister* would have hated your being here."

"My sister?"

"Yes, Rebecca. She died for you, Danton. After all she sacrificed for you, she would be horrified at your being here, trapped like an animal."

"You knew her?"

Rachel hedged the truth. Let him think whatever he needed to. "Rebecca's death was so tragic. She gave up her life for yours, Danton. I know how ill you were, and how she saved your life through blood magic. We're linked by that same blood now, you know, the reason we can talk to each other like this. The reason I know you so intimately. It would be better if we were together, though, could talk face-to-face."

No man had ever been able to resist her when she'd put her mind to it. Once she had Danton by her side, she would quickly have power over him.

"First I have to find Leah."

What was it with him and this bitch? Stopping in her tracks in front of the stairwell door, Rachel took a deep breath so as not to let her irritation with him show. "She's not on your side, Danton."

"How do you know?"

"Wasn't she the one who helped find you and bring you here in the first place?"

"Leah just wanted to talk—"

Rachel cut him off. "Leah Maguire is a tool of the military."

"No. She wasn't like them. She's different."

"That's what she wants you to think. You watch—she'll appeal to your sense of honor. She'll trick you into agreeing to do what she wants of you, and then she'll have you in a tight spot. You'll never get away. She'll convince you that you should do what's right for your country, Danton. For the people around you. That's what *I* did, and look what happened to me. I've been locked away for nearly a year because the scientists didn't know what they were doing and made me sick."

"I-I don't know. . . ."

She just about had him. "You need to think about yourself and what your sister sacrificed so that you could live. Make that sacrifice worthwhile. Meet me on three, please. We have to get out of this place as soon as we can."

Danton hesitated, and Rachel felt the heat of anger shoot through her. What the hell did she have to do to get through to this man?

"I need you, Danton." She let a small sob catch in her throat. "I can't do this alone."

Then he said, *"All right, I'll go up to three. Then what?"*

At last, Rachel relaxed and opened the stairwell door. "Just follow my voice."

As she hurried up the stairs, she realized several

other patients were heading down toward her. She waited until she was face-to-face with two men and a woman, all flushed as if they'd just sated their appetites. Sexual or blood? she wondered, noting the woman's top was ripped and all three had smears of blood decorating their flesh. She quickly hid her prurient interest and adopted a take-charge manner.

"I'm Rachel Ackart, and I'm in charge of the escape."

"Who says?" the more normal of the men asked— the other one being so emaciated he was nothing more than a bag of bones. The normal one took a threatening step down toward her . . . until she could see his eyes were completely black.

"Who do you think opened your cell door?" Rachel asked. "If you want to get out of this prison, you'll do what I say."

"And that would be?"

"Find everyone you can and send them to the armory."

The man laughed. "There's no need for weapons, not with what powers we've got."

"Then why are you still here and not on the outside?"

"She has a point," the woman said. "I, for one, would like to see daylight again."

Even in the dim stairwell, Rachel could see how pale the woman's skin looked and suspected she'd inherited the vampire's aversion to the sun. Not that Rachel would tell her so.

"We can make that happen if we work as a team. We'll blast our way out if we need to."

The trio agreed it sounded like a plan and went off to round up others like them from lower floors.

Rachel resumed her climb to three, but when she tried to open the door, she couldn't. Not that it was locked. Something heavy was pressed against it. Without thinking, she used her mind to move the obstacle and open the door.

When she stepped through, she realized the obstacle was human—a downed guard, not yet dead. He looked at her through terrorized eyes. His throat gaped open, blood oozing from a gash, and yet his lips moved and he struggled to speak.

"Help . . ."

Remembering asking for the very same thing and being given drugs to quiet her down so she wouldn't bother anyone, Rachel murmured, "Certainly."

And she stepped on his throat to walk over him and felt his windpipe give.

Smiling, Rachel headed for the armory.

Chapter 17

Anguish and despair battered Leah. Steeling herself against the electrical current still snapping and popping around her, she looked down to find herself attached to a female vampire.

Meeting her gaze, the woman let go and whispered, "Help me, please."

This escapee was young, midtwenties, her whole life ahead of her. Or would be if she weren't bleeding out. Electrical current passed along her body, arcing and sparking blue, turning her pale gray eyes dark and then light again. Andre had been able to turn himself into lightning, but Leah hadn't known the military had experimented with that power. Apparently, she didn't know a lot of things that had gone on in this hellish place.

"Didn't sign up for this . . . ," the woman gritted out. ". . . not any of it . . . tried to stop them . . ."

So she had resisted violence, and the escapees had turned against her.

Instinct told Leah to run, to get away from the woman before other vampires stumbled on them and it was too late. Instead, she knelt at the woman's side, then ripped material from one of her sleeves and, ignoring the zap she got on contact, gently pressed the cloth to the woman's bleeding throat.

"*Kill* me," the woman pleaded, her eyes filled with a pain that Leah recognized.

Innumerable times after she'd been saved from the slaughter in the cave, Leah had seen that pain reflected back at her from a mirror.

"I-I can't kill you. I won't." Leah's mind raced, searching for a healing spell she could use.

"Nothing to live for . . . *no one* . . . No more, please."

"Are you in pain?"

"Nothing I can't bear."

In truth, the woman was too far gone to be healed. Leah could feel her emotions growing fainter by the moment—she was going to die, and soon. Another death. Leah wanted to escape having to witness more tragedy.

As if the woman could sense her renewed panic, she whispered, "Don't leave me, please."

Leah looked at the result of a scientific experiment gone bad, at a woman who had no one, who was alone—and in that instant saw herself. She shook her head. "I'm not going anywhere." Taking the woman's hand with both of her own, she barely felt the weakening electrical current. "I'm Leah."

"Kim . . . thank you . . ."

Noting Kim's arm was decorated with a roughly tattooed cross—probably self-created with pen and ink—Leah hoped the dying woman could take comfort in her faith. "You'll be better soon, Kim. No more pain. You'll be free of all this . . . in a better place."

"Thank you," Kim whispered again, seeming to relax.

The current dancing along the woman's body grew fainter, and Leah could feel the life force ebbing away.

At the same time, a burst of noise in the stairwell caught Leah's attention. *Keep going,* she thought desperately. *Go to another floor.* The last thing she needed was to deal with the escapees. She couldn't panic. Couldn't leave the dying woman.

Thankfully, the noise faded once more, and Leah looked back to Kim, whose eyes were still open.

The life had already drained from them, and all traces of electrical current had vanished. Leah gently closed Kim's eyes and said a quick prayer for her soul, then got to her feet.

Now what?

The precariousness of her situation rocked her, and Leah's limbs grew heavy. She set out down a corridor she hadn't yet checked—more cells, how many were there?—but when she got to the end, there was no way out. She had to go back the way she'd come. Hardly able to move, she needed a break. Needed someplace to gather her resources. Someplace safe.

One of the cells.

It occurred to her that the escapees were likely to avoid the cells they'd escaped.

She slipped into the nearest cell, outfitted only with a bed, a small dresser, a chair, and some medical equipment.

Sitting on the edge of the bed, Leah wondered how many other escapees were like Kim—not agreeing with the violence of the break and being killed by others like her. Bad enough that volunteers for scientific experiments had been made virtual prisoners. Worse that who knew how many of them had to die.

Would anyone tell Kim's family what had happened to her?

Or would they be left to wonder forever . . . ?

Curling up on the bed, Leah pulled out her digital recorder and photos of Dad and Gabe. Her throat grew tight when she listened to another recording and felt more detached from her memories of them than ever. She ran her fingers lightly over the photographs and wondered if they all would be reunited soon. Her life would be forfeit if she didn't get out of there.

But how?

A scream shattered her sense of isolation. How close were the escapees? Had she fooled herself into thinking she was safe here?

If only she could have gotten to a working phone or intercom, she could have reached Scott, let him know she was trapped. He would do whatever it took to extricate her from this situation. She had absolute trust in him, at least where her physical well-being was concerned.

Her heart was a different matter.

Telling herself to be realistic, to recognize that she had to depend on herself alone and couldn't depend on anyone else—wasn't that the way it had been since the cave?—Leah replaced the photos and recorder in her bag. That's when her fingers brushed the bandana Scott had given her on the drive into New Orleans. She pulled it out and held it to her face, inhaled his masculine scent. Her pulse suddenly rushed through her. And an idea. Maybe she hadn't found a phone or an intercom to contact Scott, but perhaps there was another way. Dreamwalking gave her a shortcut into the Astral Plane and hopefully a direct path to Scott.

Javier, her mentor in Native American beliefs, had given her the tools. She'd used dreamwalking more than once while training with him. Yes, this could work.

The only problem was that Scott needed to be in REM sleep where dreaming occurred, and knowing him, she doubted he would fully let down his guard until the crisis was over. No doubt he would keep himself awake for days if necessary. Hopefully, she could deal with that problem first.

She would have to use magic again, and she knew what that meant—more lost memories. It couldn't be helped. What good would memories be if she was dead?

Dragging the small dresser to the middle of the room, Leah tried to ignore the sounds of a riot that seemed to come from directly above her. Her hand shook as she ripped more material from the other sleeve of her blouse, twined it with Scott's bandana, and made a circle of the two on the dresser top. From her case, she took a white candle and lit it, then set it in the circle made by the twined materials.

Frightening noises now seemed to surround her. Shutting them out, Leah moved counterclockwise around the room, projecting the thought "Keep us safe" into the walls and floor and ceiling that confined her. Then she turned and moved clockwise in silence, seeing Scott's face in her mind's eye and meditating thoughts of sleep and dreams and the narrow canyons and red mesas of the Southwest, the dream-place she'd used in the past. Finally, she stopped at the dresser, blew out the candle, and seeing Scott's amber eyes clearly in her mind, whispered, "Sleep now."

Her own eyes were already growing heavy as she settled down into the bed. She released the tension, starting at her extremities, letting each part of her body grow light, breathing slowly and deeply and expanding her consciousness until she became aware of her own aura, allowed it to expand, and then grounded herself to the earth while reaching out with her mind. . . .

Suddenly, she was walking along a wash that led her to a narrow canyon with lava-scorched walls. A snake undulated across her path, and a lizard baking on a rock watched her. High desert heat pressed down on her, drying her mouth. The sky, a brilliant clear blue, shed its magical light over the landscape, making everything seem more alive. The wash widened—tilted and twisted layers of rock striated with brown and red rose to a cliff overhead.

Leah thought herself at the top of that cliff. Magically she was there, staring at the entrance to a cave. A black hawk wheeled overhead, and wind swept across the mesa, whistling along the canyon walls and then pummeling her with its hot breath and a spray of sand. Braced against the forces of nature, she stood fast.

Staring into the dark, gaping maw of the cave mouth, she called, "Scott? Are you there?"

Though she could sense his essence, his image didn't immediately take form, which meant he was sleeping lightly but still fighting REM. Anxiety threatened to choke her.

She swallowed it and whispered, "Sleep deep," over and over, her mind stroking his, urging him give over to her will.

Finally, he emerged from the cave, his visage relaying his confusion and alarm.

"It's all right, Scott. It's Leah." The tightness in her chest released. He was there. He would help her. "You're safe with me."

She held out her hand and waited for him to come to her, coaxing him with soft words and the emotions pouring forth from her heart.

At last, his visage cleared and he stepped forward, hand outstretched to take hers. She stepped toward him. Their fingers touched and twined together, and for the moment, all Leah could think about was being held by the man she loved.

As if he knew her thoughts, Scott moved closer, his expression intense, his amber eyes glittering as he stared down into her face.

"Leah," he murmured, cupping her cheek. "I was just dreaming about you."

He slid his fingers to the back of her neck and pulled her head toward his. She could feel his pulse through his flesh, could sense his heightened emotions. For her. Her hair swirled around her face and his hand, her long skirts around their legs, as if joining them together. The breath caught in her throat as she remembered the feel of his flesh against her . . . inside her. The need to experience that again consumed her, and, for a moment forgetting about the danger, she stepped into him, raising her face.

Groaning, he covered her mouth with his, and she gave in to the hungry possession, letting him claim her with lips and tongue and persuasive hands, which he swept over her breasts and down her back to cup her buttocks.

Her eyes fluttered closed, and she sighed . . . for the moment overcome by a need that overwhelmed everything else . . . even the reason she'd resorted to using magic again.

Her heart beat hard and fast, and she wondered if he was aware of that, aware of the blood surging through her. The last time, he'd barely begun to know the effects of being turned, but now the blood hunger had to have gotten hold of him, and who knew if he could control it?

A frisson of fear skittered through her. Fear laced with excitement.

Potent.

Seductive.

Even so, Leah somehow managed to push Scott away. "We can't."

"Why not?" he asked. "You're safe here. We both are."

"No, Scott, you don't understand." Her fear returning, Leah took a shaky breath. "I never left the base. I'm still here in the complex, in the detention area. I'm trapped, and I need your help to get me out of here."

He gripped her arms. "Where do I find you? In real life, that is."

"Level Five. It's one of the corridors to the left, a cell all the way at the end."

"Too far. It'll take too long for me to reach you. Get to the staircase and come up to the sick bay on Level Three. It's near an exit. I'll come for you, get you out of there, I promise."

With that, Scott began to fade . . .

. . . and Leah sat straight up in bed with a gasp.

Chapter 18

Scott's eyes snapped open. *Leah!*

Disoriented, he looked around. The mesa with its fragrant breezes and golden canyon walls was gone. He was back in the lab again and realized that he'd fallen asleep on his feet while leaning against the wall next to BB's lab table.

Across the room, Harriman continued to hold a videoconference with a handful of other officers. The rest of the monitors still showed roving patients and scenes of carnage.

"Catch a few minutes' rest?" BB said, glancing over his shoulder as he worked. "Understandable after all you've been through. Don't worry, pal, I don't think Harriman noticed."

"Not quite sleep," Scott said, still feeling the soft electricity of Leah's touch. It had been a dream but seemed so real. In some ways, more real than reality itself. The colors had been more vivid, the smells sharper. If it hadn't been for the urgency of Leah's message, he would have liked to explore which of their other senses had been heightened. "I need you to open the riot door, BB."

BB stopped what he was doing and turned around. "What are you talking about?"

"Leah communicated with me from Level Five."

A look of confused horror crossed the scientist's face. "I thought she left a long time ago."

"She's inside," Scott said, and placed his hand against the three-foot-thick steel door. A dozen other riot doors like it sealed off the control rooms from where the patients were held. Whether the doors were a blessing or curse depended on the side on which you found yourself. If only he could send Leah a message through touch alone. Deliver a modicum of comfort to ease her fear.

"Belay that order," Harriman said, approaching. "Nobody goes in. Word from upstairs is that the situation is out of control. They're preparing to purge."

"Tell them to hold off," Scott said. "Leah is trapped inside."

Harriman shook his head. "Danton can walk through walls. They see him as too great a threat. I'm sorry, son."

"Itchy trigger fingers," BB said disgustedly. "It's like they're using the purge to erase their mistakes."

"I'm going in," Scott told Harriman, and then to BB, "Do you have any nonlethal weapons? I don't want to hurt these people if I can help it." He knew that most weapons in the complex were loaded with gold-alloy armor-piercing rounds—a mixture that had proved effective against Andre's alchemical biology and, by extension, against those injected with his DNA. But Scott didn't consider the escaped patients to be enemies. They were victims of terrible circumstance, as he was. They were soldiers, as he was. He would treat them accordingly.

BB walked to a nearby weapons locker and pulled

ut a shotgun. "This uses gold-infused rubber bul-
ets." He allowed himself a smirk. "Rubber for your
protection, you might say."

"Perfect," Scott said, taking the shotgun.

"The purge is scheduled to commence in less than
an hour," Harriman said. "There's not enough time."

"Complete autonomy, remember, Colonel?" Scott
said, checking the shotgun's breech and pocketing the
few extra rounds that BB gave him. He then used the
inhaler; he didn't want his blood thirst to become an
issue on the inside.

"I'm coming with you, then."

Scott looked at Harriman. Maybe the man wanted
to expedite Leah's rescue, or maybe he wanted to
make sure the mission didn't veer off track and put
the base in further danger. Whatever the reason, there
was greater safety in numbers. "Glad to have you
along, but we do things my way. *Minimum* force."

"Until your way stops working."

Scott ignored the dig and leveled his weapon at the
metal door. Harriman followed suit with his .45
sidearm, and White with his M4 assault rifle.

Scott then nodded to BB, who punched a code into
a wall-mounted keypad.

With a deep hydraulic hiss, the riot door slid open
slowly to reveal an empty hallway that stretched
approximately fifty feet ahead and then turned left.
Broken glass littered the tile floor. Someone—or
some*thing*—had shattered the overhead fluorescent
lights.

Scott led Harriman and White through the riot
door. They were met with the faint but sharp formaldehyde smell of scientific experiments gone bad. Glass

shards crackled under their combat boots as distant screams and howls seemed to echo all around them. "We'll communicate via throat mike," he told BB over his shoulder. "If you can track our progress on the monitors, great. We might need your eyes for advanced recon. Either way, keep us on the right path via GPS."

"Bring Leah back, pal," BB said as the door swung closed and then locked into place with a metallic *boom*.

Without light from the control room, the hallway was nearly pitch-black. Only weak fluorescents from a distant corner provided illumination, but Scott refrained from using the tactical light attached to the barrel of the shotgun. He didn't want to give away their position if he could help it.

Scott walked quickly, leading with the shotgun, and rounded the corner into another hallway. This one was even longer than the last, with open cell doors on each side.

Some of the overhead fluorescents had been shattered here as well, creating alternating pools of greenish light and impenetrable shadow. A few gurneys lay tipped on their sides among lab coats and military fatigues soaked with fresh blood. But there were no bodies. Maybe the victims had been dragged away to be feasted upon, Scott thought.

"BB," Scott said into his throat mike, "I need you to access the room cameras in sector eight."

"Nothing but static," BB's voice crackled in his ear. "Somebody got real camera shy in there."

"No-go on the cameras," Scott told Harriman and

White. "So we'll proceed in standard cover formation to clear the area."

"That's one option," Harriman said as they crept toward the doors. "Or you could turn into smoke and recon the area."

Scott tightened his jaw. His powers might provide a tactical advantage in the tight quarters, but they could also cut the mission short if he lost control of them. "I can't take the risk, Colonel. Not with Leah's life at stake."

"It's not a risk, son. It's a prudent course of action."

"Not when we don't have the luxury of calling for evac or reinforcements if things go bad," Scott said. "Now let's keep moving."

Before they could continue, a man appeared from a door far down the corridor. He wore a white examination gown and hobbled toward them, crossing through the pools of harsh light and deep shadow.

White immediately trained his M4 on the man and tightened his trigger finger. Scott batted the barrel aside before White could fire. White took a step toward Scott in challenge.

"Stand down, soldier," Scott said. "That's an order. This man could be an innocent trying to escape."

White glanced at Harriman, who nodded. White stood down but continued to glare at Scott.

Scott ignored him and turned his focus on the approaching man. "Stop and identify yourself!"

The man didn't respond, and continued to hobble forward.

Scott could see the man's features more clearly now. The right side of his face was normal, but the left side was badly disfigured and looked like a runny watercolor painting. His chest and left arm were no better, nothing more than mudslides of purplish flesh. His left leg looked as though it had been curdled by flame, with the outside arch of the foot barely scraping the floor.

Scott felt a pang of empathy. He could just as easily have been that man. He could still become that man. "Name, rank, and serial number, solider!" he tried again.

"Stop or we *will* open fire!" Harriman called out, leveling his .45. White smirked as he took Harriman's side and brought his M4 to bear once again.

Maybe the hobbling man couldn't hear the command or cared more about reaching them than he did about safety. Either way, he kept coming. Scott knew that Harriman wouldn't offer another chance before firing, so he placed himself in his line of fire.

"Are you crazy, Captain?" Harriman growled. "Move aside!"

"If the man wanted to attack, he wouldn't have exposed himself."

"He might be out of his mind!"

"He also might know a faster way to Leah. Cover me."

Scott placed his shotgun on the floor and approached the man. When he was only a few feet away, the man stopped finally. "Please help me. . . . I'm not like the others." The words came out halted and slurred from between his deformed lips. "I was waiting for rescue. . . . Please . . ."

Scott's heart broke for the man. The guy wasn't violent or crazy; he'd merely been thrust from one terrible situation to another. "I'm Captain Scott Boulder."

". . . First Lieutenant Mike Brubaker, Seventy-third Infantry Division . . ."

"We're trying to reach someone in sick bay, Lieutenant Brubaker. A woman."

The man began to tremble as he whipped his head from side to side. "There isn't anyone left. . . . Everybody's dead. . . . Only *they* remain."

Scott knew full well who *they* were: patients who'd been transformed into psychotic killers or vampires who could turn innocents into monsters. "You hearing this, BB?"

"Roger that," BB replied. "I'm trying to verify his claim about sick bay, but the camera is out of commission there, too."

Scott closed his eyes as terrible images thundered through his mind. Leah running in terror, doing her best to put up a fight . . . "Jesus, BB, give me some good news."

"You're in a safe area. One of the only safe areas remaining, from what I can tell."

"Can you still lead us to sick bay?"

"I'll do my best, but cameras are being taken out left and right. The patients must know we're watching them. By the way, you don't have much time."

"I know, I know," Scott said.

"I . . . I can lead you," Brubaker said, ". . . if you promise to get me out of here."

Scott paused. Although it occurred to him that Brubaker might be leading them into a trap, he decided it was worth the risk. The man could already have done them harm if he'd wanted to.

Scott indicated for the hobbling man to lead the way and then motioned Harriman and White forward.

"At the first sign of trouble, we put the guy down," Harriman said.

White stared at Scott and said nothing, but his expression said it all: *You're a pussy for letting the guy live.*

Scott met the man's gaze with his own unspoken message: *Happy to disappoint.*

Despite Brubaker's hobble, he moved surprisingly fast.

Scott trailed close behind, followed by Harriman and White. They headed down a number of hallways, some streaked with blood, others strewn with smashed medical equipment and more tattered uniforms. But all otherwise empty. Sometimes the echoing screams they heard were distant, sometimes they were so close that Scott reconsidered using his powers. If they were attacked by a superior number of enemies, he might have to use them, and pray he could deal with the consequences.

At one point, Scott noticed that White lagged behind to gather wristwatches, wallets, and other personal objects dropped by slain victims. Harriman didn't seem to notice the behavior, instead keeping his focus on Brubaker.

Scott stopped, allowing Harriman and Brubaker to walk a few more steps ahead, and then yanked White into a side corridor. "What the hell do you think you're doing?"

White scoffed. "You public sector boys are all the same." The man had a Bostonian accent and clipped his words as though each were leaving a bad taste in his mouth. "Holier-than-thou patriots. Gung-ho warriors of freedom. Such bullshit."

Scott ignored the jibe. "I'm not about to let you desecrate the memory of these people. Now empty your pockets."

White kept his gaze on Scott as he pulled two handfuls of booty from his assault vest and dropped them onto the floor. "You're missing the point, Captain, and don't even know it."

"Just do as you're ordered."

"This is what it's all about," White said, indicating the wristwatches and wallets with a nod. "This is what it's always been about."

"Maybe in your world."

"My world is the only world there is . . . or haven't you been paying attention? Look around. Look at this *place*. Your own people have been bought and sold like these wristwatches, and for what?" White shook his head. "Better to consume than be consumed, wouldn't you agree?"

Scott regarded White incredulously. The man was a true mercenary. "I caution you to remember why you're here, White."

"I know exactly why I'm here, and who I'm fighting for," White replied. "The real question is: Do you? And more important: Would you do it again?"

Scott turned away in disgust. He'd had enough of the man's pessimistic view. "Shut up and fall in. That's an order."

As Scott caught up to Harriman and Brubaker, he felt his disgust grow. Under normal circumstances, Scott would have tossed White from the team. The man's greed made him a danger to others and to himself. Scott only hoped Harriman could keep White in check.

Scott stepped in line with Brubaker. "Where are we, soldier?"

"Almost there," the man slurred. "But we gotta be careful. . . . We're at the edge of a safe area."

"I meant to ask," Scott said. "How did you end up here?"

Brubaker glanced at him, muddled features tightening in shame. "I needed the money . . . simple as that. . . . Got a wife and four girls . . . couldn't make ends meet. . . . They offered a hefty bonus to become a guinea pig. . . ."

Scott nodded. He knew the incentives. Thirty pieces of silver for your soul. "You were taking care of your own, Lieutenant. There's no shame in that."

Brubaker shook his head, misshapen flesh rippling horribly. "My Karen doesn't know. . . . She thinks I'm overseas on a mission. . . . She was proud when I left. . . . What's she gonna think now? I'm a monster. . . ."

Scott gritted his teeth. Project 24 had chewed up too many good men. After the matter with the Philosopher's Stone was resolved, he would do everything he could to end the program. "The part of you that loved your family enough to make the sacrifice hasn't changed," he said, thinking about how Leah had accepted him despite everything that had happened. "Your wife will realize that."

As the man continued to lead, Scott thought about the contrast between Brubaker and White. Both had been motivated by money, but beyond that, there was a world of difference. A difference worth fighting for.

Presently, Brubaker led them through a large storage area that held dozens of liquid nitrogen canisters and pallets of scientific supplies. As they continued, Scott could feel the slightest razor's edge of blood thirst. He fingered the inhaler in his leg pocket and did his best to ignore the sensation.

Harriman stopped him. "How are you doing, son?"

"Fine."

"Thirst coming back?"

"Nothing I can't handle." Scott glanced at his watch. "We've got to keep moving."

Looking up, he noticed that Brubaker had continued without them and soon disappeared into a pool of shadow created by a series of smashed overhead lights.

Scott, Harriman, and White moved quickly to catch up. They passed through the same patch of darkness, but when they emerged on the other side, Brubaker was nowhere to be found.

"Perimeter," Scott whispered, and the three men immediately formed a tight circle, backs to one another. Weapons out. Ready to fire on anything that moved.

But nothing did.

Brubaker had disappeared like he'd never existed.

"We should have taken the man out when we had the chance," Harriman said.

Scott glanced at his watch. "We don't have time to wait for something to happen and can't continue with our rear flank exposed." He turned on the tactical light attached to the barrel of his shotgun. "Follow me."

As Harriman and White switched on their own lights, Scott led them into the shadowy area they had just passed through. The circles of light illuminated more broken glass and shattered medical equipment. But still there was no trace of Brubaker.

Scott heard a soft wet noise moments before he saw the growing pool of blood on the floor.

As Harriman and White approached, Scott raised his light. There was blood dripping from a hole created by a missing ceiling tile.

"Colonel, get back—" Scott began, when a flood of viscera poured from the hole. He leaped away, but not before it splashed across his uniform and into his mouth.

Scott reeled, gagging, as the metallic taste of blood rushed across his tongue and triggered an explosion in the pit of his stomach—a deep, edged wanting that blew past the anesthetic effect of BB's medicine.

Scott fumbled in his pocket for the inhaler as a pair of men and women draped in gore-streaked scrubs leaped down through the hole.

Chapter 19

On her way to meet Scott, Leah was nearly up the first flight of stairs when the brutal sound of a life-and-death struggle echoed down at her along the stairwell, followed by a scream and a fine spray of blood.

Slowing, she stared down at her bare arm, now dotted with red, and knew she couldn't use this stairwell to get to sick bay. Too dangerous. She would need to find another way. Her stomach knotting, her legs growing heavy with dread, she took the last few steps up to Level Four, cracked open the door, and listened.

All seemed quiet.

Thinking there must be another stairwell in one of the corridors off this one, Leah set out to find it. She had just spotted a sign leading her to another set of stairs when she heard voices coming from around the corner.

"What kind of freedom is this?"

"Don't think there are any guards left," came a reply. "But we're still trapped. The cage has just gotten bigger."

They were coming toward her. Trapped between these escapees and the ones in the stairwell, Leah froze even as her heart sped up and pounded against her ribs. She could barely breathe as she looked around for a place to hide.

Nowhere.

Unless it was in plain sight . . .

Glamour, a trick of making others see what you want them to see—though Leah knew the principles, was familiar with the technique, she'd never actually tried the spell before. Unfortunately, she didn't have time to set up the magical elements the way she should. She would have to do without, do the best she could using her mind as her only tool. That would affect how strong the illusion might be, how long it would last, but she had no choice. She had to try or die.

Swallowing hard, Leah took a deep breath to keep at bay the panic threatening her.

Clearing her mind, she visualized the shape of a woman's body in a dark void. She concentrated on white light limning that shape, enveloping it. Imagined dressing the woman's body in the tunic and pants many of the escapees wore. Imagined the light changing, crackling, turning to pure energy—the way lightning had surged off Kim, the woman who'd died.

Then she imagined stepping *into* the electrified body as if she were putting on a costume . . .

. . . and opened her eyes as the vampires turned the corner.

Suddenly, one of them stood before her, his every vein and artery visible through pale, translucent skin. The other two, one of them badly deformed, stood slightly behind, as if in deference.

"You're going in the wrong direction," the leader said. "No food this way."

Leah shrugged and, wondering if he could smell the

sweat of fear on her, said, "I'm looking for the woman who released us."

"Rachel? Can't help you. Why don't you come with us instead?"

Feeling the energy surrounding her grow fainter with her sudden panic, Leah shook her head. "I've already been that way. I want to thank the woman . . . um, Rachel."

"You can do that later."

He reached for her and Leah jumped back, her stomach churning with fear. Instinct made her focus her thoughts to intensify the electrical illusion around her body. The charge crackled and sparked with her roiling emotions.

"No, don't," she warned him. "You'll get nothing but pain from touching me."

The vampire's hand stopped and then pulled back. "Let's go down a floor," he said to his companions, who seemed disappointed but didn't argue.

They passed her even as the current protecting Leah began to flicker and die out. Her knees felt like rubber, but she forced herself forward and around the corner. By the time she reached the door to the stairs halfway down the corridor, the glamour spell had worn off. She ducked into the stairwell and steadied herself before hurrying up to Level Three.

Once on the landing, she stopped to catch her breath and tried to think out her route, but never having been to this section of the containment area, she was disoriented. Indeed, when she left the stairwell, she saw that the corridor didn't end where the Level Four corridor did. It went on and snaked around another corner.

Certain that was not the direction to sick bay, she was about to head the other way when movement farther down caught her attention.

The wall itself seemed to move . . . and then a man stepped through. Her eyes widened. *Danton!*

About to call to him, she hesitated. He might run from her in fear. She needed to talk to him, to get through to him, to ask him for his help.

His expression was so intent, and he seemed very focused. He stopped a moment, then tilted his head as if he were listening to something.

Or some*one*.

Reminding her of Rachel on the digital recording. Was Andre talking to Danton, too?

Fear knotting her stomach, Leah knew she had to stop him before he made the biggest mistake of his life.

"Danton, wait, please."

He started and his eyes widened. "Leah. I was looking for you."

"Well, good," she said, moving toward him. "I've been wanting to talk to you." She checked him over and was glad to see that he seemed to be in one piece—the escapees hadn't gotten to him. "You must be awfully confused with everything that's gone on since you got here."

Danton nodded. "So many deaths. How the hell do we get out of here? What's going on?"

"These people volunteered for a medical experiment with the vampire's blood, and it had bad results for many of them. Some were simply sick, while others became very dangerous, so they had to be kept in a secure area until a cure was developed."

"But all the doors were open."

"One of the patients—a woman named Rachel—somehow used her powers to kill a medic and a guard before escaping. She's the one who opened all the cell doors."

"Don't put the blame for this mess on Rachel," Danton said. "She was abused, tortured—"

Hearing his defensive tone, Leah grew cautious. "You've *seen* Rachel?"

He grew quiet, and Leah suddenly realized it hadn't been Andre talking to Danton but Rachel Ackart—with Andre undoubtedly somehow controlling her. It wouldn't do to put Danton off by trying to convince him that Rachel was dangerous. She took a different tactic.

"Rachel needs help, Danton."

She felt his inner turmoil calm a bit.

"I know. She told me. She just wants to get out of here, Leah. Me, too."

Leah briefly thought about letting Danton go to Rachel so that she could follow him and find the woman herself, then decided it would endanger him. "Come with me, then. I'll get you to someplace safe."

"What about Rachel?"

"We'll see to her, Danton."

"You'll let her go, then?"

"That isn't up to me." Leah knew the military would never let someone as dangerous as Rachel go free, not with all the deaths she'd caused. "Come with me now, please. Scott will get us out of here."

"Scott?" Danton's visage darkened. "You mean the guy who knocked me out."

Trying to negate the fear and loathing she felt leach

off Danton, Leah said, "Scott wasn't trying to hurt you, Danton."

"You could've fooled me."

"We were ordered to find you because you took the Philosopher's Stone. We need it back."

"What if I don't have it anymore?"

His whole demeanor changed. He stood stiffly, but as if he were ready to fight. Was he serious? Did he really not have it? Or was he playing with words to make her think so because he didn't trust her? Leah knew she needed to appeal to Danton's innate decency. Losing the Philosopher's Stone was dangerous. And unthinkable.

"Even if you don't have it on you, surely you must know where the Philosopher's Stone is. Securing it someplace safe is imperative for the good of everyone, Danton. I know you're an honorable man and that you wouldn't want more people to get hurt than already have been. Would you?"

Danton's expression turned suspicious, and he backed away from her. "She said you would say that."

She? Rachel? No, Andre had known . . .

"The Philosopher's Stone is dangerous, Danton," Leah said, allowing her concern to color her tone. "You have to come with me so we can find it. In the wrong hands—"

"Forget it."

Danton backed off an additional step and then turned and walked straight through another wall.

"Danton, wait—"

But, of course, it was too late. He was already gone.

Not willing to give up so easily, Leah knew she had to follow.

She ran down the corridor and opened the nearest door to a short hallway. She paused at each door with a window, hoping to spot Danton again. It wasn't until she reached the last doorway that she caught a glimpse of him as he came through one wall, then went through another.

Away from her.

Leah flew out the door at the end of the hall, made a right turn, and headed down another long corridor. Oddly, there were no bodies, no blood, no broken lights. The corridor was pristine. Untouched by battle.

Passing a door, she glanced into a window. No Danton. The next. No Danton. The next . . .

Had he gotten away, then? Zigzagged in a different direction? Found an exit?

Was she on a fool's errand?

Realizing she was getting farther and farther away from sick bay, where she was supposed to meet Scott, Leah fought a growing sense of panic. It would be all right. Scott knew she was trapped. He would find her, no matter what.

And she *had* to find Danton before the evil let loose in this place found him. Certain he was an innocent in this massacre, she had to catch up to him and talk to him before he could be tainted by half-truths.

She sped up and got to the end of the corridor in time to see Danton in plain sight, heading in yet another direction. One with fitful lighting and several discarded bodies—heavily armed guards. Instinct made her more cautious, yet still she followed.

At a darkened area, Danton turned another corner.

Leah slowed as she reached the intersection—she heard voices—and carefully looked around.

Thankfully, she was cautious, for surrounded by darkness, Danton stood mere yards ahead of her, frozen in place as though he were trying to assess the situation. He was so caught up in the drama a dozen yards ahead of them that he didn't notice her.

Dozens of escapees gathered in a large room, and they were passing around weapons and ammunition. Dear Lord, it was the armory. In their midst, a blonde—Rachel—seemed to be in charge.

The sight took away Leah's breath, and she slid back around the corner. How could she get to Danton now? Too late. She couldn't just walk silently to him, place her hand on his arm, and indicate that he should come with her. After what had been done to him, it would take some fancy talking to regain his trust.

And if she tried talking to Danton, Leah knew she would draw the attention of every escapee in earshot.

Now they would be even more dangerous, she thought—those responsible for the slaughter. There were probably explosives in the armory as well, which meant the escapees could blast their way out of the complex. Then what?

Leah couldn't let that happen.

She had to chance that she could get Danton to come with her and, somehow, to help her.

But rounding the corner once again, she realized she'd waited a moment too long—Danton was on the move again, heading straight for the armory.

Chapter 20

"Found the C-4, Rachel!" one of the mutants yelled.

"Good."

Her mind spinning with the reality of what they could do with such firepower, Rachel took a look around the armory—a single room about thirty feet wide, fifty long. The center of the room held a half dozen tables with benches for briefings along with a small canteen table, home to a big coffee urn and bottled water. The long wall to her right held racks of supplies and uniforms. The one to her left, open cabinets stocked with handguns, assault weapons, and explosives—all available to them now.

Standing across the room from the doorway where the computer was located, Rachel took a quick count of the patients who had joined her—nearly thirty so far—a very small army.

And still no Danton.

Where the hell was he?

She didn't have forever to wait. The military was probably already executing some kind of counter-measure. At least they wouldn't call for reinforcements—not to a facility with a top secret project.

Thinking Danton had lied to her, Rachel decided she couldn't wait any longer.

"What else do we need to blow up this hellhole?" she asked.

Not to mention everyone who worked here—every person responsible for the experiments that had eventually imprisoned the scientific volunteers.

"We need a detonator for the plastic explosive," someone said.

Suddenly distracted, she said, "Then find one." Her senses overwhelming her, Rachel let her thoughts veer in a different direction.

Danton . . . he was close by. . . . she could feel him . . . as if her blood recognized his. . . .

Her mood shifted to one of elation.

She moved across the room toward the open doors and stared into the darkened hallway.

"Danton, I can feel you. I know you're there. Please show yourself."

Indeed, mere seconds later, a man tentatively stepped out of the shadows. Elation waning, Rachel frowned. At first glance, he was a disappointment. He was thin . . . not very tall . . . certainly not well muscled. His caramel-colored skin had an ashen gray sheen. And the way he was looking around, as if aghast at the sight of so many malformed patients, made her doubt he could do anything to help. No sense of power in this Danton.

Surely Josef had his reasons for wanting her to contact the man. Danton must have some special knowledge or power, since Josef was convinced he could get her out of here. *And* help bring Josef back from the dead.

She asked, "You *are* Danton Dumas?"

His expression wary, he nodded. "I am."

"Thank God."

"God has nothing to do with what's happened to us."

The way he was looking at her, examining her with those dark eyes as if he wanted to trust her but wasn't sure he could, alerted Rachel.

Sensing he was looking for some kind of a connection, she pulled her features into an expression of pain, moved to his side, and touched his arm. "You're right, of course," she whispered. "Men, not God, have played this cruel trick on us."

Men who would pay, she thought for the hundredth time, starting with the head scientist, BB. The C-4 would come in handy for more than getting out of the complex. She wondered if there was enough to blow up everyone left behind.

"What's going on here?" Danton asked.

"We're simply trying to find a way out."

"With weapons?"

"We may need them."

Danton looked around the room. "Anyone who stood in your way is already dead."

"Not everyone. And we acted out of self-protection," Rachel assured him, adding a quiver to her voice. "The government we served betrayed us, Danton. We're simply trying to free ourselves."

Danton's tension was transparent. Rachel could tell he wanted to believe her, but he needed a bit more prodding. She drew closer to him—close enough that her breast brushed his arm—and looked up into his dark eyes.

"We're all in the same boat," she said softly. "We

all need each other, right? It's us or them, and I fear they won't let us go without a fight."

"If we stay out of their way, no one else has to die. There are some people who work at this facility who are innocent. Who wouldn't want to see anyone hurt."

About to protest that every person in any way responsible for their incarceration—responsible for making them no better than lab rats—*deserved* to die, Rachel remembered Josef telling her they needed Danton to cooperate and that he wouldn't be convinced that violence was necessary. And he was undoubtedly worried about the bitch Leah.

"But we have to stop the scientists from further experiments," she said aloud.

From developing a cure. She *wanted* her powers. Wanted *more*.

Josef had assured her Danton could give her more, that he had powers she could not imagine and could easily share them with her. But first she had to get free of this place. Get Danton alone. She knew how to handle a man so he would give her what she wanted—whatever powers he had, plus a way to bring Josef back from the dead.

"Rachel, do you have plans of the whole complex so we can see the safest route to take?"

Safe—she'd just wanted her and Josef to be safe, to spend their lives together entwined in scientific genius. They could have been great leaders, revered by the world. Now look at her fate.

"The computer," she said, gesturing toward it, even as her mind started to drift off in search of her lover. "The schematics are up."

Baden-Baden . . . a good memory . . . something to hold her through the coming hours.

Try as she might, Rachel couldn't latch on to the memory, couldn't feel Josef. She then tried to return to their initial meeting at the Eagle's Nest. Nothing.

Fearing Josef had been torn from her again, she felt a moment's panic. "Aaahhh!"

"Rachel, what is it?" Danton asked, sounding alarmed as he turned away from the computer. "Are you in pain? Is there anything I can do for you?" Danton asked.

"Pain, yes." Realizing she'd drifted off for a moment, she improvised quickly, touched her forehead, ran shaky fingers through her hair. "I can't make it stop. Not until I am free from this place." She grabbed on to the emotion, intensified it until her eyes filled with believable tears, something she'd learned to do at age four to make her father do what she wanted. "Help me, Danton, please."

Once he helped her get free, she would make him give her these new powers Josef promised. And then Josef himself. She would have the man, wouldn't have to rely on memories . . . or a disembodied voice. She would have everything she wanted—freedom, power, and a man with whom to share both.

Danton placed a hand on her arm. "First you have to promise not to hurt anyone else."

Before Rachel could think of a way of allaying his fears, an excited buzz went up around the room.

"Look what we found out in the hall, spying on us."

Rachel turned to the armory entrance to see two

men drag in a woman with short red hair wearing a ripped blouse and calf-length skirt.

"Leah," Danton said. "Tell them to let her go, Rachel. Leah's one of the innocents. She'll want to help us."

"You know this person? Bring her here."

The man was unduly rough, but the redhead didn't fight him. Her gaze found Danton and locked in on him.

"Danton, I need to talk to you."

"You can talk to *me*," Rachel said, feeling the woman's green eyes bore into her. "I'm in charge here."

"All right," Leah said. "The violence has to stop."

Remembering she wanted Danton's cooperation, Rachel kept her voice reasonable. "It does, but how do you suggest we get out of this complex? The military isn't simply going to open the doors and let us walk out. Do you know of some secret exit not on the schematics?"

"I wasn't suggesting you leave," Leah said, "but start negotiations—"

Rachel stepped closer to Danton, slipped a hand between his body and arm so she attached herself to him. "You see, Danton? Didn't I tell you this woman was trying to fool you? She wants to keep us prisoner."

"No, that's not what she's saying." Danton looked to Leah. "It isn't, is it?"

The redhead stared at him, then said, "No one can leave here, Danton. Not until we sort things out."

Chapter 21

"Fall back!" Scott grabbed Harriman's shoulder and yanked him away from the four vampires. The creatures advanced—eyes red, flesh a sickly, curdled yellow.

Brubaker's severed head lay among the guts that colored the floor, eyes and mouth wide open, spinal column trailing from the stump.

White ignored the command and opened fire. The gold-alloy rounds from his M4 punched bloody holes through one of the male vampires, killing him instantly.

"Hold your fire!" Scott cried. Despite the attack, he still saw these creatures as soldiers who had volunteered for Project 24 to serve their country. BB was working on a cure. They could be healed. To lose faith in them would be to lose faith in himself.

A female vampire leaped at White. The man pivoted sharply and fired, blowing her head apart in a meaty spray.

"I said, hold your fire!" Scott rushed forward, clutched White by the arm, and whipped him toward the door. The man glared at Scott as he nearly tripped over his feet, and then bolted to the opposite side of the storeroom, where he joined Harriman.

Scott realized the vampires were attacking to sate a thirst they could not understand or control. It was a desperation that Scott knew all too well, a desperation he now felt as he jammed the inhaler between his lips and sucked in spray after acrid spray.

But he could still taste the blood that had splattered into his mouth and feel the terrible urge to feed hum through his veins.

Scott moved to follow Harriman when the two remaining vampires slammed into him from behind, jarring the shotgun from his grasp. They fell into a heap. The female vampire then rolled on top of him, hissing and shrieking.

"We can help you!" Scott yelled, but the woman was beyond listening, insane with blood thirst. *I can't let this happen to me, too. . . . I won't . . .*

Scott pressed his forearm into the woman's throat as she strained to sink her broken, bloodstained teeth into his face. Her breath smelled like a mass grave and kicked his own blood thirst into overdrive, causing the razor-sharp need to course through his body like a living thing.

Gagging, Scott struggled to hold the thrashing woman at bay. From the corner of his eye, he saw Harriman fire his .45. The remaining male vampire went down as blood sprayed from his throat.

BB's voice crackled in his ear. "Scott, you there? You've got more hostiles headed your way!"

As his adrenaline redlined, Scott felt the DNA-charged power surge through his muscles. He shoved the woman away, careful to use as little of his enhanced strength as possible to make sure he didn't injure her. She slid across the floor and slammed into a row of liquid-nitrogen canisters, which toppled with a series of clangs. Scott then jumped to his feet and retrieved the shotgun.

"Behind you!" Harriman yelled.

Scott threw a glance over his shoulder. The woman was already up and charging. He racked the shotgun and fired, sending a cluster of gold-laced rubber bullets into her chest. She jerked violently, fell to the floor, and lay still. Down, but not dead.

At that moment, a dozen more patients rushed into the room, appearing like diseased phantoms. The patients snarled as they bolted for him, clearly out for blood.

Scott ran but was careful to stay between Harriman and White and the patients. He refused to let the patients be cut down, regardless of their transgressions. They were victims. They didn't deserve to die.

Harriman aimed his pistol. "Get down!"

"I said, hold your fire!" Scott yelled, and veered to the liquid-nitrogen canisters lining the wall. He hefted one of the canisters over his head and then flung it into several others that were close to the charging patients. The canisters exploded and sprayed liquid nitrogen across the room, forming a barrier.

The patients scattered, howling in pain and confusion, which gave Scott enough time to lead Harriman and White out the opposite door. They kept running toward sick bay, which Scott knew was located in an adjacent sector.

The battle had lasted only minutes—but minutes they could hardly spare.

As they ran, Scott cursed himself for using his powers. Things could have spiraled out of control. He'd gotten damn lucky. "Where are we, BB?" he asked.

"Turn left, second doorway."

Scott continued down a short hall, then kicked

open the sick bay door as his bloodlust continued to hammer in his chest like a second heartbeat. He prayed that Leah would know how to control the thirst, since the inhaler had become ineffective.

He entered, leading with the shotgun, but Leah was nowhere to be found. "She isn't here, BB!"

"Okay, okay," the scientist said with alarm. "Give me a couple of minutes to track her down!"

Scott knew that Leah wouldn't have moved unless absolutely necessary—or unless she'd been taken. He conjured her in his mind's eye as he tried to send her an unspoken message. He knew he lacked the magical ability, but it was all he could think of to do. *Hold on, baby. We're coming.*

Scott walked toward Harriman and White, who kept watch near the door. "Colonel, we've got to keep—"

Harriman cut him short with a punch to the jaw. "Don't ever pull a stunt like that again," he growled. "Those things were out to kill us."

Scott recovered quickly and stepped forward. White blocked his way. "Those 'things' are *soldiers*, Colonel."

"Not anymore. They're hostiles and will be treated as such."

"I won't let you use deadly force against them," Scott said. "It's that simple."

"You aren't giving us any choice, son."

"Excuse me?"

"You're refusing to employ your powers. We have no choice but to resort to more lethal means."

From a battlefield perspective, Harriman was right. A soldier used the force at his disposal without quarter until an enemy was defeated. But Scott knew there were other options. There were always other options. Leah had taught him that.

Before Scott could respond to Harriman, BB's voice crackled in his ear. "Leah's in the armory, but she's not alone."

"Rachel?" Scott asked, swallowing thickly as his blood thirst surged again.

"Rachel and a peanut gallery from hell. Looks like they're gearing up for an attack."

"We're heading for the armory," Scott relayed to Harriman, trying to hide his condition. If Harriman knew, he'd assume command, and Scott didn't want to think about how many lives might be lost if that happened. "I need your guarantee, Colonel, that we'll continue to do things my way."

"After what we've been through, I can't make that promise, son," Harriman said. "If the situation were reversed, neither could you."

With BB's guidance, Scott led the team quickly to the armory. When they reached the door, Scott held up his fist, signaling Harriman and White to stop behind him.

He heard muffled conversation coming from inside and recognized Rachel's voice. Danton was there, too.

And Leah.

Scott felt overwhelming relief that was quickly undermined by dread. He looked at his watch. They had barely ten minutes before the purge. He slid to the edge of the door. "BB, what's going on in there?"

"Bad guys all over the place," BB replied. "No way to get in without being seen."

"They armed?"

"Some."

"Where's Leah?"

"Far left corner. Rachel and Danton are speaking with her."

"Is she facing this way? Can I signal her?"

"She's got her back to you."

Scott closed his eyes, took a series of slow, deep breaths. The blood thirst felt like a separate, pulsing presence that threatened to eclipse everything he needed to be to save Leah. He struggled to maintain focus as sweat poured down his neck. "Give me some good news, BB."

There was a moment of dead air before BB said, "Leah is alive, Scott. That's more than we can say for a lot of people in there."

"You look like shit," Harriman said from behind him.

"I'm fine," Scott lied. "Leah is inside—"

"Not even your powers can give us the advantage now," Harriman interrupted. From his tone, it was clear he was assuming command. "There are too many hostiles. Too many variables." He looked at his watch, and his expression darkened. "Full breach. It's the only option if we want to get Leah out in time."

Scott shook his head. "If we go in firing, this'll turn into the O.K. Corral."

"I'm not about to let your sympathy for these people compromise our lives or this mission. Not this time, son."

Scott knew Harriman was proposing a last-ditch tactic. Hit hard, hit fast, and try to take advantage of the chaos. He'd used the strategy himself during Special Ops missions in the past, with mixed results.

Sometimes it was successful. Just as often it led to disaster.

"I'm asking you to reconsider, Colonel. There's got to be another way."

Harriman looked at him with a hint of sadness. "I know why you insisted on this mission. Frankly, it's similar to the reason I decided to come with you. But this isn't open for discussion. I'm giving you a direct order. We go on my mark."

As Harriman motioned White forward, all Scott could think about was Leah getting caught in the cross fire with dozens of patients whose only mistake had been stepping up when their country needed them.

He couldn't let it happen. Wouldn't.

Before Harriman could give the command, Scott set the shotgun on the floor, placed his hands on his head, and then walked into the armory.

Up close, the mutated patients appeared even more horrible, and the odor that had greeted him when he'd first entered the complex assailed his nostrils with renewed intensity—a noxious blend of ammonia, formaldehyde, and God knew what else that seeped from their very pores.

"Rachel Ackart!" Scott yelled.

Every head turned his way. Some froze, stunned by his audacity, while others took a few menacing steps toward him.

Rachel and Danton glared while Leah regarded him with amazement, as though she couldn't believe that a man would go to such lengths for her. Scott hoped she knew that nothing would have kept him away, and that he would do much more for her if given the chance.

"Stay back!" Rachel said. "One step closer, and I'll have you torn limb from limb!"

"I'm not here to hurt you," Scott said, raising his hands in a conciliatory gesture. "I'm here to tell you that you need to put down your weapons before it's too late."

"Too late for what?"

"The military is about to burn this place out."

"Bull!" Danton said angrily. "You'd never sacrifice yourselves."

"It's the truth."

"What do you know about truth?" Rachel asked. "You're one of *them*. One of the animals that kept me in here." Her anger was contagious and began to spread through the crowd.

"I know enough. We were exposed to the same genetic code."

"You're a liar," Danton interjected. "If that was true, you'd have used your power to catch me in New Orleans."

So his opting for restraint had come back to haunt him. Scott grimaced at the irony. Realizing he had no choice but to prove himself, Scott focused on his right hand while visualizing a galleon at sea disappearing into thick fog. *My hand is nothing. . . . My hand is nothing. . . .*

He felt a familiar tingling in his wrist and then felt the weight of his palm and fingers fade as his hand dissolved into a static cloud of gray mist. Taking a breath, he prepared for whatever chain reaction the demonstration of power might trigger in his body but felt nothing. With a bit more focus, his hand rematerialized.

"I understand what you're going through, Rachel," Scott went on as the blood thirst continued to slice mercilessly at his insides. He knew he wouldn't be able to control himself for much longer. He would need to feed soon. "My body is changing, too. In ways I can't control. At times, it feels like I've become someone else."

"Some*thing* else," Rachel whispered. "I've become something else entirely."

Scott felt a sort of connection with her now. They both knew the terror that often accompanies unwanted, irrevocable change. Nearby, Leah stood absolutely still. She understood what he was trying to do and waited, biding her time.

"I don't know what the future holds or if I'll be around to see that future at all," Scott said. "But I do know that I can have a profound impact on the present." He took a step closer. "Tell these people to lay down their weapons, Rachel. If you hurry, you can save their lives."

Danton glared at him, eyes blazing with what looked like jealousy, and then turned to Rachel. "We can't let him turn us into prisoners again!"

Scott returned his focus to Leah, who stared back intently. He held out his hand to her and nodded. She stepped away from Rachel and Danton, who were too consumed with each other to notice. Miraculously, the crowd didn't react either, apparently content with taking its cue from Rachel.

Scott kept his hand outstretched as Leah approached. He wanted nothing more than to carry her far, far away from this place. . . . Suddenly, a gouging pain tore through his abdomen. He'd let his guard down, and the blood thirst had welled up like a storm surge over a levee. With a grunt, he went down on one knee.

A patient whose body was little more than a mass of tumors lunged for him. Scott didn't know if the patient was taking advantage of his weakness or simply trying to keep him from falling. In the end, it didn't matter.

The patient was blown off his feet by a hail of gold-alloy rounds.

Scott whirled as Harriman and White charged into the room, guns blazing. They'd interpreted the patient's act as a threat and decided to take matters into their own hands.

The crowd broke into a riot—screamed, howled, and attacked one another in rage and confusion.

Scott tried to keep a bead on Rachel, but it was impossible through the chaos. He grabbed Leah by the wrist and pulled her to him. "You okay?"

She nodded, hugging him tightly. "Are you?"

Before he could reply, a patient bowled into them. Scott dodged the patient's desperate blows and then delivered a jab to his jaw, which took him down. Still clutching Leah's hand, Scott rushed to the door, quickly incapacitating any patient who got in their way with a few well-placed punches.

Across the room, Scott saw a female vampire leap at White. White fired at the woman point-blank, cutting her in half. He continued to fire haphazardly into the crowd, full-auto, with an expression of sadistic glee. Some rounds flew wide and sparked along a pyramid of ammunition boxes stacked against the far wall.

Jesus . . .

Scott pulled Leah into a dead run as the pyramid detonated with a hiccupping *boom*.

Flame streaked across the armory, immolating several patients where they stood. The blistering heat touched off more boxes of ammunition, which ignited with rolling, thundering blasts in a precursor to the napalm purge, which was only minutes away.

Danton ran from the flames, leading Rachel by the hand. Scott saw White give chase before a ball of flame engulfed them all, obliterating his view. When the flames rolled past, they were gone.

"Take cover!" Scott yelled to Harriman, who stood with his back to a wall as he reloaded his .45.

Scott yanked Leah from the room moments before a jet of flame rushed past them. Too fucking close. And then Scott caught a glimpse of his watch. The battle had wasted the remaining time they'd had left. They'd never make it back to the control room before the purge.

Scott pushed Leah into an alcove and pressed his body against hers, shielding it. He knew his toughened body would never be able to withstand napalm, but there was a chance—a slim chance—that he could absorb enough heat to save Leah's life.

Scott wrapped his arms around her narrow waist as she clung to him. He could feel the soft weight of her breasts against his chest as he guided her deeper into the alcove, trying to expose as little of their bodies as possible to the coming heat. She pressed herself more urgently against him in reply, and he closed his eyes, nearly giving in to the sensation.

BB's voice crackled in his ear. "Scott, I don't see

you and Leah on the inbound monitors. You've got less than ninety seconds before things light up!"

"We aren't going to make it."

"What the are fuck you talking about?" BB's voice rose in pitch. "I can lead you out of there! It isn't too late!"

But Scott knew it *was* too late. There was too much ground to cover in too little time. "BB, listen to me. Rachel Ackart and Danton Dumas are dead. If the officers in charge tap into the armory camera, they can see for themselves and stop the purge."

"What if they don't?"

"We've got one minute, pal. Please hurry."

"Jesus. Hold on!"

The line went dead.

"What did BB say?" Leah asked.

"He said it'd be no problem," Scott said. "No problem at all."

"I can sense your emotions, remember?" she said. "Besides, if we were safe, you would've let me up."

"Maybe I like holding you like this."

Leah shifted so that her face pressed against his cheek.

Scott's passion surged along with his bloodlust. He could feel the beat of her heart, the pulse of her throat against his, the silky rush of blood through her veins. He traced his lips and tongue gently along the curve of her neck, lightly nipped her flesh. She moaned softly and interlaced her fingers with his.

If these were indeed his last moments, he wanted to spend them with her, and he wanted them to feel like forever.

Chapter 22

Pitch darkness.

Moving through solid earth, Danton saw nothing but felt everything: abject fear, his body scrape-sliding through dirt and pillowed bedrock, the burning pain of his muscles as he struggled to climb toward the surface and freedom while he pulled Rachel in tow.

He'd transferred his power to Rachel by touch, and now they both had the ability to pass through solid matter, though he wondered if she was in shock since it felt like she was hanging limply behind him, much heavier than she should be.

Like a lifeguard pulling an unconscious swimmer toward shore, Danton continued to drag Rachel up a punishingly steep grade toward the surface. But the steeper the grade, the faster they'd be free, so he struggled—step by agonizing step—terrified that he'd become disoriented, that his burning muscles would give out, or that he might lose focus and cause them to rematerialize under tons of earth.

A bolt of panic shot through him, nearly breaking his concentration. Had Rachel been injured? Was that why she wasn't moving?

He pushed away the fear. No, she was fine. After the ammunition boxes had detonated in the armory, they'd fled the firestorm side by side. He couldn't recall any wounds on her body. No burns or blood or torn clothing.

"Do you trust me?" he'd said as a soldier rushed toward them, followed by a massive, roiling fireball.

"Yes, Danton," she'd replied. "I trust you."

And then he'd pulled her through the armory wall.

Rachel was fine, he told himself again, needing to believe it was true. In a strange way, he felt devoted to her even though they hardly knew each other. She'd inspired hope in him when all he'd felt had been despair since Rebecca's death. He hoped he could reciprocate the gesture in some way. Maybe help her get past the trauma of what she'd endured at the hands of the military.

Danton continued to wade up through dirt and rock, carefully pulling his precious cargo and doing his best to ignore the gouging pain in his arms and legs. Suddenly, he felt the soil change consistency— from dry, impacted earth to gummy, shifting silt.

His heart leaped. Louisiana topsoil! The last dozen feet were like slogging though tar, but he knew he was close to the surface now. And then the darkness smash-cut to blinding white light as he felt a humid, salty breeze rush across his face, and his full range of movement return.

Panting, Danton opened his eyes. He was in the employee parking lot outside Miescher Laboratories, hidden from the front gate by rows of cars and SUVs. Wiping the dirt from his clothes, he heard a soft moan. Rachel was beside him on her hands and knees. He clutched her arm lightly and helped her to her feet.

"Are you okay, Rachel?" he asked.

"You did it," she said softly, still shaken from the experience. "Your sister would be so proud, Danton."

Danton couldn't help but smile as he regarded Rachel's ratty hair and muddy scrubs. She was a mess but still utterly gorgeous. "We're free, but not out of danger. We're in the lab's parking lot. We need to—"

He lost the power of speech when she slumped against him for support. Her body felt so good against his. ". . . We need to . . ." And then he fell silent as she burrowed her face into his neck.

"There was someone," she breathed.

Closing his eyes, Danton became lost in the tickling sensation of her lips against his skin. "Someone . . . ?"

". . . behind me. . . ." She wavered, still weak, but began to regain her bearings. "I had your hand, and someone had mine."

Danton pulled away in alarm. "Someone had your hand?"

Just then, he saw a dark figure rise up from behind a nearby car—the soldier who'd chased them in the armory. The man must have grabbed Rachel's hand at just the right moment and traveled up through the earth with them. That would explain why Rachel had felt so heavy.

Clad in a khaki jumpsuit and holding an assault rifle, the soldier stumbled toward them. Before Danton realized what he was doing, he let out a cry and charged, but the man collapsed before the battle was joined.

Danton stopped short. "Wow, I didn't know I had it in me."

Rachel moved quickly past him and crouched by

the unmoving soldier. She rolled the man's head to the side to reveal a ragged wound in his throat. "He's been bitten by a vampire," she said, standing again. "We shouldn't be here when he wakes up."

"You mean we're going to leave him?"

"We don't have a choice."

"We can't let the military do to him what they did to you and me," Danton said. "They'll turn him into a guinea pig. Or worse."

"He tried to kill us, Danton."

Danton knew it was true, but he couldn't leave the soldier behind. Not when he was a vampire himself. Helping him deal with his vampiric transformation was, well, the *humane* thing to do. "He needs our help just like you needed mine, Rachel. We can't abandon him. Besides, he might appreciate the gesture and help us in return."

Rachel looked at Danton evenly and then nodded, finally, when she realized he wouldn't give in. "We need a car."

"Exactly what I was thinking."

Danton pressed his right hand through the driver's-side window of a yellow, old-model hatchback in front of them and unlocked the door. As Danton climbed behind the wheel, he made a mental note to notify the owner after this mess was over, then passed both hands up through the steering column and felt for ignition wires. Soon, the car sputtered to life with a burst of purple exhaust. "Let's put our friend in back," he told Rachel.

"Already on it," she said.

Danton turned to see the unconscious soldier floating in a standing position above the ground with his boots a half inch from the asphalt. Telekinesis, Danton realized with awe. So Rachel had powers, too. Something else they had in common. Suddenly, he didn't consider himself such a freak anymore. "That's a handy trick."

Rachel guided the soldier into the hatchback and then climbed into the passenger seat and placed her hand on his knee. "Let's hope they think we're dead and don't come looking for us."

"Let's hope," Danton nodded, feeling his leg tingle where Rachel touched it.

He put the car into gear and then drove from the parking lot in another burst of purple exhaust. After navigating a deserted side road, Danton picked up speed, entered the interstate, and merged into traffic heading for New Orleans.

Rachel sat silently. She stared out the window, lips moving slightly, lost in her own dreams. Or nightmares.

He understood the impulse to escape from reality. He'd felt like crawling into a hole after Rebecca died—and then felt like crawling into a deeper, darker hole when he'd realized his body was changing. If it hadn't been for Lilly Fry, he might have done just that. Lilly had given him the space and time he'd needed, and he'd do the same now for Rachel.

After glancing back at the unconscious soldier, Danton thought of Leah. He wished he could have pulled her from the armory, too. But part of him couldn't quite get past her decision to work with Scott Boulder. The man was military, a professional killer. So what if he'd been infected by Andre's DNA?

As they entered the city limits, Danton realized

they couldn't go back to his apartment. If the military were looking for them, they'd go there for sure. "Rachel, we need a place to stay." Given her military experience, he knew she'd choose an appropriate safe house. "Any suggestions?"

She turned to him, eyes still distant. "My sister owns a pied-à-terre in the city."

"Are you sure you want to involve another person in this?"

"She's out of the country."

Rachel glanced out the windshield at the passing city skyline, and pointed to an upcoming exit. "Get off here."

Danton followed Rachel's directions through the French Quarter to a side street lined with oaks. They stopped in front of a three-story building adorned with a brick façade and white wooden balconies. Given the area and architecture, Danton judged the building to have been built in the mid-1800s. No doubt a former residence for slaves, it had since been converted into an upscale apartment building.

Danton cut the ignition, climbed from the car, and opened the hatchback. "Our boy is still out cold."

Rachel nodded as she lifted the man effortlessly with her mind, again making him float vertically an inch or so from the asphalt.

After stowing the man's assault rifle out of sight, Danton took a blanket from the backseat and hung it over the soldier's bald head like a shawl to hide his bloodied neck and uniform. He and Rachel then walked on either side of him with their arms around his shoulders. From a distance, it would look like they were guiding an intoxicated friend home after a long night on Bourbon Street.

"Again, nice job back there," Danton said as they entered the building and headed down a hallway. He was becoming more and more impressed with Rachel. Intelligence, compassion, beauty, resourcefulness . . . He felt a flutter in his chest.

"*Danke,*" she whispered.

"*Sie sind willkommen.*"

She raised an eyebrow. "You speak German?"

"*Ja, Fraülein.* Believe it or not, I'm freakishly proficient in languages, including computer languages and mathematics. I can pick them up in no time."

She regarded him closely. "Impressive."

"Did you study German in college?" Danton asked.

"An old friend taught me," Rachel said, looking away. "A very old friend." She stopped at apartment number two. "We're here."

"Be right back." Danton walked through the door into a small living area tastefully decorated with antique French furniture, toile de Jouy, linen velvets, and alabaster. He recognized the Creole style, and it made him feel at home. Rebecca had had similar tastes.

He unlocked the door and let Rachel in. The soldier floated in dutifully behind her. They entered a half bathroom, where Rachel dumped the man on his butt inside the shower stall.

"Should we take him to a hospital?" Danton asked.

"No ordinary hospital is equipped for what he's about to become," Rachel replied. "He has a much better chance if we take care of him here."

"How do you know so much about his condition?"

"I was a captive for quite some time, Danton. I lis
tened and learned as much as I could," she said
squeezing by him in the confined space. "We'll dea
with him after he wakes up. In the meantime, I'm
going to take a shower and check the closet for
clothes."

Danton followed her out, then closed the bath
room door and wedged the back of a chair under
neath the knob. Just to be safe. He turned to ask
Rachel if she was hungry, but she'd disappeared into
the master bedroom and closed the door.

Sitting on the sofa, he decided that he'd made the
right choice in picking Rachel over Leah. Leah would
certainly have left him by now in favor of Scott Boul
der while Rachel seemed to care about him. He real
ized that he felt safe with Rachel and hoped she fel
the same about him.

Contentment aside, however, he felt growing dread
He wanted to believe they'd escaped the influence o
the Philosopher's Stone but had a cold, nasty feeling
they hadn't. Not by a long shot.

Chapter 23

The last-minute order to halt the purge came through with seconds to spare. Reinforcements armed with gold-alloy bullets and other of BB's weapons arrived to round up the couple of dozen patients who'd survived the explosion and get them back into containment.

At Harriman's orders, Leah and Scott retreated from the nearly destroyed armory and headed directly for the infirmary. Scott hung on to her hand like he wouldn't let it go.

"You saved my life," Leah said. "Again. I owe you."

"We're part of a team, Leah. No owing involved."

For a moment, she was happy—until Scott squeezed her hand too hard and she sensed he was fighting an internal battle. He tried to let go of her, but she hung on to him, wanting him to know she was with him and unafraid. They passed pools of blood and splatters on the walls, and she felt Scott's struggle with the thirst increase.

So when they reached the infirmary and BB said, "Good news, I'm pretty sure I've got it right this time—the cure, that is," Leah went weak with relief. "I was close before," BB said. "Just needed to adjust the ingredients of the recipe, so to speak."

"Thank God," Scott said.

Leah breathed easier. Scott needed this good news. She was so happy for him. And after taking the cure, he would have no reason to keep holding her at arm's length.

On the move, BB indicated they should follow. "I'm just glad I can finally do something for these poor souls. Well, hopefully take away the perverted powers they were given. Nothing I can do about repairing cellular damage. All these months . . ." He shook his head, and regret was clear in his tone.

Realizing the head scientist had a guilt-inspired vulnerability, Leah impulsively reached over and hugged his narrow shoulders. "Good work, BB."

A blush creeping up his neck into his fire red hair, BB led them into an unoccupied area separated from the rest of the room by a military tan curtain. There was an exam table and all the usual medical paraphernalia, either attached at the wall or sitting on a wheeled cart.

"Hop on up, pal." BB indicated the exam table. "I'll get a doc to check you over, give us a heads-up on your vitals. Then someone will see to those cuts and scrapes."

"Forget everything but the cure."

Scott sat but didn't relax. His body stiffened and his features pulled into a scowl, and Leah knew he was fighting the thirst even now.

"You should be the last one to take the cure, Scott," BB said, "after we see the results on others firsthand. You know . . . just in case. We could be left with a nightmare if it worked on you but not on them. Any clue as to how many are still alive?"

"No idea."

"There are dead everywhere in the corridors," Leah said, purposely distancing herself from the horrific images that had burned a place in her mind. "And now in the armory. But they've been teaming up in gangs—I ran into a few. There could be others hiding out anywhere in the complex."

BB nodded. "Saw some of that action on the monitors. My assistants are preparing a distribution system—the cure in the form of a spray. I plan to discharge it into the ventilation tunnels and turn on the air full blast. Particulates should hit every corridor and every room on every floor, all practically at once."

"So it eliminates the blood thirst for sure, right?" Leah asked, watching for Scott's reaction.

"You bet. About an hour after spraying the rats, we set out blood for them, and they had no interest."

Scott nodded in grim relief. "I want to be first, BB. We owe a debt to these people. Call me a human guinea pig, whatever. Just let it be me."

BB shifted from one foot to the other as Scott locked gazes with the scientist. In the end, Scott's natural power won out, because BB capitulated. "All right. If you insist. Be right back."

He left the area, leaving Leah alone with Scott.

"At last something for *you* to be thankful for," she said. "A small reward for what you just did."

"I only did my duty."

Suddenly, his features collapsed into a grimace, and she knew his blood thirst was getting worse. Several times on the way back from the armory, he'd used his inhaler, and she'd realized it wasn't working. His clothes and skin splattered with blood made things doubly difficult for him. She touched his arm and sensed a bit of the torture he was feeling.

"Perfect timing on BB's part," she said.

Scott tried to grin at her, but the expression fell short. "I barely remember what it's like to feel normal."

"Sorry, son, but you won't be able to feel normal for a while longer," boomed a deep male voice.

Leah turned to see Colonel Harriman coming up behind her.

"How long will the cure take to work?" Scott asked him, sounding surprised.

"That's not what I meant. It's not a matter of how long. You can't *take* the cure, not just yet."

"I don't understand. If the remaining inmates have no powers, where's the risk?"

"The Philosopher's Stone. You still need to find it. No cure, and that's an order."

Sensing the anger growing in Scott, Leah tried to reason with Harriman. "Scott's vampiric powers aren't going to help find the Stone."

"No, but they may be necessary to protect it. We don't know who else is looking for it, and if Andre really is out in the ether somewhere, there's a certain risk. The two of you are our best defense against the bastard."

Scott asked, "Are you telling me I can *never* take the cure?" even as BB returned, vial in hand.

"I'm saying it's not in our best interests now—not until we have the Stone in our possession. That's all."

Leah could see pain reflected in Scott's eyes as he

nodded in defeat. Then he grimaced, and his entire body stiffened.

"What's wrong?" Harriman asked. "You told me you weren't wounded."

Scott choked out, "Blood thirst."

"The inhaler?"

"The inhaler doesn't work anymore," Leah told the colonel. "I saw him take it several times, but it didn't seem to do anything. He needs blood."

"I'll get it," BB said.

"I'm not drinking any damn blood. I can't."

"You *can* drink it and you *will*," Leah said. "You'll do what you have to for now. The blood thirst is like a fever. I can see it in your eyes, your face, your body. You can fight with everything you have, Scott, but you might not remain strong enough to control it. You would never forgive yourself if you let it get the best of you."

His features pulled even tighter. "I would kill myself before I let that happen."

Leah shuddered at the thought. Knowing Scott, he would do something so noble. "Let's not go there, all right?" she begged him. "I promise you I will find a way to help overcome your blood thirst, but in the meantime, you have to be able to function if we're going to find the Philosopher's Stone."

"Seriously, you think you can do something to help?" Harriman asked.

Leah nodded. "Using magic." Harriman didn't know Andre had forced his blood on Scott and in turn she'd saved Scott's soul and kept him from becoming a vampire in fact. "I'm not sure what I can do yet. It would take a very powerful spell. I can research what I have to do when we get to New Orleans."

She could consult with a Voodooist . . . or read through a Voodooist's spell books. As far as she knew, Danton's sister Rebecca's books were still in her quarters above Magic Nights.

"Listen to her, son," Harriman urged. "She's making sense."

Scott swallowed hard and made a last effort to control whatever demons he was fighting. And then the fight went out of him. His emotions washed over Leah, and she knew the disappointment had left him devastated.

"All right." He nodded to BB. "Get the blood." Then he turned back to Leah. "You have to leave."

"Why?"

"I may have to drink the damn blood, but I don't need you here to see me do it."

"Scott, I—"

"Just go, Leah. For once, don't argue with me."

Leah backed away from Scott. He wasn't even looking at her. He sat staring in the other direction, both hands white-knuckling the edge of the exam table.

"When you're done, you'll find me in the lounge."

Scott didn't say anything.

Her throat tight, Leah couldn't help worrying as she did as he asked and left the area. Scott had put his own life in danger to rescue her, but now that he needed her, he wouldn't let her help him.

The lounge held no solace. Desperately needing to be free of the blood on her clothes and skin, Leah went into the ladies' locker room. Maybe a shower and changing into fresh clothes that she'd stored here would make her feel better.

But she couldn't wash away the nightmare she'd just survived. Awful visions filled her mind.

The bodies . . . the blood . . . the savagery.

As she dressed in a fresh rose-colored skirt and rose-embroidered white halter top, she prayed nothing would go wrong with the cure. BB had a point. It really was too bad that he hadn't found the right combination of drugs even twenty-four hours ago. Some of the escapees had been beyond saving, perhaps even before the break. Others were innocent— like Kim, the woman Leah had stayed with until she'd died.

And Danton.

What a horrible waste of life. She remembered he'd been working toward a PhD in linguistics, a branch of anthropology, so they'd had that in common. He hadn't asked for what his sister had done to him. He'd fought the blood thirst on his own. He'd been confused, looking for answers. And before he could get them, his life had been snuffed out.

Not that she was placing blame.

Tossing her ruined clothing in the trash, Leah returned to the lounge and threw herself into a chair with frayed brown upholstery, where she would wait for Scott.

Death came so easy to some. Sometimes she thought the dead were the lucky ones. They weren't left behind to remember the horrors.

Memories . . .

Leah pulled the photo of Dad and Gabe and the digital recorder from her bag. She started the recorder and brushed the images with her fingertips as she listened to her own voice.

"*When Gabe was twelve and I was nine, he used to bug me by walking around calling himself a preteen and saying that he was ready to start dating, as if that put him light-years beyond me. One day when I got really tired of it, I called his bluff. I told this girl Sandy that Gabe really liked her—which he did—and brought her home to talk to him. Gabe was horrified. He didn't know what to say, and Sandy left. Afterward, I suggested he stop bragging until he was old enough to follow through, and he threatened . . . he threatened . . .*" A short pause was followed by her recorded voice saying, "*I don't remember what he threatened to do to me. . . .*"

Leah clicked off the recorder and felt even more alone than she had before turning it on.

She'd lost her family, not only in the flesh but also the real memories—the strong feelings she'd once had for them. She had those feelings for Scott, but he only wanted her when it was *safe*. If you cared for someone, you took chances, not just to protect them but to be with them, to share the bad times as well as the good.

Leah was beginning to think she should get used to being alone. She could do it. That she'd been so self-sufficient in the face of danger, had survived for so long in a hostile environment—all without resorting to violence—amazed her. She'd gotten through several horrible situations physically unscathed.

Alone.

Maybe that was her destiny. Obviously, Scott didn't trust himself in a relationship with her any more than he trusted himself with his vampiric powers. Maybe it would be this way between them forever.

Leah sighed.

She would help Scott tame the blood thirst as she'd promised. Would help find the Philosopher's Stone and secure it so its power was out of Andre's reach forever. But once those things were done, Team Ultra's purpose was fulfilled. Her work here would be finished. And Scott apparently didn't need her the way she wanted to be needed.

So she would go back to her apartment in Albuquerque, would work with her mentor, Javier Estes. Would find her place in the world once and for all.

Alone.

Chapter 24

Scott hated to send Leah away, but he didn't want her to see what he'd become. Not like this, not this time. She'd seen him drink blood during his first battle with Andre, but those had been extreme circumstances. He'd been forced to feed on corpses to regain his strength.

They were in a controlled environment now. Somehow, sating his blood thirst in this matter-of-fact context made it all the more horrifying. He didn't want to make it any more obvious to Leah that he was more monster than man. Taking a cue from Leah, Harriman had left the room as well to give him a few moments of privacy.

"The blood," Scott said, clenching his teeth. "I need it, BB."

"Coming, pal, coming," the scientist said, flinging open a large steel refrigerator. He quickly scanned the interior, which was crowded with racked vials, beakers, and petri dishes, then pulled an opaque plastic bag from the top shelf. The kind that blood banks used. "Shit, I don't have catheter needles or tubes. I'll have to go up to the main lab."

"No time," Scott said. "Give it here."

Pulling a short spout from the top of the bag, BB hurried over and handed it to Scott. The plastic felt slick and frosty. Scott stared at the red-black blood within and felt bile flood his throat even as his thirst kicked into overdrive. "Bon appétit," he rasped, and then tilted back his head as he lifted the spout to his lips.

Scott felt his nausea build as the viscous blood rolled slowly toward the spout. When the blood chilled his lips, he retched and spit out what little had actually made it into his mouth. He tried again with the same result.

His gag reflex was working in opposition to his thirst. It was impulse versus instinct, his humanity at war with the creature within. He wondered why he'd been able to drink from corpses during his run-in with Andre, and decided it was because he'd been crazed in the midst of battle. Or maybe it was because his human side was finally waging a counteroffensive against the transformation. Either way, his body's rebellion brought him some comfort. It meant he wasn't altogether lost to this curse. Not yet. "You got a pill or something I can take instead, BB?"

"I've got freeze-dried capsules and chewables in all sorts of fun shapes and colors, but they aren't nearly as potent as the pure thing. And if it turns out that Leah can't help you control your thirst, you're gonna need all the potency you can get." BB thought a minute, then cocked an eyebrow. "Wait, I've got an idea." He rushed to a computer desk, poured the coffee from a smiley-face thermos, and then emptied the blood bag into it and brought it back. "Might be easier if you can't see it coming."

Scott took the smiley thermos with trembling fingers. "Guess it'll have to do."

He tilted his head back again. Without the visual, he was able to keep his nausea at bay until the cold, coppery blood was already sliding down his throat. He retched once but forced himself to focus on consistency rather than taste to keep from retching again as he swallowed. Soon, the razor-blade pangs of blood thirst subsided.

"You good?" BB asked.

"Do me a favor," Scott said, wiping his mouth with a towel and then handing the thermos back to BB. "Spike it with scotch next time."

BB nodded in relief. "This whole out-of-control blood thirst thing scares me, man. Like special sauce on burgers scares me. Like catching the garter at a wedding scares me, you know?"

"You're telling me."

Presently, Harriman walked in with a file folder. "Are we done in here?"

"In a manner of speaking," Scott replied, feeling "done" with the mission, "done" with the secrecy surrounding it, and more than "done" with the atrocities committed in the name of national security. "Your actions today were unacceptable, Colonel."

"White gave his life to save your ass, son. Don't forget that."

"Due respect, sir, but I was close to achieving a cease-fire. Dozens of lives could have been spared, including his."

"You don't know that for certain."

"And you don't know that it could have been otherwise."

Harriman crossed his arms. "I'm not about to debate my decision with you, but I will say this: You and Dr. Maguire have the luxury of doing what you see fit and leaving it at that. I don't. Every decision I make affects hundreds of people, and I make my choices accordingly. I couldn't take the risk that Rachel Ackart would escape from this base. The result could have been catastrophic, especially since she was in contact with Andre Espinoza, as you said yourself. And if that meant initiating a breach, so be it."

Scott heard echoes of his father in the man. His father hadn't served in the army, far from it—he'd been an alcoholic who could barely hold down a job. Nevertheless, the man had bullied him and his mother with didactic rationales and dogged protocols. The old Harriman wouldn't have fired on his own soldiers. The old Harriman would have found another way. Any other way. This mission had changed the man for the worse. Despite what Harriman had done for him in the past, Scott felt the issue drive a wedge between them.

Now more than ever, Scott wanted to leave the military and start a new life—a *normal* life—with Leah. But he couldn't just yet. "You've got information about the Philosopher's Stone?"

Harriman approached like the conversation had never happened. "Next best thing. Intelligence compiled this report on Danton Dumas. Fortunately, the guy led a relatively uneventful life, so it shouldn't be tough to connect dots that need connecting. Abusive parents, doting sister. He was studying linguistics at Tulane before he was diagnosed with leukemia. You know the rest." He handed Scott the folder. "When you decide how to proceed, let me know. But decide fast, Captain."

Scott watched Harriman leave and then opened the folder and skimmed the documents within. There were plenty of photos showing Danton and Rebecca together. They had clearly loved each other. Despite everything that had happened, Scott was glad that Danton had been able to find some solace in family. Scott wished he'd been able to find the same with his parents, especially his father.

He also found himself checking the control room door periodically, hoping that Leah would walk in. Finally, she did.

"We've got a lead," Scott told her.

"Is that so?" she replied, not looking at him.

"Would you look at the time?" BB said hurriedly, sensing the tension. "I've, um, got to pull something out of the centrifuge." The scientist then hurried out the door and left them alone.

Uh-oh, Scott thought. Apparently, Leah was angrier than he'd been led to believe. "Danton went to graduate school with a girl named Lilly Fry. She was a good friend, maybe even his best friend. She helped him with his studies after he got sick, brought class notes to his bedside, that sort of thing." He waited for Leah's response, and when there was none, he said, "Lilly lives and works in New Orleans."

"We should go to Magic Nights first," Leah said, still not looking at him. "I can look through Rebecca's books, maybe find a spell that will make sure your blood thirst doesn't become an issue again."

Scott didn't know if she was talking about the issue created by his blood thirst in the complex or here in the control room, and decided she'd probably intended it that way. Although he knew she felt hurt, he also wished that she could be more understanding. He was doing the best he could under the circumstances. Either way, an apology was in order.

"Leah, about my sending you out of the room—"

"Are we heading to Magic Nights or not?"

Scott frowned. Well, maybe she wasn't ready for an apology quite yet. Regardless, she was right about Magic Nights.

He ushered Leah from the room, and they walked in silence, heading for Harriman's office to let him know their plan of action. He couldn't imagine being happy without Leah and hoped the misunderstanding wouldn't cause an irreparable rift between them.

He also hoped that finding the Philosopher's Stone this time would end his association with Project 24. But something inside told him that things couldn't possibly be that easy and that Andre Espinoza was even more dangerous dead than alive.

Chapter 25

Andre waved his hand, and the stone and wood and glass of his father's alchemical lab scattered like beads of fallen mercury around him and then faded away into nothing, leaving him alone—a robed, solitary figure in the boundless white of the Space Between.

He needed full concentration. No petty comforts or distractions.

He'd instigated Rachel's escape from the military complex by using her memories of Josef Neumann. But now that she was free, she would no longer be under the influence of sedatives, which had helped make her mind malleable. In addition, she might choose to become independent now that she had tasted freedom—choose her own path to power and vengeance—regardless of what she'd felt for Josef. Rachel had Danton after all and might simply usurp his powers and end things there.

If she did that, Andre knew he would become stranded in the white abyss for eternity.

Thus far, he had used Rachel's passion for Neumann as a guide for which memories to employ. Now he would have to influence a range of emotions. Guilt, desire, arrogance, ambition, entitlement—they would all need to come into play if he wished to control her.

Closing his eyes, Andre tapped into Rachel's mind

again, where his fear was confirmed. Freedom from
confinement and barbiturates had cleared Rachel's
thoughts significantly. Her consciousness no longer
appeared confused but more like her beloved Black
Forest—a formidable place that held more sunlit
possibility than tangled darkness.

His salvation would lie in that darkness.

He delved into it, sifting through the crackling duff
and casting aside duller memories of Neumann until
he found one that glimmered. It was a memory that
took place inside a German hilltop fortress during the
days following Operation Overlord.

Andre projected the memory onto the whiteness
around him, so that he could better determine the
time to intervene. Perhaps sooner and more strongly
this time.

He watched as Rachel crept along the inside wall of
Fort du Roule clad in a white silk robe that billowed
in the humid night breeze. The soft, wet sound of her
bare feet sinking into the muddy grass was accompanied by the distant, thundering roll of Allied bombs
striking the town's coastal fortifications. Normally,
Cherbourg was a jeweled spectacle at night, but the
city had gone dark in defense against the air raid. An-
tiaircraft batteries flashed angrily from that darkness,
sending streams of staccato-white tracer rounds into
the night sky.

She and Josef had moved the lab here by command
of the Führer so the potion that Josef had developed
could be used to strengthen SS troops and help repel
the Allied invasion. Rachel had been ordered to prevent that from happening and hurried toward the
southern wall of the fort to meet French Resistance

fighters who would help her steal the potion, destroy the lab, and escape.

Suddenly, the southern wall exploded, and then a squat, mechanical shape lumbered through the smoking breach with a grinding roar. A Sherman tank, she realized incredulously, as a dozen American GIs streamed through the breach behind it.

Rachel ran in the opposite direction, struggling to maintain her footing on the slick grass as her mind raced with panic. The mission had been called off in favor of an all-out assault. Why in God's name hadn't she been notified? These soldiers would not know she was a spy!

She scrambled through the bunker door, but before she could close it behind her, four GIs stormed through, guns trained. "Don't shoot!" she cried in English.

"Ma'am?" said a red-haired GI in a Texas twang. "Are you American?"

"Yes!" Rachel said, fearing the soldiers wouldn't spare her unless she could convince them she wasn't an English-speaking German.

However, before she could continue, there came a thundering flash within the bunker. The red-haired GI went down. Several more flashes took down the rest.

Neumann stepped from the shadows with a smoking Luger pistol in his right hand. He was also dressed in a white robe. "Gretchen."

"Oh, Josef," she said in German, and rushed toward him.

"Stay right there." Neumann trained the gun on her. She stopped. "Josef? What are you doing?"

"There is no need to continue this masquerade. I know you're a spy, Gretchen. You left signs so obvious that I can only assume you wished to be caught."

"Josef, that's nonsense!"

He knelt and pulled one of the GIs into a sitting position against his knee. The soldier wasn't dead after all and stared at Rachel with pleading eyes. It was the red-haired GI who had spoken to her earlier. Just a boy.

"Tell me the truth, Gretchen," Neumann said. "Tell me, and I'll spare his life."

"Josef, we must hurry—"

"Tell me!"

Rachel met the gaze of the wounded soldier—and Andre could see in her expression that she considered herself the key to stealing Neumann's formula. The one who had infiltrated enemy lines, taken the risks. If these men died to protect her secret, so be it.

"I am not a spy," she said.

"Damn you," Neumann snapped, and shot the GI in the head. Dropping the corpse, he clutched her wrist and pulled her from the bunker. There were explosions all around them, followed by the *rat-a-tat* of small-arms fire as American soldiers engaged Germans within the fort.

"We have to save the formula!" she cried.

He clutched her by the shoulders. "To hell with the formula. All that matters is you and me!" As if to punctuate his point, an explosion rumbled deep within the fort, perhaps in the lab itself.

Andre noted that Neumann was clearly still in love with Rachel despite her duplicity, and that Rachel was terrified of losing everything she had worked for.

A moment of heightened desperation for them both. Perfect to exploit.

Andre quickly took over Neumann's body and then, as Neumann, slapped Rachel. Hard.

Rachel's head whipped to one side. "Josef . . . !"

Andre slapped Rachel again and felt her mind pinwheel as she grew lost in a flurry of emotions: her reticence to betray the man she loved, her loyalty to the Allied command, and her willingness to sacrifice others to accomplish her goals.

"Gretchen! Look at me!" Andre/Josef kissed her cheek even as he tightly clutched her wrists. "I just saved your life, and now it's your turn to save mine. Do that, and I'll return everything you've lost, plus much more. Do you understand?"

Rachel seemed confused, and then her expression cleared. "Yes, Josef."

Andre felt a sense of triumph. He had her. "You need to collect a few items in order to bring me back. A spell book. A part of my body—Danton's sister is buried with my fingernail in a pouch hung from her neck. Most important is the Philosopher's Stone." He then dictated a list of alchemical ingredients that would allow him to implant the Stone within his body without magic.

"The Philosopher's Stone," Rachel said.

"Danton has it. Do whatever you must to get it from him. Scott Boulder and Leah Maguire may try to stop you again—"

Her expression hardened, but as she looked at him, her eyes sparkled with ambition and desire. "Let me take care of them for you, Josef. Let it be my gift to celebrate your rebirth."

Andre nodded, knowing that he no longer had to worry about spending eternity trapped in the Space Between. He had won Rachel completely and would take more away from her than she could possibly imagine.

Chapter 26

Seducing Danton to her will should be a no-brainer, Rachel thought as she searched her sister's closet in vain for something soft and shimmery. Though they'd looked alike—which would fool the landlord into thinking she was the late major Wallas Ackart—her sister had been no femme fatale. The closest thing to sensual that Rachel could find was a pair of royal blue silk pajamas. They would have to do.

Or the top would.

Rachel slipped into it, leaving several buttons undone to show her cleavage. Then she rolled the sleeves halfway to her elbows and gazed at herself in the dressing table mirror. When she moved just the right way, Danton would get a glimpse of nipple.

Rachel smiled.

It had been too long since she'd sated herself in a sexual frenzy. Now that her mind was free of drugs, she felt every part of her come alive, and she was eager for it.

She fluffed out her blow-dried hair and among her sister's things found a ruby red lipstick and a bottle of jasmine-scented perfume that surprised her. As she put on the lipstick, she regarded herself in the mirror, wondered if Wallas had ever enjoyed her own sexuality. Wallas had always seemed asexual, as if the only thing she enjoyed was the power she got from her military rank. Rachel realized she didn't care. She had no feelings other than contempt left for the sister who'd betrayed her by having her locked up and drugged.

"Rachel, are you all right in there?" Danton asked, his voice muffled through the bedroom door.

"Perfect," she murmured, positioning herself— pajama top half off one shoulder—before opening the room to him.

Danton stood there, eyes widening as he took in the transformation. "Wow."

She smiled, stepped closer so her body warmth scented with jasmine would have an even greater effect on him. "I'm glad you approve." She stretched like a cat, making her full breasts draw upward, threatening to spill from the opening of the shirt. "This feels so good, sating the senses after being repressed for so long."

His eyes glued to her breasts, Danton appeared dazed and flushed despite the ashen cast to his skin.

Too bad she wouldn't have an experienced partner—Danton was obviously not very skilled with women, perhaps even a virgin. Too bad he wasn't Josef, who knew exactly what made her head spin. Her old lover would be with her soon enough, though. She would think of Josef while she was seducing Danton into sharing his powers with her . . . after which, she would make him help her bring Josef back from the grave.

Rachel moved in on him, placed a hand on his chest. "You needn't feel shy with me." She slipped her hand upward and wrapped her fingers around the back of his neck. "You saved my life, Danton, and I haven't properly thanked you yet."

And then she kissed him, eased her tongue into his mouth. He hesitated and then tongued her back. He wrapped his arms around her, shoved her against the doorjamb. Inexperienced, perhaps, but certainly enthusiastic.

So easy, Rachel thought, as she broke the kiss and slipped away from him, giving him her most seductive expression. "Shower first."

Danton whipped into the bedroom and into the shower. Rachel smiled. She would give him a few minutes.

And herself.

She closed her eyes and called up Josef's face, searched for the memory of Baden-Baden to inspire her.

What came to her instead was her last hours in Cherbourg . . . Josef's face twisting as he screamed. . . .

Rachel shuddered and forced the memory away before it could develop fully. Later, after she had what she wanted, she would be better equipped to deal with whatever put a chill down her spine. Of course, once she did what she had to, she would never feel the same way again. The thought put her on edge, yet the promise of more power was too heady to withstand.

Danton would resist, of course. He was a noble one. Such heroic potential. But in the end, he would gladly take what she offered. Corrupting him would be the most enjoyable thing she'd done in years. He was clay, hers to mold. Jaded after so many decades, she needed to add spice—a little pain, even—to satisfy her sexual appetites. She wondered how far she could push Danton the first time.

Taking a deep breath, Rachel entered the bedroom and stood for a moment in the bathroom doorway. Danton was scrubbing himself as if he were willing to remove his skin to rid himself of the last few days.

She moved closer, at the same time unbuttoning the pajama top, until finally, Danton realized she was there, flesh exposed by the parting silk. Hunger tensed his features as he reached out and pulled her inside the shower, pressed her against the tile wall, and kissed her again.

As the water beat against them, Rachel explored the planes and sharp angles of his body, dropped one hand lower between them and cupped his testicles.

"I want you, Danton, want to be with you always," she murmured, now sliding her hand along the length of his hard penis to the soft tip.

"I want you, too, Rachel." His hands were everywhere, exploring her, making every cell in her body come alive after too long a sleep.

"Then take me."

"Here?"

She rubbed her hardened nipples against his chest. "Yes, I want you now . . . and I want to taste your blood."

"What? No!"

Suddenly, Danton backed off, away from her. Though he was still fully aroused, his mind was getting the better of his lower parts. Rachel sighed. Having suspected his nobility would interfere, she'd prepared more lies.

"Don't you want me?"

"You know I do, but . . . not like that. Why would you want tainted blood?"

"Nothing about you is tainted to me. You're special—look how you saved me. We could be together for a long, long time, but only if you share your blood. What they did to me in there . . . I'm afraid I won't live long."

"You're just tired and weak from being locked up."

"No, it's more than that. I heard them."

"We'll take you to a doctor—"

"My blood isn't any more normal than yours. Any doctor would alert the Centers for Disease Control. They'll find me, lock me up again until I die."

She could tell he believed her, that his resolve was weakening.

Still, he said, "You don't understand, Rachel. You'll need to drink blood to live."

"But at least I *will* live. And we'll be together. I asked for your help, and you came for me. Don't let me down now."

She moved to him, stroked his engorged penis. "I need your blood, Danton. Then we can be together always."

Rachel reached out of the shower to where she'd left a straight razor on the back of the sink. She'd wondered if Wallas had actually used it on her legs—or if it belonged to some mystery lover. Whichever, it would be put to better use now.

As to her own sacrifice—giving up real food for a dependence on blood—that was a small price to pay to acquire Danton's powers.

She shoved the straight razor between them. "Your blood . . ."

"I can't do that to you."

Thinking that perhaps this once she had failed, Rachel thought to cut him herself and drink him dry. But Josef had told her only Danton could help bring him back, so she couldn't kill him. Or alienate him. He had to make the decision to let her drink himself because he was a necessary part of her life.

"Then I die," she whispered dramatically. "Save me, Danton, please. I need your blood, need *you*. . . ."

His hand shook when he finally took the razor from her. His eyes were crazed with a mixture of his own need for blood, sexual lust, and the choice he had to make.

Rachel pressed herself more fully against him and, raising her leg and wrapping her thigh around his hip, opened herself and guided him in. Crying out, Danton ground into her, moaning.

She whispered in his ear. "Now, Danton, now, please."

Hands shaking, Danton slashed his own wrist. Not wanting to give him a chance to change his mind, Rachel latched onto his flesh, covering the wound with her mouth, and drank.

Lights pinwheeled behind her eyes, but the pain was exquisite torture. Indeed, the sensation was like nothing she'd ever before experienced. Her body became electrified, a bolt of white-hot sensation, and yet she reveled in it as she slammed Danton against the wall with her hips. He came almost immediately, and they both slipped to the shower floor, water beating down on them.

Panting with a need greater than any she'd ever experienced, Rachel could barely move in her triumph—knowing that Danton Dumas would do everything she wanted.

Her body hummed with renewed potency, Rachel thought as she pulled herself up from a place that had been filled with dark dreams—scenarios of power and pleasure so unlike the nightmares she'd experienced in the detention area. Danton's blood rushing through her had been so powerful that she'd passed out. And then Josef had come to her again, had set her corporeal body on fire, had left her wanting. . . .

Wanting . . .

Thinking she could use Danton to satisfy her cravings, she left the bed and found him settled in the shadows of the living area. Fully dressed, Danton sat at a small table, forehead furrowed as he scribbled something on a pad of paper.

"You seem awfully intent."

He glanced at her, his expression wary. "Mm-hmm." Kept scribbling.

Curious now, Rachel crossed the room and circled him so that she could see over his shoulder. Candles and some kind of powder in a small bag as well as the pad of paper sat on the table. Danton wrote in some other language. He moved his body as if he were trying to hide it from her, but not before she saw the words—French, Rachel guessed, but mixed with something more exotic.

"What are you writing?"

He didn't answer.

"Danton?" she asked, putting force into her question.

He reluctantly said, "A spell."

"Spell? As in magic?"

Finally, he looked at her. "To heal me." He unwound the bloody cloth he'd wrapped around his wrist.

Rachel started when she saw the gash oozing a puddle of dark red blood. And then her body reacted. The pain started deep in her stomach and spread along her nerves. Blood . . . she needed more. She licked her lips and was thinking of the best way to seduce Danton into feeding her hunger when his guarded expression stopped her.

Asking him for more blood wouldn't do, not the way he was looking at her. His cooperation was more important at the moment. The hunger wasn't that bad. She could control it, could wait a while longer. Danton needed to be hers, and she knew he'd only conceded in the throes of his sexual frenzy. Afterward, he'd acted guilty, as if doing whatever it took to please her was wrong. No matter what she'd said, he'd been inconsolable.

There could be no further disagreement between them until he helped her bring Josef back.

"This spell of yours will work?" she asked.

"I hope so. I saw my sister write spells a couple of times. As I told you before, I have an incredible flair for languages. I even remember the cadence she used when reading her spells."

Danton set down the pen and lit the candle, then sprinkled the powder across the gash. After which, he began to read the strange-sounding spell. Unable to understand the language, Rachel stared at the wound. She could swear it was looking better, the flesh less ragged, in the process of healing by the time he finished.

"Well?" she said. "How long before you know if it worked?"

"It's working now. It feels better already." Danton flexed his hand, and indeed, no blood bubbled up. The wound looked to be half closed.

Amazed, Rachel tried to touch his hand to look closer, but he pulled it away and stared at her, his expression closed.

"I'm glad it's working," she said silkily, hoping to regain his trust. She wondered what else he could do. She sat back and gave him a smile meant to warm him. "You are so clever. What other spells do you know?"

"None, really. Rebecca was the one into Voodoo. She was always reading those books of hers. She even had a copy of *The Grand Grimoire*."

Rachel had heard of the handbook of black magic. Her interest immediately picked up. "You still have access to these books?" Josef had suggested a spell to bring him back, but perhaps the grimoire held something even more powerful.

"If the military didn't destroy all Rebecca's things, they should still be in our quarters above Magic Nights."

"We can't let anyone else get hold of them," Rachel said, her mind whirling with the possibilities. "What if they try to use them to capture us?" She could see the spark in his expression that told her she'd gotten

through to him. "I'll get dressed, and then we'll go ge
anything that's left and bring it all back here."

Danton's blood added to her own made her power
ful, more powerful than Scott Boulder. She'd tol
Josef she would take care of the bastard and his bitch

With magic added to the mix, she wouldn't fail th
man she loved.

Chapter 27

Reluctant as she was to revisit the quarters above Magic Nights—the scene of so much violence—Leah knew she had to search Rebecca's spell books for an answer to Scott's blood thirst. It was the least she could do for him.

The gentlemen's club itself was closed for the foreseeable future. With both Rebecca and Danton dead now, the property undoubtedly would be mired in the courts for some time. If it weren't the part of Bourbon Street where clubs showcasing beautiful women reigned supreme, some developer would probably try to turn the building into condos.

The military had access to the place; therefore, Scott had no trouble getting them inside. He took the lead in case they ran into trouble.

"Looks just the same," Scott said, waving to her to catch up to him. Though he was dressed in civilian clothing, his tan linen jacket concealed a shoulder holster.

Indeed, the bar was in the same mess it had been after their battle with Andre and Rebecca had ended. Leah narrowed her focus on Scott and the courtyard ahead and hurried to catch up to him. The scent of camellias, roses, and wisteria calmed her, as did the sound of water splashing from the large fountain at its center. Her feet skimmed the glass mosaic footpath as she followed Scott to the cast-iron staircase and climbed to the second floor.

"Man, what a mess," Scott said as they stood before the open doorway. "You'd think someone would at least have boarded up the place to keep out transients."

When he'd been in pursuit of Andre, Scott had smashed through the wood and glass French doors as easily as if they had been made of paper.

"The gate is locked, so no one can just wander back here." Leah took a deep, calming breath and then led the way inside. "And the vibe is bad, so I don't think anyone would really want to break in."

"Vibe?" Scott rushed in after her. "Is someone here?"

Leah shook her head. "No humans, but evil doesn't dissipate so easily. The entire property needs to be cleansed both of Andre's presence and of the dark magic Rebecca practiced."

Leah looked around. The inside appeared broken as well—furniture overturned, Rebecca's valuables scattered—proof of the violent supernatural struggle that had taken place between Scott and Andre.

Focused on the opposite wall and the altar where Rebecca had practiced her Voodoo, Leah moved through the purple and red decor and stopped before the plaster images of Catholic saints surrounding black cross candles, pots of herbs, and vials of oil. Leah swept her gaze over the shelved collection of books on Voodoo and black magic, but instinctively she knew the one that lay open on the altar was the very one she needed. It must have been the last book

Rebecca used when she cast her spell to make Andre immortal. Leah checked the cover.

"This is it," she told Scott. *"The Grand Grimoire."*

"What kind of information do you expect to find?"

"I'm not sure yet. This is a collection of old spells—black magic." Even touching it put her on edge. Not that the book itself held power. But what lay between the pages was dangerous work for any practitioner. "I need to find an applicable spell that I can reverse—hex, binding—probably I'll use a combination of two or more spells."

She started paging through the big book.

"Andre didn't use magic on me," Scott said, coming up behind her.

His nearness seared Leah with wanting, and she fought her own emotions. She loved him, yes, but she couldn't do this anymore—want what she couldn't have; it would make her soul-sick. She needed to keep her mind on her purpose.

"Andre used blood magic as a way to complete his own transformation into the vile creature he became," she told Scott. "That dark spell was responsible for the blood thirst he passed on to you, so in response, we need to use some form of blood magic to rid you of the craving."

"Wait a minute. I'm not drinking your blood, Leah, so you can just forget that."

His abhorrence of the idea washed over her.

"Don't worry. I wouldn't think of suggesting any such thing. I have something quite different in mind." Finding a spell in the book that might work for the situation, Leah opened her bag and pulled out a pad of paper and a pen. "I'll write my own spell based on what I find. In the meantime, you need to bathe."

Ritual baths were often part of enhancing a spell, especially in tandem with an anointing oil. Leah figured Scott could use all the enhancement she could find. A quick look through Rebecca's things unearthed a plastic bag labeled "Uncrossing Salts." Opening the packet to smell the contents, she thought it contained hyssop and rue and a variety of other herbs. She resealed the packet and handed it to him.

"While I prepare the room, use this on your body. Downward strokes only help drive away an evil condition. Make the water as hot as you can stand to get your blood flowing freely."

Scott scowled. "You're going to bleed me?"

"No bloodletting involved," she assured him. Still, she didn't feel ready to discuss her plan, which wasn't yet fully formed. "You simply have to trust me."

"I'll agree to anything that will rid me of this insane urge to feed, as long as no one else gets hurt."

"Of course."

Relieved, Leah went back to writing her spell, thoroughly aware that Scott stood there for a moment and stared at her as if he wanted to say something— his uncertainty palpable—before retreating to the bathroom. Even when he was out of the room, she didn't breathe any easier. Trying to separate her emotions from what she was doing was one of the hardest things she'd ever had to do.

She forced herself back to work.

Hesitant to use anything contained within the pages of *The Grand Grimoire*, no matter that she was adapting the spells to what she needed, Leah knew it was necessary. If Scott weren't in such a desperate state of mind, she would never use the book. She wouldn't even attempt the spell now. Here. She'd promised to help him, and Rebecca had anything she might need at hand. If she could take care of the blood thirst, even temporarily, he could carry on with a clear mind. Though she couldn't heal him, she could try to keep the nightmare of his blood thirst at bay until he could take the cure.

Nevertheless, she couldn't help but worry the black magic that lay within the grimoire's pages could somehow taint her by association. She felt different somehow just touching the paper on which the spells were written. She caught a glimpse of a love spell guaranteed to bind her lover to her.

For just a second, she was tempted . . . could almost see them happy together. . . .

Leah shook away her foolish imagination—she would never actually use black magic against anyone, certainly not against the man she loved. Doing so would violate everything she believed in.

Trying not to be upset by the cloud of doubt that descended on her, Leah went back to her preparations. From the bathroom, the pipes protested and the water rushed seductively, and she had to steel herself against thoughts of Scott and what he was doing and keep her concentration where it belonged. After gathering together the tools she needed from Rebecca's supply, she moved a chair and small table to the wall and lifted some things scattered around the floor to make enough space.

On her knees, she chalked a circle large enough to hold Scott's length and then drew an X through the middle. The Devil at the Crossroads represented an area outside of the normal, an appropriate place for magical rituals. Taking a container, she sprinkled salt in the four corners of the room to help cleanse it of unwanted influences—the residue of evil she'd felt when she'd entered—then collected the tools she needed and brought them into the circle.

After which, she prepared herself, placing several objects she might need in her skirt pockets, including a vial of holy water.

A few minutes later, Scott left the bathroom with nothing but a towel wrapped around his waist. Caught by the sight of his lean, muscular, nearly nude body, Leah simply stared breathless for a moment.

"You really think this will work?" he asked, his gaze narrowed on her, his features tight.

She could feel his anticipation. And his dread if it didn't work. "I think it will. You need to lie down in the middle of this crossroad."

Scott complied as Leah picked up two lengths of rawhide.

"What do you plan to do with those?"

"Tie your hands together. And your feet."

His eyebrows rose. "Bondage?"

A shiver of desire washed through her, but Leah tried not to let that affect her. She had to stay focused. "It's symbolic. You're now bound by the blood thirst, and I plan to remove the bindings as part of the spell."

Leah would swear he seemed disappointed, yet physically aroused if the bulge under the towel was any indication. Knowing what she was about to do, Leah couldn't deny her own desires. They'd only made love that one night, and she'd longed to be with him ever since.

Even though the spell was serious business, she couldn't help but take pleasure in thinking about Scott's flesh pressed against her . . . in her. Sex magic could be a powerful weapon against evil. Flushing, she tied his hands together over his head, then tied his ankles, after which she lit four candles, placing two white candles a yard apart above his head, two black candles similarly below his feet.

Remaining silent, he didn't take his eyes from her as she worked.

"I'm using an element as a ritual tool," she told him. "Air represents blood." She lit a cone of incense in a small container and then blew the fragrant smoke over every part of his body. "I want you to inhale and exhale deeply. Close your eyes and think of a white light surrounding you and draw it in."

When Scott did as she asked, Leah set down the incense and picked up "Uncrossing Oil" and rubbed it on her palms. Straddling him, she started at his forehead and stroked his face, ears and neck, then worked her way down his body.

"Break the spell that binds this man to blood. . . . Grant him the power to resist the evil that gives him thirst. . . . Let the thirst be removed. . . ."

His flesh tightened, and her fingers on his belly elicited a groan from him and his breathing deepened, but he didn't open his eyes, not even when she separated the towel, exposing him. Trying to deny the physical effect touching Scott had on her, Leah continued her path downward along his thighs, over his knees, all the way to his feet.

"Lend my hands the power to remove the addiction . . . to banish it from his body. . . ."

As she moved back over him, Scott shuddered, and Leah felt her own center heat and liquefy.

"Burn the binds that hold him. . . . Blow them away and free him. . . ."

His eyes were open now, watching her. He pushed up, instinctively finding her entrance. She slid down his length, reached back to untie his ankles, then forward to untie his wrists.

"I call darkness to take back this man's blood thirst."

When something frightening tried to flick to life inside her, Leah hesitated a moment. It tried to envelop her . . . smother her. She willed the feeling away.

"As he finds release and the blood retreats," she said, oddly breathless, "so it will be with his dark need."

Scott's coming during her spell would reject the original blood magic.

At least she prayed it would work.

Chapter 28

Their tongues intertwined, Scott rolled on top of Leah and used his knees as leverage as he thrust into her, concentrating not on the tactile pleasure now but on the sparkling force of the magic that surged through him to clear away his terrible thirst like fire through overgrown brush. With each passing moment, the craving continued to wither away, to blacken, to crumble into ash until he no longer felt the agonizing desire to feast on blood, no longer craved the coppery taste or viscous sensation on his tongue.

When Scott finally came—together with Leah, clinging tightly to her and she to him—he threw back his head and felt the last vestige of blood thirst dissipate completely, abruptly, like a tendril of ash gray smoke torn apart by strong wind.

At first, the absence filled him with panic. In many ways, the urge had made itself a part of him, and now that it was gone, he felt a vacuum. A deep and endless chasm. But then hope and light rushed in, and he no longer felt like an imminent threat to those around him.

He kissed Leah deeply again, cradling her face with both hands as though it were a precious jewel. "Thank you," he murmured into her mouth.

"It worked, then?"

He nodded. "It's gone. No more craving."

"I'm glad." Leah untangled herself from him and then, licking her fingertips, extinguished the candles.

Confused by her silence, Scott watched her pack up the spell components. She couldn't possibly still be angry about what happened at the lab, he thought. Surely she understood the circumstances, especially now that they'd gone through the considerable—albeit pleasurable—effort to remove his blood thirst.

"You okay?" he asked.

"Fine."

"I'm going to the bathroom. Need anything?"

"No."

Scott shrugged, thinking her silence might be an aftereffect of the spell, and then left the room. Despite himself, he smiled as he walked down the carpeted hallway to the bathroom. Reveled in the new calm—the new *freedom*—within his body. The blood thirst was gone completely, replaced by his body's normal cravings. In fact, his stomach grumbled, and he realized he hadn't eaten normal food in days. He fantasized about biting into a bacon cheeseburger and taking a long draw from a frosty bottle of beer.

Now that the blood thirst had been removed, maybe—maybe—he had a chance at a normal life with Leah after all this was finished. He turned the possibility over in his mind. He could leave the military once and for all, and they could move to a small town together. Have a litter of kids. He could open a jazz club, and she could pursue her anthropology at a local university. They could act like regular people again. Maybe.

Admittedly, they still had a fair amount to do before the mission was over, but it gave him something to look forward to.

As Scott continued toward the bathroom, his thoughts turned to Harriman. He still couldn't believe how cavalier the colonel had been about the decision he'd made in the complex. Had it been a defensive reaction? A way to deal with the horror? Scott hoped so. He wasn't ready to write Harriman off just yet. The man had meant too much to him over the years and had been a positive, paternal influence when his real father clearly hadn't been up to the job.

Turning a corner, Scott entered the bathroom. He turned on the light, flipped up the toilet seat, took a piss. He then washed his hands and regarded his stubbled face in the mirror as memories unfurled like the legs of a spider.

Scott had been just two years old when his father walked out. The man had returned periodically after that, but only when he needed money. Inexplicably, his mother had let him into the house every time and never failed to fall prey to his verbal and emotional abuse.

Scott remembered his father vividly: barrel-chested with thick arms and hands as big as dinner plates. The man would polish off a case of beer every night without missing a beat and could yell for hours about how things should be done. His father had made that point particularly clear once when Scott was seven years old. . . .

"Is it dead?" Scott said, looking at the carcass of an orange cat that lay in the street outside their house.

"Sure is."

"How'd it die?"

"Who knows? Probably did something wrong," his father said, breath heavy with beer. "Pick it up."

"I don't want to."

"Mind what I tell you, boy."

"I'm afraid."

"I said, pick it up."

Scott stepped away, but his father grasped his hands and thrust them toward the cat. Tears welling, Scott slid his palms under the animal's body. The fur felt waxy and stiff. As he lifted, the cat drooped like a bag of broken sticks.

"Let this be a lesson, Scott," his father said. "If you're not careful, the same will happen to you."

Logically, Scott knew he'd been too young to influence his father's behavior, but there were times when he blamed himself. If only he could have said something . . . maybe then the man would have quit drinking. Been a positive presence in his life.

Scott shook his head. Ridiculous. Nevertheless, in that context, what Leah had told him while they were chasing Danton in New Orleans made some sense. *I trust you, Scott. Even if you don't trust yourself.*

But he did trust himself, didn't he? he wondered as he left the bathroom and headed downstairs. Careful not to tread on debris with his bare feet, he moved to the bar, where several bottles remained despite the absence of staff and patrons.

Come to think of it, there *was* a fundamental part of him that didn't trust the integrity of close relationships—or his ability to function within them. Maybe that's why he'd chosen to lead teams of men into battle. Subconsciously, he could have been trying to reinforce that kind of trust in himself. When it came to relationships, he always felt like he was waiting for the other shoe to drop, waiting for some unknown variable to come and tear things apart—which was probably why he found it tough to commit to Leah on any real level.

In this case, however, his concern was justified. BB's warning about the unpredictability of his DNA powers haunted him. Talk about one hell of a dropping shoe. The only thing he trusted was that his body *couldn't* be trusted. His powers might metastasize into something horrible—like those poor souls in the underground lab. If that happened, he might inadvertently hurt those around him.

Walking around the bar, he pulled a bottle of Oban scotch from the shelf and twisted off the top. A small toast to the possibility of a new life was in order, certainly. Even if it was a distant possibility.

He was looking for a highball glass when he saw a flicker of movement reflected in the amber liquid. Leah. Maybe the tension between them was finally gone.

"Want me to pour you some?" he said, turning, and then saw that it wasn't Leah at all. For a moment, the sight didn't compute. "I saw you die" was all he could manage.

"We see what we want to see," Rachel said as Danton stood beside her.

Scott suddenly understood how Rachel had escaped the armory. Last he remembered, Rachel and Danton had been holding hands as they ran like hell from a fireball. Danton must have pulled her up through the earth to freedom.

But Rachel appeared much different now. Scott saw pure malevolence in her eyes, an expression far beyond the hopelessness that had possessed her in the complex. It was as though she'd cast aside whatever humanity she had left to further her own goals—or, God forbid, the goals of Andre Espinoza, who might still be in contact with her.

Scott quickly considered the odds. He was buck-naked. Vulnerable. The SIG was upstairs. But the concerns slowed him for only a second. Clearly, Rachel would not spare anyone who got in her way, which meant he couldn't let her get to Leah.

Scott vaulted over the bar, smashing the bottle against the wood as he did, turning it into a jagged weapon. But he never landed on the other side. He felt himself freeze midleap—his body sharply canted, knees together, one hand pressed flat against the top of the bar, the other clutching the neck of the broken bottle.

Telekinesis, he remembered too late.

He remained in stasis for a moment only before he was pitched violently back. He smashed into the shelved liquor bottles, then dropped to the floor. But he was up in a flash, even though his back and legs bristled with glass shards.

"*Lea—*" Scott yelled, but the cry caught in his throat as he was jerked off his feet. He dangled midair, unable to breathe, as though an invisible noose had snared him. He clawed his throat as Rachel tightened her grip.

"Danton . . . Help . . . ," Scott rasped, but quickly realized that his plea fell on deaf ears.

Danton had changed, too. Earlier, the guy had been

merely distrustful, but now he clearly saw Scott as a pawn of the military. As the embodiment of the pain suffered by Rachel and the other patients in the complex, the one responsible for dozens of needless deaths, including the death of his sister.

Scott tried to suck air into his lungs as red stars crowded his vision. He refused to leave Leah at the mercy of these people. The red stars turned black. He was dying.

With no other choice, Scott closed his eyes and tried to concentrate past the crushing pain in his throat, tried to visualize a galleon at sea disappearing into deep fog. *My body is nothing. . . . My body is nothing. . . .*

He felt his muscles and bones and the weight of his core slowly melt away into mist as the glass embedded in his back and legs jangled to the floor. With the transformation came freedom from Rachel's telekinetic grasp, but he knew he couldn't maintain the form for long. He was weak from lack of oxygen and blood loss.

Streaming up through a crack in the ceiling, he found himself back in the upstairs bathroom. There, his body took form on the floor, curled into a fetal position. His back and legs were streaked with blood. His head reeled. Gripping the sink, he struggled to stand. Tried again to call to Leah, but his ravaged throat could produce only a croak.

Outside the bathroom, he heard thumping footsteps on the stairs. Rachel and Danton were charging for the bedroom.

Scott staggered to the door on watery legs, clutched the doorknob for support. He could only hope that

Leah had heard the commotion in the bar. He lurched from the bathroom, head still reeling, and lumbered down the hallway, leaving a trail of bloody foot prints.

When he turned the last corner, he had a clear view into the bedroom.

Leah was at Rebecca's altar, clutching the grimoir under one arm. Her other arm was outstretched defensively toward Rachel, who was across the room. Lamps, candles, books, picture frames, and a myriad of other objects swirled around Rachel, propelled by the telekinetic power of her mind.

Scott tried to pick up the pace, wanted desperately to attack Rachel's flank while her attention was elsewhere, but his legs betrayed him. He collapsed, landing hard on his elbows, just as a picture frame whipped free from the vortex and streaked toward Leah with lethal force.

Scott cried out, the sound a mottled rasp, knowing there was no way he could protect Leah. All the hopes and dreams he had for them slipped away as the missile—a fucking picture frame!—homed in, its chrome edge glinting in the candlelight like the blade of a guillotine.

But when the frame flew to within a yard of Leah, it whipped back toward Rachel and struck the ceiling above her in a shower of glass. Rachel screamed in frustration, flinging a marble ashtray, an African figurine, a metal trash can, and a portable radio at Leah in rapid succession. But each time, the object boomeranged back toward Rachel, who was forced to deflect it away.

Leah must have been using magic to protect herself. But how long could she keep it up?

Scott scrambled back to his feet. He still had a chance to take Rachel down but would have to use his power to do it. Fear clawed at him as he prayed he wouldn't doom himself and Leah by doing so.

He imagined his arm consumed by crackling light, which triggered a searing-hot surge of voltage down his bicep. He held out a hand as black hairline filaments arced between his fingertips and then prepared to direct a bolt of lightning at Rachel—when Danton stepped through the wall beside him and touched his shoulder blade.

Scott felt his entire body tingle as though every muscle had fallen asleep simultaneously. And then he dropped through the floor. One moment he had a clear view of the bedroom, and the next he found himself twelve feet above a storeroom on the first floor, in free fall.

He twisted, trying to land flat on a stack of boxes, but was too dizzy to pull it off. Instead, his head slammed against the edge of a beer keg, and he crumpled to the floor in a heap.

Chapter 29

Danton made sure Scott had dropped all the way through the floor and then rushed into the bedroom.

Rachel stood on one side of the room, surrounded by an array of swirling objects. Leah stood on the other, using her own magic to cast away whatever objects Rachel flung at her.

"Rachel, stop it!" Danton yelled.

Shielding his head with his forearm, Danton charged through the vortex. This wasn't part of the deal. They'd come to Magic Nights to retrieve *The Grand Grimoire,* not kill anyone who got in their way. Danton felt several objects thud against his arm and waist before he reached Rachel, grabbed her by the shoulders, and spun her roughly to face him. "Stop it! You'll kill her!"

Rachel glared at him, eyes blazing. "Let go of me!"

The intensity of Rachel's reaction caused Danton to step back, but he resumed his effort, grabbing her by the shoulders again and shaking her this time. "Stop it!"

And then, as though she were just realizing where she was, the anger drained from Rachel's eyes. She looked at him plaintively as the swirling objects clattered to the floor. "Danton, what are you doing?"

"I can't let you do this, Rachel."

"Do what?"

Suddenly, Danton noticed how quiet it was in the room. He turned and saw Leah on the floor. There was a heavy candle next to her head—one of the objects that Rachel had been manipulating. Danton's breath caught in his throat until he noticed that Leah's chest was moving slowly up and down.

"I wasn't trying to kill her," Rachel said.

Danton whirled. "Could've fooled me. You certainly tried to kill Scott Boulder."

"Boulder was different. He would have killed us first if given the chance."

Danton paused. She may have been right about that. Boulder had made the first move with the broken bottle. Then again, he could merely have been acting to protect Leah.

"I wasn't trying to kill her, Danton," Rachel repeated. "I wouldn't dream of it, especially since fate was kind enough to put her in our path."

"What are you talking about?"

"We *need* her." Rachel stepped close, bringing her face inches from his. He could feel her soft breath on his mouth. "You saved me from that awful complex," she whispered. "The least I can do is return the favor."

Mere mention of favor caused his head to swirl with images from the shower. "You've . . . done pretty well so far."

Rachel smiled coyly. "I'm talking about something more. Much more." She took his hands in hers. "I'm talking about removing my blood thirst, and making you human again."

Danton's heart leaped. After all that had happened,

humanity seemed like an abstract notion, an unattain able dream. He would do nearly anything to make tha dream a reality. To put this nightmare behind him.

Even so, he felt a pang of guilt when Rachel men tioned blood thirst. He should have tried harder tc prevent her from sharing his tainted blood, but i seemed there was precious little he could do to resis her charms. The way he felt around her . . . mascu line, capable, *wanted*. Plus a gnawing lust, which didn't help matters.

"I want to become human more than anything," he said. "I think you know that. But why do we neec Leah? We can study the grimoire ourselves. As I men tioned before, I'm proficient with languages. These arcane summonings aren't much different."

"I know how good you are," she said, tracing her fingers along his arm as she brushed her lips against his ear. "But we don't have much time. Leah is profi cient in *magic*, which is different. She'll know exactly what to do."

"We could have asked for her help."

"She wouldn't have agreed, Danton. Oh, she migh have made promises, but in the end, she would have notified the authorities."

Danton nodded, knowing it was probably true They had no choice but to take Leah along. Still Danton worried about her. He believed that Leah hac a kind heart and lived according to a different philos ophy than Scott Boulder. "Fine, but we don't hurt her Understand?"

"Of course."

Rachel stared at Leah, concentrated, and Leah's body began to rise off the ground.

"No, let me do it," Danton said.

Stooping, he lifted Leah gently from the floor and then followed Rachel downstairs and out a side door to the car, where he placed Leah carefully into the backseat. He then just as gently bound her wrists and ankles before slipping behind the wheel. Rachel was already in the passenger seat.

As he drove them to the White Fish Grill, Danton considered the way Rachel had changed since leaving the underground complex.

Part of him trusted her well enough, but there was another part of him that was wary. There was no denying she was different now that she was free. Inside the complex, she'd gone out of her way to make sure he stayed safe and had shown genuine concern for the mutated patients. Now she seemed to have little regard for anyone but herself. He realized that part of her change could be due to his tainted blood, and he felt guilty again for allowing that to happen. But another part of her transformation seemed to have deeper roots.

Danton wasn't sure what was happening, or whose side she was truly on, but it seemed she might say or do anything to get what she wanted. Maybe the change was temporary and she'd snap out of it. He hoped so.

When they arrived at the White Fish Grill, Danton parked in back behind a Dumpster. When they climbed from the car, he said to Rachel, "Let me go in alone."

"We're more effective as a team."

"Not here," he replied, suspecting that her desire to collaborate was less about partnership than lack of trust. "Your presence will only raise questions."

For a moment, he saw the anger return to Rachel's eyes. "If you aren't out in a few minutes, I'm coming in after you."

"Fine." Danton jogged to the restaurant's alley door. Yes, Rachel would attract unwanted attention, but more important, Danton didn't want Rachel anywhere near Lilly, who would be working today. Since Rachel had become unpredictable, he didn't want to put Lilly in danger.

Cracking open the alley door, Danton peered into the White Fish Grill's kitchen. Several cooks crossed hurriedly through the room carrying all manner of cooking implements and prepared dishes.

When the coast was clear, he rushed through the door and peered into the brimming lobster tank where he'd hidden the Philosopher's Stone. No matter how hard he tried, he couldn't see any sign of it. *Shit.*

Rolling up his shirtsleeve, Danton plunged his hand into the tepid water, pushing away dozens of scuttling lobsters until he felt the gritty bottom of the tank. He groped blindly, hoping—praying—that he'd feel the smooth, warm edge of the stone or suddenly spot its glowing crimson core.

"Danton! There you are!"

Danton yanked his arm from the tank and whirled to see Lilly approaching. As usual, she was wearing her whites and was all smiles. "Hi, Lilly."

"Where have you been these last couple of days?" she said, her usual shyness taking a backseat to concern. "I was worried."

"I've, you know, been around."

"I don't want you to think you have to run away," she replied as she pushed her thick-framed glasses up the bridge of her nose with her thumb. "I want you to know that I'll do my best to understand whatever it is you're going through, and that you're welcome to stay here for as long as you need."

"That's great, Lilly. Thanks," Danton said as he peered back through the alley door. He could see Rachel waiting across the street. "But I didn't run away. I'm right here."

"I can see that," she said, turning beet red as her shyness returned. She indicated his dripping arm. "Did you lose something?"

"No."

"Then why were you reaching into the lobster tank?"

"I was hungry," he replied lamely.

"Why didn't you say so? Sit down and I'll make you something to eat!" She whisked him to a back room where the kitchen staff took their breaks, sat him at a small table, and then bustled off.

Realizing he was no longer in view from the alley door—and Rachel—Danton took a breath to calm his nerves. *Panic never helps.*

It seemed like Lilly was always there when he needed her. God knew he didn't want to involve her in this mess, but the Philosopher's Stone was gone. Possibly thrown out as garbage. Possibly taken as found treasure. Lilly might know . . . but would he be putting her at risk by asking?

"Normal or jalapeño corn bread?" Lilly called from the kitchen. He could hear the soft, echoing scrape of pans as she put his meal together. "We've got a fresh batch of each!"

"Normal is fine!" he called back, and glanced at his still-dripping forearm. Thanks to the healing spell, there was no sign of the cut he'd made with the straight razor. But there was no telling when Rachel would demand more of his blood or demand that he do something far worse.

The truth was, he didn't want to be the person that Rachel wanted him to be. Yes, he could have killed Scott Boulder at Magic Nights—the guy might even have deserved it—but he'd chosen to drop him through the floor instead. Closing his eyes, he wondered how he'd gotten into this mess. He wished he could go back to a simple life filled with research papers and Lilly's corn bread.

Still, there was something about Rachel. It was like a connection had been forged between them. And now that Rachel had consumed his blood, he felt an even stronger connection to her, almost as though they were two sides of the same person.

"Here we are." Lilly bustled in and set down a feast on the table in front of him: a dinner plate the size of a hubcap crowded with steak, grilled shrimp, collard greens, and seasoned French fries. Next to it was a bowl of seafood gumbo with a wedge of corn bread half submerged in the middle.

The mélange of savory and spicy smells filled Danton's throat with bile. Even though he didn't crave blood at the moment, the terrible thirst caused his body to react against normal food.

"You didn't have to go to all this trouble," he rasped.

"No trouble at all. It's my pleasure," she said, nervously smoothing her white apron with both hands

before sitting across from him. She smiled and nodded, clearly anxious to know what he thought of the
meal. "I've already had lunch, Danton. Go ahead and
eat in front of me. I don't mind."

He raised a spoonful of gumbo to his lips, hoping
he could swallow it without retching, but felt his nausea threaten to explode. He let the spoon drop back
into the bowl with a *plunk!*

Lilly's face fell along with it. "I made the wrong
dishes, didn't I?"

"No, it's not that. I guess I'm not as hungry as I
thought."

"I knew I should have asked what you liked," she
said, pushing her glasses up her nose. "But I had to go
and make what I *thought* you'd like instead."

"The food looks delicious. Really."

"Then what is it? What's wrong?"

"Lilly, I—" Danton began, but couldn't say the
words as the war between pleasing Rachel and protecting Lilly raged inside him. He looked down at the
table. *Lilly, I've lost something important, don't you
see? I don't want to involve you, but my very life
might depend on finding it.*

She laid a hand on his wrist. "Danton, look at me."
He kept looking at the table, concentrating hard on a
crack in the wood instead, unable to answer. He
didn't want to involve her, God knew he didn't, but
he felt like he didn't have a choice.

He glanced back at the alley door. Rachel wasn't
there, but he knew she was close.

And then he felt Lilly squeeze his wrist. He looked
up. Such a bold move must have been difficult for her,
but she'd done it just the same. She blushed, let go of

his wrist to smooth her apron. "Danton, I know what you're looking for."

"You do?"

"Remember when you were sick? When I brought you your books?" she asked, as though she hadn't just dropped a bomb in his lap.

His mind raced. She couldn't be talking about the Stone. How could she know? "Lilly—"

"That wasn't the first time I did something like that for someone," she went on. "I took care of my father when he had pancreatic cancer. He lasted only four months from the day he was diagnosed."

"I'm sorry, Lilly. I had no idea." Danton could feel Rachel's patience with him slipping away and knew he should act quickly to get the Stone—but he couldn't help but listen quietly to Lilly as she spoke. Her soft, lilting voice held such normalcy and comfort. It filled him with peace—and confusion, too. He didn't know where he belonged. Part of him wanted to cling to Rachel despite what she'd done because she was different. A monster, like him. And part of him wanted everything that Lilly could offer.

"Thanks," Lilly replied. "I've never told anyone about it, I'm not sure why. Anyway, my father said some strange things to me under the influence of medication. Things I'm sure he never wanted me to hear. Affairs he'd had during his marriage to my mother . . . transgressions at work . . ." She shrugged. "Those things didn't make me stop loving him. In fact, I was honored that he felt he could unburden himself to me. If you want to know the truth, I believe the mere act of saying those things allowed him to move on from whatever he *thought* he should do in penance, right or wrong, and die in peace."

"Did I say something under medication?" Danton whispered. "When I had leukemia?"

"You were always very respectful."

"That's not what I asked."

Lilly regarded him, shyness all but gone. "You said one thing in particular that I remember, but I don't want to embarrass you by repeating it."

"You won't embarrass me. I promise."

Now it was her turn to look down. "You told me you wished you could have better protected your sister growing up. I don't know the context because you didn't go into detail, but you were very insistent about that."

Danton nodded, remembering there were many things about his life growing up that he wished he could have changed. "I'm not embarrassed, Lilly. I'm just sorry you had to hear it."

"Don't be," she said, meeting his gaze again. "And don't think you have to be sorry about unburdening yourself now either."

Danton withdrew his hand slowly from hers and stood. He felt like he could talk to her all day, all year, always, for the rest of his life. But he was out of time, and out of choices. Rachel was waiting. "Lilly, about what you said before . . . You know what I'm looking for?"

"The red stone," she replied. "Am I right?"

He stared at her blankly.

"I found it yesterday afternoon and put it in the Lost and Found box," she explained. "I wasn't sure that's why you were here, but it wasn't hard to put two and two together given your odd behavior." She smiled.

Danton felt like kicking himself. Lost and Found. Unbelievable.

"I can get it," she went on. "But something tells me that you don't really want me to. Am I right?"

Danton didn't know what to say. Of course she was right. He wanted to forget this shitstorm had ever happened, but there was no way he could leave the Stone with her. As bad as things might get for him after he possessed the Stone, he couldn't expose Lilly to that kind of risk.

"It's okay," Lilly interjected, pushing her glasses back up her nose with her thumb. "Really, whatever it is, it's okay."

He took a breath. "I've done some things recently that I'm ashamed of, Lilly. And I'm not sure that I won't do something else that I'm ashamed of before the day is over."

She nodded. "It's okay, Danton."

"I don't think it is okay. But I don't think I can stop myself." He shook his head again. "By the way, you're right about the Stone. I do need it. I need it now, and I need it more than anything."

Lilly left the room and returned a moment later to hand him a heavy brown takeout bag with "White Fish Grill" on the side in bold black letters. "I need you to do one more thing for me."

"Anything," she whispered.

He leaned forward and kissed her on the cheek. She emitted a gentle sigh. "I need you not to follow me."

With that, he turned and walked toward the alley door. He glanced once over his shoulder and saw that

Lilly had taken a couple of steps after him. She maintained eye contact, her glasses off now, until he exited and closed the door.

Danton ran back across the street to Rachel.

"I was just about to go in after you," Rachel said, taking the bag. When she looked into it, the red glow from the Stone reflected in her eyes. "Very good, Danton. Very, very good."

Danton nodded absently as they climbed back into the car. While driving to the cemetery that held Rebecca's crypt, he found that he could hardly focus on what Rachel was saying. Something about an object interred with his sister that was essential to casting spells from the grimoire. He also found that he could hardly stay focused as he led Rachel through the cemetery, unlocked the crypt, and then waited outside for her to reemerge from its inky depths with her prize. Even the cold grief that washed over him as he stared at his sister's engraved epitaph—"Here lies Rebecca Dumas, Beloved Sister, Guardian, and Friend"—could distract him only for mere moments.

He couldn't keep focused on anything at all, except Lilly.

The way she'd tried to ease the fear she'd sensed in him. The way she always had.

Lilly had made him feel more human than he'd felt in days. Maybe just as human as he'd felt before the transformation. His mind swirled.

Should he continue on his present course even though it grew more insane by the minute?

He didn't know what to do or what he wanted. All he knew for certain was that, suddenly, he cared very much about what Lilly might think of him after it was all over.

Chapter 30

"Keep your mouth shut and get inside," Rachel said, pushing open a door to reveal the interior of a living room.

Though her hands were still tied in front of her, Leah was on her feet. Barely. She'd regained consciousness several minutes ago, had a headache, and was a little muzzy. Still, she had noted that the apartment building to which Rachel and Danton had brought her was located at the edge of the French Quarter. If she could get away, at least she knew where she was.

"What is it you want from me, Rachel?" she asked as the blonde shoved her inside by the arm. "Talk to me. Maybe I can help you."

"Oh, you'll help me—" Rachel stopped, and her grip on Leah's arm tightened. "What the hell? Danton?"

They were standing a yard away from what was left of a door that had been shattered. Leah could see inside enough to know the room beyond was a bathroom.

"I'm on it." Danton rushed by them and seconds later exited, his expression grim. "Gone. What do we do now?"

"Check the rest of the apartment."

Danton did as she asked, sticking his head through a couple of doorways, but when he rejoined them, he said, "Nothing."

"He's probably gone out to feed."

"If he's out there killing people, I have to stop him." Danton headed straight for the front door.

"Leave it be. You won't find him." Rachel's growing irritation was evident from her tone. "And we have plans to make."

Danton appeared torn, and even from a distance, Leah could feel his internal struggle. And his resistance to Rachel, a fact that gave her hope that she could win him over yet to the side of good.

In the end, he looked directly at *her,* then said, "All right," and closed the entryway door.

Giving Leah the distinct impression he was staying to protect her from Rachel. "Danton—"

Before she could plead with him to listen to reason, Rachel was pushing her again, saying, "You can wait in here," and popped her through an open doorway.

Still a bit off balance, Leah stumbled inside the darkened room and stopped only when her knees hit something soft. Eyes adjusting, she realized it was the bed. With the frilly curtains drawn, early evening light barely dappled the connecting walls, so she got the hazy impression of an old-style New Orleans boudoir with a big canopy bed in the middle of the room.

"Don't get stupid," Rachel said, quickly patting Leah's body as if searching her for some weapon. "If you scream for help or try to get away, you'll *wish* you were dead long before I actually kill you." She glanced over her shoulder, then back at Leah. "I understand you're the noble type and wouldn't want to get someone else hurt, so add Danton to that threat. Get in my way, and I'll make you watch as I rip him apart."

Then she slammed the door in Leah's face. And locked it.

Wondering if she could come up with a spell to get her out of this mess, Leah abandoned the idea. Rachel would go through with her threat, might even torture Danton and kill him if she didn't heel, and Leah couldn't let that happen. She'd sensed that a real decency remained in the man, and he'd only confirmed it first by protecting her from Rachel, then by wanting to go after some other vampire to prevent any more deaths. It wouldn't take that much to win Danton over, to get him to work with her against Rachel, she just knew it.

Another vampire, though . . . And if he was out feeding, who knew if he might be making even more dark creatures. Leah felt sick at the thought and wished there was some way she could warn Scott. If Rachel hadn't taken her bag, she might be able to reach him through another dreamwalk. . . .

Suddenly, a moan startled her, so deep it sent shivers up her spine.

"What the hell?"

More groans came from the floor on other side of the bed near the windows.

Who was back there? Had they taken someone else prisoner?

"Hello?"

No answer.

What if someone was hurt? Needed help?

Leah swallowed her hesitation and fumbled for the bedside lamp only to have her stomach knot in fear when she turned it on and light danced through dozens of long crystals hanging from the shade, illuminating the lavender bedding smeared with darkening blood. And when she knelt on the bed to look over to the other side, she saw blood on the man who lay there—a man apparently regaining consciousness. Evidently, he'd gone out to feed and come back here to sleep, starting on the bed, ending on the floor. His face and the front of his black uniform were covered with gobs of viscous fluid.

Leah flew back and almost tumbled to the floor on the opposite side of the bed. She knew this guy, Harriman's bodyguard—she'd seen him disappear behind a wall of fire, and they'd assumed he'd been killed along with Danton and Rachel. It seemed the man wasn't dead after all. . . .

. . . *Or was he?*

No matter that she tried, Leah couldn't stop her heart from racing. When he made growling sounds deep in his throat—he sounded like a wild animal—her blood pumped double-time.

Calm down, she told herself. *Calm down before you set yourself up as a target.*

Peering over the bed, she could see the bodyguard's muscles jerk—he was undoubtedly awakening.

A scream boiled in her throat, but she forced it down. She had to get out of here, but he was blocking the windows and Rachel had locked the damn door. She shook the handle anyway, called, "Rachel, he's in here—let me out," then realized the more noise she made in trying to get herself rescued, the faster Harriman's bodyguard would come after her.

Tied-together hands trembling, she worked at her skirt pocket where she'd stuck that vial of holy water earlier, in preparation for releasing Scott from the blood thirst. Apparently, the folds of her skirt had hidden it from Rachel's search. When the vamp came after her, she could toss the contents on him.

But would that stop him or even slow him down? Though BB hadn't gotten it to work on Andre's flesh, he had said the transition could differ for individuals. With her bag confiscated, what else could she do, trapped with a vampire in this tiny space?

He moaned and turned and turned again, thrashing out a bloody arm on top of the bed as if truly awakening now.

Clutching the vial of holy water in one hand, Leah remembered how she'd used glamour to disguise her identity when she'd been locked in the detention area.

If the bodyguard thought she was another vampire, would he leave her alone? Was there some way she could keep him in line until Danton or Rachel opened the door?

Suddenly it came to her—the only person the bodyguard had answered to in his mortal life had been Harriman. The colonel might be the only one who could control him now.

The bodyguard grunted and started to unfold himself.

How long could she sustain the glamour? The first time she'd tried it, she'd had mere minutes of protection, and there was no reason to think that without the proper preparation she could sustain the illusion for longer.

Knowing she had to try or die, Leah cleared her mind, this time quickly visualizing a man's body in a dark void. White light limned and enveloped the silhouette. She dressed the body in the neatly pressed khakis Harriman favored. Imagined the weathered face taking shape. The snub nose. Carefully trimmed gray hair. She imagined stepping into the wiry body and standing ramrod straight.

She said, "You're a mess, soldier."

With a snarl, the bodyguard looked down at himself, at the gooey substance covering the front of his black uniform. He scooped some up and sniffed it, then licked it off his hand, the very act making Leah's stomach lurch.

"You'll stand down until I give you your orders," Leah/Harriman said, just as she heard intense voices coming from the other room. It sounded like Danton and Rachel were arguing. "You will retain control, son," she said, backing toward the door, "as befitting a soldier of the U.S. Army. Is that understood?"

The vampire's brow creased and his eyes gleamed, sending a frisson of fear straight up Leah's spine.

"You wandered off base in a daze, soldier. You fought like a hero, though. When this situation is resolved, I'll see that you get a commendation."

He wasn't buying it. Because she didn't sound authentic? Was the glamour fading? Panic made Leah intensify her mental effort even as the bodyguard's stance changed, grew challenging. He cocked his head and looked at her more intently, as if he were sizing her up for a meal.

"That's enough, soldier! At attention."

He adjusted his stance as if judging how best to attack, and Leah felt the glamour slip even as she fumbled trying to free the vial of holy water of its cork. She finally opened the vial, but he vaulted over the bed and grabbed it from her so hard that the glass smashed to bits in his hand.

"Aaahhh!"

The bodyguard cradled his smoking hand, spreading the holy water from one to the other. He screamed repeatedly in agony as his hands smoked, and he lurched toward her. Leah thought this was it—the end—when suddenly Danton melded through the door and got between her and the angry vampire.

"Get back now!" Danton yelled, though the bodyguard had at least fifty pounds and who knew how many years of combat experience on him.

To Leah's horror, the bodyguard picked Danton up before the smaller man could react to protect himself and practically threw Danton back through the wall even as Rachel walked through it. Her face flushed with anger as she assessed the situation.

"Don't touch this woman," Rachel ordered in a clipped military tone. "I need her."

The bodyguard let out a savage growl and wiped a bloody hand across his mouth.

"You'll feed, but not on her." Rachel's voice was calm . . . smooth . . . intent and deadly. "If you so much as touch her, you're done, soldier. Do you understand?"

The vampire bodyguard clearly didn't like taking orders from Rachel. He roared at her and tried to shove her aside, but his hand went through her. Then she swiped a hand toward him, and he flew up against the wall.

"Don't make me destroy you," Rachel said, her low, threatening tone making Leah's mouth go dry.

For a moment, the vampire looked as if he wanted to carry out the threat in return. Rachel stared at him, eyes glittering, exuding power from every pore in her body.

And then, amazingly, the vampire backed down.

Rachel stepped back and took something from her pocket. "I'm going to allow you to feed, but you will stop when I tell you. Is that clear?"

Without waiting for an answer, she slashed at the inside of her arm and held it out. Blood spurted at the vampire, and he latched onto the wound with a savage growl. Leah's stomach lurched when Rachel threw back her head, her face wreathed in something that looked like ecstasy.

Leaving Leah to wonder which would be worse—death or whatever it was that Rachel had in mind.

Chapter 31

Scott threw on his clothes and shoulder holster, then bolted outside to the Humvee, cranked the ignition, and peeled out. As he slalomed through traffic in the French Quarter, blaring the horn and stomping the gas and brake intermittently, he snatched up the dashboard mike and radioed Harriman at the lab.

"What's going on, Scott?" Harriman said when he came on.

"Rachel Ackart and Danton Dumas are alive."

There was a moment of crackling silence. "Are you sure?"

"They took Leah."

"Do they have the Philosopher's Stone?"

"Unknown."

Just then, a street performer clad in a gold jumpsuit and glittery blue Mardi Gras mask stepped directly into the Humvee's path. Cursing, Scott veered right, barely missing the guy, but passing close enough to ruffle his rainbow-colored wig.

"How long since you made contact?" Harriman asked.

"About thirty minutes," Scott replied. "I'm on my way to the White Fish Grill to talk to Lilly Fry. She's the only lead we've got."

"Ackart and Dumas couldn't have gone far. I'll meet you at the grill to coordinate our pursuit."

Scott's stomach tightened. It was bad enough that he'd allowed Rachel and Danton to get the jump on him. But Leah had also suffered for his mistake.

He screeched to a stop in front of the White Fish Grill. Ignoring the cars that honked behind the double-parked Humvee, he stormed through the front door of the crowded restaurant and strode past the hostess on his way to the kitchen.

He stopped a young, blond-haired waiter who emerged from the service area with a tray of steaming seafood. "I'm looking for Lilly Fry."

"Lilly, yeah," the waiter said. "She's in back—"

Scott didn't wait for the guy to finish. Drawing the SIG and holding it discreetly against his thigh, he entered the kitchen and quickly scanned all quadrants of the room. He knew even gold-alloy bullets wouldn't be much use against a woman who could manipulate objects with her mind—or against a man who could manipulate the density of his body. Then again, he might take them by surprise and get in a lucky shot.

He spotted Lilly in a small break room. She stared down at a table covered with plates of food. Moving across the kitchen, Scott stopped in the doorway to prevent her from escaping. "Lilly Fry," he said. She looked up, eyes red from crying. Fear clouded her face when she noticed the gun, but she maintained her composure nonetheless and said nothing. "Ms. Fry, I'm Scott Boulder, here on behalf of the U.S. government. I'm looking for Danton Dumas."

Her expression remained neutral. "What's he done?"

"I don't have time to explain, but it's critical that I find him as soon as possible."

"You want the red stone, too, don't you?"

Scott's blood ran cold. Clearly Danton and Rachel had already gotten what they'd wanted. "When was Danton here, Ms. Fry?"

"Not long ago," she whispered.

"Where was he going?"

Lilly shook her head, eyes filling with tears.

Rachel and Danton would try to flee the city, Scott thought. Or worse, they'd try to use the Stone as soon as possible. Probably the latter, since they'd abducted Leah. God only knew how they might use Leah in their sick rituals. Lilly's carelessness could have cost the life of the woman he loved. "Do you have any idea what you've done?"

"I—"

"No, I don't think you do," Scott interrupted. "The Stone is an object of enormous magical power. In the wrong hands, it could be devastating. Lives are at stake." He knew how the notion might sound to a layperson—he'd rejected the idea of magic himself not long ago—but Lilly seemed to take it in stride.

"You're wrong about that, Mr. Boulder," she said.

"I can assure you that I know what I'm talking about, Ms. Fry. Now I want you to think very carefully about where Danton may have gone." He took a step closer while making sure Lilly noticed the gun again. He hated to threaten her, but Leah's survival was at stake.

"I didn't mean to say you're wrong about the Stone," Lilly said. "You're wrong about Danton."

"You don't know the facts of this case."

"Maybe not, but I know *him*." She shook her head as tears spilled down her cheeks. "Danton has been through so much, Mr. Boulder. That's what *you* may not know. Leukemia, the death of his sister. Tragedies that would have made a lot of people cynical and bitter. But I saw firsthand how Danton became more kind and compassionate through it all. In fact, he tried to take care of me while I took care of him. He's that kind of person. That's how I know he wouldn't do anything to hurt anyone."

"People can change," Scott agreed, thinking about Danton's terrifying new abilities—and his own. "But sometimes for the worse in ways you can't easily see."

"Not Danton. At least not in the way you're implying. I did notice that something was wrong when he came by, though. He wasn't his usual self. So pale and afraid. He wouldn't tell me what was wrong, but it was obvious that he didn't know what to do." Her expression crumpled with the weight of the memory. "He looked so lost."

Scott nodded. He knew Danton's pain all too well. He knew Lilly's pain, too, from watching Leah. "Lilly, we don't have much time—"

"You asked if I realized what I'd done. My answer is yes. At least as much as I could realize without knowing about the Stone," she said with plaintive defiance. "Why did I let Danton leave? Because he asked me to. Simple as that. Believe me, I wanted to follow him, more than anything. Letting him walk out of here alone made me feel so frantic, so out of control. But I let him go."

Scott nodded again, realizing there was no way Lilly could know how much he understood. He'd been infected, contaminated, transformed. In the process, he'd lost every ounce of control that most people took for granted. Part of him wanted to scare the information he needed out of Lilly, but a deeper part of him knew that he had to let her talk things through for a few moments longer.

"I wanted to follow Danton and see who or what was causing him so much pain," she continued. "Honest to God, I would have helped him confront whatever it was on the spot. I might not look very strong, but I would have fought for him tooth and nail if I had to." She paused as though surprised at her own resolve and then nodded slowly as the realization took hold. "Yes, that's right. That's absolutely right. I would have fought for him tooth and nail, no matter what."

Scott regarded her with growing respect. This young woman had no military training or enhanced abilities, yet she'd been prepared to battle an unknown threat regardless of personal consequences. "You trusted yourself," he said, echoing the comment Leah had made to him that morning on the streets of New Orleans.

"I guess you have to in a situation like that. I mean, what else can you do?"

You can let fear take over, Scott thought ruefully. You can tell yourself you're pulling punches to protect the people around you when you're really trying to protect yourself. Scott holstered the SIG and sat across the table from Lilly. The example this girl had set was extraordinary, as noble as anything he'd experienced on the battlefield. Suddenly, he felt incredible shame. He'd been acting like a selfish coward.

"I would have done anything for Danton," Lilly said simply.

"I understand," Scott said, and realized he meant it in a way that would dictate how he conducted himself from now on. After all that had happened, he was ready to take a cue from this brave, selfless young woman and use every power at his disposal to try to right so many terrible wrongs. Lilly was right: What else could he do? And then, after this was all over, maybe he could convince Leah to give him another chance at a future together.

Lilly sensed the change in him, which caused her defensiveness to drain away. "Please help Danton, Mr. Boulder," she said. "He's a good man and worth saving."

Scott remembered that Leah had made a similar comment about Danton when they'd first captured him. Thinking back, he realized that Danton had always been reticent to inflict harm. Even at Magic Nights, the guy could have tried to kill him but hadn't. Danton had been a victim of circumstance like he had been. But while he was surrounded by people like Leah and BB who had his best interests at heart, Danton had fallen under Rachel's corrupting influence and could still follow the wrong path. "I'll do what I can, Lilly. You have my word. But first, I need to know where he went."

"I don't know," she said, shaking her head. "I don't even know if he's out there all alone. Do you?"

If Lilly wasn't already romantically involved with Danton, she clearly wanted to be. Telling her about Rachel would only inflict pain when she had already suffered enough. "Did Danton mention anything about the Stone?" he asked, avoiding the subject.

"Only that he needed it immediately."

Scott nodded grimly. That meant Rachel and Danton intended to use the Stone as soon as possible. He took small comfort in the fact that Danton might try to protect Leah, but Rachel had considerable power and was willing to kill to achieve her goals.

Scott heard a noise grow in the distance—the telltale thupping of a Black Hawk helicopter. Harriman was on his way. "Thank you, Lilly," he said, standing. "I'll be in touch."

Scott moved quickly back through the dining area and exited the restaurant as the Black Hawk hovered overhead. The rotor wash whipped grit and garbage across Bourbon Street. Traffic came to an abrupt stop as drivers gaped at the spectacle.

After waving the Black Hawk to land in a nearby abandoned lot, Scott leaped aboard to find Harriman and BB waiting for him. BB's thick red hair poked out from underneath a white flight helmet.

"Rachel and Danton have the Stone," Scott yelled as the Black Hawk lifted off.

Harriman nodded as he passed Scott a black tactical jumpsuit, then showed him a handheld tracker. On it, a tiny green blip moved rapidly across a map of the French Quarter toward the Botanical Garden. "We picked up White's GPS signal a few minutes ago," the colonel said. "Satellite imagery places him in a yellow hatchback with three other passengers."

"Rachel, Danton, and Leah," Scott replied as he shrugged free of his jacket and put on the jumpsuit. "I thought White had been killed in the armory."

"We couldn't explain it either. And then we saw this."

Harriman pushed a button to bring up White's vital signs as transmitted by the GPS chip: heart rate, body temperature, blood pressure, and respiration. All flatline. Yet the guy was moving.

"I sent a rapid-deployment team ahead of us," Harriman said. "We'll be able to strike wherever the signal stops."

Scott nodded and watched the multicolored city rush past two hundred feet below. Clearly, White had been transformed into a vampire or zombie and was in league with Rachel. That would make it all the more difficult to bring Leah back alive.

Chapter 32

"You'll need to go inside and take care of the alarm," Rachel told Danton. She could do it herself, but she didn't dare take herself out of the picture, not even for a moment, even though the vampire Danton claimed had been Harriman's bodyguard was overseeing Leah.

Though it was dark, she checked to make sure no one else was around. It wouldn't do to have interference now that she was finally ready to carry off Josef's plan.

All clear.

At her signal, Danton melded through the door to the Conservatory of the Two Sisters, a central part of City Park's Botanical Garden.

Rachel pressed the grimoire and its promise tightly to her breast, the Philosopher's Stone fastened to the high waist of her full-legged black slacks. Her sister's closet had held a few surprises after all. She'd paired the slacks with a long-sleeved white silk blouse open at the throat that reminded her of an outfit she'd worn in Baden-Baden. She'd clustered her blond hair around her shoulders in tight curls, and her face was artfully adorned with what makeup she'd been able to find.

Hopefully, Josef would appreciate the effort she'd gone through to be the woman he remembered.

"What do you want from me?" Leah asked, her voice even.

"You should be asking what you're going to do—but don't bother." She would reveal her plan as she saw fit.

A lily pond lay outside the domed building with arched windows, and long rectangular greenhouses stretched out to either side—giving the illusion of a calm oasis in the midst of hurricane-twisted live-oak stands. Beyond lay the seething urban jungle of New Orleans, which Rachel would soon rule with a will of iron. She hadn't lived for the better part of a century, experimented with her own life multiple times, to take a backseat to anyone ever again.

Except perhaps to Josef . . . when it suited her.

"Rachel, we need to talk," Leah said, just as Danton opened the door.

Ignoring the other woman, Rachel nodded to the bodyguard, who picked up Leah's soft case with its tools of magic in one arm, the box of scientific instruments in the other, then pushed Leah herself inside. The thug had been reduced to little more than a rabid animal, but somehow his instincts to obey a higher command remained intact, and Rachel took full advantage. As terrifying as he could be to others, in *her* mind, he was nothing. Just another man to control.

The question was, why did Leah seem so calm when she ought to be begging for her life? Did Leah know something she didn't?

"Which way?" Danton asked.

"Follow the sound of the water."

Their way lit only by low nightlights hidden beneath the fronds of ferns, they turned out of the reception and orientation area into the glass conservatory wing of living fossils, an exhibit of prehistoric plant life. The primordial setting gave off an eerie low glow that danced through the fine spray of water misting the greenery.

Feeling a connection with the fossils—she, too, had lived practically forever—Rachel smiled wryly and made her way toward the waterfall. The adjacent lagoon was lit by underwater lights so that the clear water luminesced and burbled like some strange, live jewel. Here she would draw upon the poisonous cycad plants Josef had deemed necessary as part of the equation that would return him to Earth.

They stopped before the lagoon with its lush ferns and rocky outcroppings that evoked a swampy prehistoric landscape. The air grew heavy with warmth, visibly rising mists, and a volatile fragrance that nearly took away Rachel's breath. The scent was harsh and somewhat overwhelming. Or perhaps it was her anticipation that made breathing more acerbic.

Suddenly having been able to "see" the equation that had allowed her to keep her youth, Rachel had already written it down. Now before the pool that looked so much more inviting—and, yes, mystical—than the tank she'd used in the Eagle's Nest lab, she removed a small notebook from her slacks pocket.

"I need you to rework the equation," she said, handing the notebook to Danton.

"Rework it to what?"

He seemed something of a savant with all languages, even mathematics and science. "To reverse the formula so that it will grow cells and quickly age them."

"What kind of cells?"

Rachel opened the front of her silk shirt and pulled free a soft pouch that she'd taken off Rebecca's remains earlier. From it, she removed the fingernail covered with dried blood.

He recoiled from the horrific-looking object. "You want to grow that into what?"

"Someone who was lost to me long ago."

"Science can't do that."

"Perhaps not science alone, but with help from the grimoire . . ."

Rachel looked to Leah, whose face registered her horror. Ah, at last the little bitch realized her purpose. She was able to feel Leah's resistance now as a tangible thing. She asserted her silent will on the woman and smiled when Leah looked away, her defenses seemingly crumbling. Behind her, the bodyguard gazed on, his features hardening, his eyes gleaming as if he wished she would resist openly.

"Get busy," she said to Danton, though she could feel his reluctance to do so as she shoved the fingernail into his palm. When he didn't immediately respond, she wrapped his fingers around the nail, then lowered her voice so only he could hear. "I thought you wanted to be human again, Danton." Apparently, her hold on him was starting to slip, but still she had in her power what he wanted most. "Bring Josef back to me and he'll reward you."

The reminder was enough. Danton sat down on a small cement bench near the waterfall, placed the nail in a petri dish that he set before him, then opened the notebook. As he read, his expression grew intent and his lips moved, though no sound passed them. Mists from the water encircled him, softening his sharp edges, making him look somehow ethereal in this primitive setting.

To Rachel, Danton looked every bit the modern-day sorcerer capable of pulling Josef straight from the primordial ooze.

With some additional help, of course.

She placed the heavy grimoire on a high rock and opened it to the spell she thought might do. Then she turned to Leah, a green-tinged ghost so faint the woman nearly disappeared into her surroundings.

Rachel relished her fear. "You may start reading as well."

"What if I refuse?"

Voice lowered, Rachel said, "Remember the consequences to your friend over there," then turned her back on Leah, signaling to the bodyguard to follow her.

The woman was too weak, too terrorized, to do anything but comply. Indeed, a glance back assured Rachel that Leah was moving to the grimoire. She would do exactly as instructed.

Then again, Leah's lack of begging and pleading might have something to do with Scott Boulder. Had she somehow drawn him and Harriman here with some covert piece of magic?

Not willing to chance it, Rachel told the body-guard, "We can't afford to be interrupted. See to it that we aren't. Seek and destroy anyone within a mile of here. Devour them. Spare no one."

The vampire's eyes glowed red with anticipation as he slipped away unnoticed through the mists.

Rachel watched him go and for a few moments savored her imminent victory. Revenge on those who had turned on her would be sweet, but not as sweet as being reunited with the only man who had ever been powerful enough to engage emotions that swayed her from her purpose.

Danton was on his knees now, the box of measures and weights and containers and chemicals emptied on the bench in front of him. Rachel cut the cone from a cycad and split it in half—its contents the very ingredient Josef had insisted on her adding to the formula.

"I'll take it from here," she said, and Danton stepped back without a word.

Rachel compared the two formulas and decided the reversal appeared as it should. Excitement energized her as she removed the Philosopher's Stone from her waistband and set it on the bench, then once again used the tools of her chosen profession to dole out the proper ingredients into the beakers.

"Hey," Danton suddenly asked, "where is he? Harriman's bodyguard?"

"I sent him to take care of his master to stop any interference." If Rachel had expected Danton to be shocked, she would have been disappointed.

"He's been gone a long time. Maybe I'd better see what's keeping him."

"I need you here."

She quelled the flicker of annoyance that rose in her when he argued, "And maybe I can find Scott Boulder while I'm at it. I owe him, you know?"

So Danton wanted some revenge—he was growing

a spine, which would come in handy for her, assuming he survived the night. "Don't be long." Perhaps the guard had taken care of Boulder already, but he had also been gone longer than she'd expected him to be. It wouldn't hurt to find out what was going on.

Danton glanced at Leah, who was setting a lit candle in place near the waterfall, and said, "I'll just take a quick look around, and then I'll be back to get my due."

Rachel waved him off. Poor deluded vampire. He would never be human again, not when she needed an army of her own.

"How did he die?"

Rachel snapped out of the reverie and realized Leah had left the book and was only steps away from her. "What?"

"This man you want to bring back? How did he die?"

"You're not as clever as you think. I know you're a spy."

Suddenly hearing Josef's voice whisper through her, Rachel went rigid.

"If you want me to bring him back, I need to know how he died."

Suddenly, she could see her Nazi lover again, as he was in Cherbourg, pulling one of the GIs into a sitting position against his knee . . . just a boy.

"Tell me the truth, Rachel, and I'll spare his life."

It hadn't taken but a moment to make up her mind. If the boy had died to protect her secret, it had simply been the price of war. No choice to make.

Still, the splinter of memory rattled her. She said, "Josef Neumann died in the war, of course."

"But how?"

"Isn't it enough to say that Josef was killed by Allied forces?"

"An explosion?" Leah asked. "A knife wound? Rubble falling on his head? I have to work that information into whatever spell I write."

Leah stared at her, an off-putting intelligence gleaming from her eyes. The greenish glow of her face brightened into a mask. Was she hiding something? Could she possibly know the truth? Rachel wondered. Is that why she wouldn't stop pushing? Or were the details really requisite to bring Josef back from the grave?

Rachel considered her options. She could try revising the spell herself, but her area of expertise was science, not magic. She would have only one chance, and if she got it wrong, Josef would be lost to her forever.

And she would fail at her mission, one she'd sworn to complete. Unthinkable.

"All right." Rachel tried to remove herself from the disturbing scenario. "It was Cherbourg, the Allied invasion. My mission was to secure Josef's formula and destroy his work, so that Hitler would not use it on his troops."

It didn't matter how she fought it. Agreeing to tell involved her, sucked her back into the mire of emotion that was not the universe of a scientist. . . .

Once more, she was back in Cherbourg and Josef was clutching her by the shoulders, saying, "All that matters is you and me," as an explosion rumbled deep within the fort, perhaps in the lab itself.

She'd never denied her attraction to Neumann. Perhaps she was even in love with him. She hesitated to betray him, and yet . . . she had her loyalty to the Allied command.

A glance behind her told her it was too late. The work was already destroyed. For that, she could take credit. She still needed the research.

"The formula," she said.

"You can't go back. You'll die."

Surely he wouldn't have left it behind—not under the circumstances—not even for her. "Do you have it on you, Josef?"

His gaze narrowed on her, and his lip curled as his grip tightened on her wrist. "Of course I have it." Relief poured through her until he said, "But your Allies will never get it. They've sent a woman on a fool's mission."

Choking, Rachel stumbled then, and when she fell, Josef couldn't hold her weight. She sprawled face-first over a body. An American GI, his pistol across his chest between them, held in a death grip. His eyes were still open.

Accusing . . .

"Come," Josef said, his voice clipped now as he held out his hand. "We need to get behind German lines."

Rachel's eyes filled with unshed tears. She couldn't go with him. Couldn't go back without the formula. Couldn't fail her mission.

"Don't worry, Rachel, my love, I won't betray you."

Her gaze was drawn to the dead soldier's pistol.

"Rachel, now."

"Yes, now," she agreed, grasping the pistol and wrenching it from the dead man.

"Rachel, no, you can't."

She twisted so she could see his face one last time. "Good-bye, Josef, my heart. . . ."

Fear leached from her lover—he obviously believed she would turn the gun on herself and end her own life.

Rachel aimed the gun at him instead and fired.

And when he came at her, she fired again.

Over and over and over until she was covered with his blood . . .

Chapter 33

Scott jumped from the Black Hawk after it landed on the fifty-yard line of Tad Gormley Stadium in the east end of City Park.

Harriman and BB leaped out behind him, and then Harriman took the lead. "Our spotters put Rachel and Danton in the Conservatory," he told Scott, pressing his ear mike with two fingers for better reception as they jogged from the stadium. "We've been in contact with Keesler Air Force Base in Biloxi. A Predator drone is en route."

"Wait," Scott said. "We're calling in an air strike?" He knew the Predator well from his missions in the Persian Gulf. It was an unmanned, remote-controlled aerial vehicle roughly the size and shape of a glider that was armed with Hellfire missiles. Since the Predator could strike from an altitude of twenty thousand feet, targets couldn't see or hear it. One minute they'd be pissing in the sand, and the next . . .

"We can't give Rachel and Danton a chance to use their abilities against us," Harriman said. "They're too powerful."

Scott had debriefed Harriman about Magic Nights before landing. Now he deeply regretted the timing of his report. "Colonel, Leah is—"

"Not this time, son," Harriman said as they ran

double-time through a grove of old-growth oaks. The trunks looked like the legs of giants in the dark, and the thick foliage blocked the starlit sky. "We tried it your way in the complex, and two hostiles escaped. Worse, they secured the Philosopher's Stone and turned one of our own men against us."

"This is Leah we're talking about, Colonel. She helped us defeat Andre Espinoza. She helped save several lives, including mine. Is this how you mean to repay her?"

"I didn't make this decision lightly, son. The risk is too great. I'm sorry."

Scott grabbed Harriman's shoulder, stopping him. BB stopped a few steps behind to give them space. "It's not just Leah," he said. "I believe Danton is ready to switch sides. Go through with the air strike, and you'll take out two friendlies."

"You've already conveyed Lilly Fry's point of view," Harriman said. "But I shouldn't have to tell you that we can't abort a mission based on the judgment of an emotionally charged young woman. Or on the judgment of an emotionally charged soldier either, for that matter."

There it was again, Scott thought, gritting his teeth. Harriman had first leveraged his feelings for Leah to justify his involvement in the mission and was now using those same feelings to remove him from it.

"Leah's worth to this mission far supersedes what I may or may not feel for her." He was prepared to say anything now to stop the air strike.

"You don't believe that any more than I do," Harriman replied. "One of these days you're going to have to put the people you've taken an oath to protect before your own selfish interests."

"Have you forgotten that Leah and Danton are among those people?" Scott asked.

As they continued forward, Harriman pointed through the trees to a distant canvas tent illuminated by work lights. "The rapid-deployment team is here to make sure we keep civilian casualties to a minimum. But that's where their involvement ends. The drone is being controlled from Keesler Air Force Base, and they won't abort the attack without my direct order."

Given the Predator's airspeed, Scott knew the strike would occur in less than thirty minutes. "The Stone will be destroyed," he tried, making a last-ditch effort.

"Not according to BB."

Scott glared at the scientist, who raised his hands plaintively. "I had no idea he planned to do this!"

"You're to retrieve the Stone after the strike, Captain. The team will provide assistance if you need it."

"And if I refuse?"

"I suspect your sense of duty will compel you to protect the citizens of New Orleans in any way you can."

Before Scott could reply, Harriman stopped midstride and pressed two fingers to his ear. He listened for a few moments and then turned to leave.

"Where do you think you're going?" Scott said.

"I've been ordered back to base to debrief my superior officers."

"Now?"

"We all answer to someone, Scott. Apparently, you caused a host of problems when you let Rachel and Danton escape." Harriman jogged away and then called over his shoulder, "Let's work together to fix those problems and move on."

As soon as Harriman was gone, BB rushed up carrying a metal briefcase and an M4 assault rifle. "Colonel Asshole is more like it," BB said, and offered Scott the weapon. "I shouldn't have told him anything about the stone. I'm sorry."

"Not your fault," Scott replied, taking the M4 and trying like hell to push away his worry for Leah. Success would depend on staying focused. "This loaded with polyalloy rounds?"

BB nodded as they moved out from underneath the oaks onto a concrete path. The full moon cast them in silvery light. "Got something else, too." The scientist opened the briefcase to show Scott what looked like a black leather dog collar nestled in black foam. "High-pitch frequency emitter. Lock this baby around Rachel's neck, and it'll blast her inner ear. She won't be able to tie her shoes, much less spin-cycle you with her mind."

Scott pulled the collar from the foam and realized it wasn't leather after all but flexible steel. "Does this only work around the neck? That might be tricky."

"Best I could do on short notice. But it's money-back guaranteed to drive your psychic vampire nuts."

Scott slid the collar into a pocket. As they hurried toward the tent, he considered reasoning with the rapid-deployment team. It was possible that Harriman had been bluffing about their capability to control the drone. Slim chance but worth a try. "You should catch the next flight out with Harriman."

"I'm coming with you," BB said.

Scott shook his head. "You're more valuable in a support role."

"I'm always behind the lines. This time I want to be where the action is. I want to help you get Leah back."

Scott threw a glance at BB. The scientist was a good man, always ready to help even when doing so risked his safety. He had as much to learn from BB as he did from Lilly Fry. There were true heroes all around him. It was time he became one himself. "You *are* helping me get back Leah, but I'm going to have to insist that you withdraw. We can't afford to lose you."

BB glared, clearly hurt by the rebuff. And then, slowly, he cracked a smile. "I *am* helping, aren't I?"

"You always do, pal."

BB's smile grew wider. The tension was gone as quickly as it had come. "Okay, fine. But I can't believe you're asking me to travel with Harriman again."

Scott smirked. "That bad, huh?"

"The guy scares me, man. Like animated syrup bottles scare me. Like people who don't wash their hands after they go to the bathroom scare me, you know?"

"I hear you."

BB nodded, face still etched with concern, but walked away just the same. Scott watched the scientist disappear among the shadowy oaks before he continued to the tent, which he judged to be about a thousand square feet in size. Approximately two hundred yards to his left stood the glass dome of the conservatory, majestic against the starry sky. Scott thought he could see an orange flickering within one of the greenhouses. Candlelight, maybe. *Leah* . . .

He didn't have much time.

Scott pushed through the tent flap. He expected to see members of the rapid-deployment team bustling around green-glowing computer consoles that offered a bird's-eye view from the Predator as it streaked toward its target.

What he saw instead stopped him cold.

For a moment, Scott could only stare. On the battlefield, he'd been exposed to every kind of bodily trauma. Bullet wounds. Shrapnel wounds. The pulverizing effect of high artillery. But this was different from anything he'd seen. Unhinged in its brutality.

He couldn't identify a single intact body. The carnage looked unreal, like dolls that had been pulled apart by a petulant child. And the blood . . . It painted the canvas walls in hideous Rorschach patterns above a ruddy stew of organs that coated the grass, thick as mud. And within that stew were decapitated heads, dismembered arms, stripped lengths of spinal cord, legs twisted off at the knee, and seemingly countless other jumbled pieces that had been chewed on and chewed through.

At the center of it all, a man in black combat fatigues knelt over the wrenched-open body of a soldier. *White*.

Harriman's ex-bodyguard rooted through the dead man's chest with both hands, tearing free chunks that he jammed into his mouth. Scott wrestled his fear, terrified that witnessing the display might reawaken his blood thirst. But all he felt was a rush of adrenaline, followed by the corresponding surge of superhuman strength.

White threw a glance over his shoulder and howled in crimson fury. Scott noticed the man's eyes—black and bottomless with no trace of humanity. The transformation had erased the old White completely.

Scott didn't hesitate, not this time. Fuck the risk. Leah was worth it.

He summoned black lightning from his core and cast it at White, but the crackling bolt passed harmlessly through the man's body to strike a computer monitor in a shower of sparks. White had inherited Danton's density control!

The man howled again, then gripped the dead soldier by a rib and loped away, boots sucking gory muck as he dragged the corpse through the wall of the tent like a lion making off with a killed gazelle.

Jesus . . .

Scott let him go and rushed to the main computer console. A decapitated soldier sat at the table with tangles of purple intestine at his feet.

Pushing the man aside, Scott went to work. He punched in every top secret code he was privy to at his rank, but none gave him access to the drone. Harriman hadn't been bluffing.

Beside him, a blood-spattered monitor displayed a map of the Predator's progress. The thing was just outside New Orleans, having already traveled most of the way from Biloxi. Under the map was a digital countdown to its arrival. Scott synchronized his watch for twenty minutes, twenty-four seconds.

There was still time to get Leah out of the conservatory.

He sprinted for the tent door when something locked around his ankle. He pitched forward, landing hard in scarlet jelly as the M4 slid from his grasp.

White's bloodstained hand had reached up through the earth to snare him. The fingers were strong as steel. Couldn't be shaken.

Scott felt his leg go numb in the same way his body had gone numb before Danton had sent him through the floor at Magic Nights—and then his leg sank into the ground to the knee. White was dragging him underground like a shark dragging a seal underwater.

Scott turned his leg to smoke, freeing it, then leaped to his feet. White sprang up through the ground after him, eyes wild. Scott discharged another bolt of black lightning. This time White didn't have time to dematerialize. The bolt struck him squarely in the chest and pitched him back across the tent.

Scott ran again for the door, shot a glance at his watch. The clock was ticking. . . .

Suddenly, White streaked through the tent wall to Scott's right, barreling into him. They fell into a heap. Scott felt his strength surge, but White was just as strong.

They rolled through the bloody muck, locked in a death grip, when Scott suddenly found himself on the bottom, elbows pinned beneath White's knees. Scott grunted as White locked one hand around his throat, then passed the other hand through his stomach—and solidified it.

Scott shrieked in agony and then screamed again as

White pushed in the other hand. He could feel the man's fingers slide against his stomach and intestines groping for something to tear free. Scott tried to turn to smoke, but his concentration blew apart under the pain. He coughed a streamer of blood as White glared at him with crimson saliva swaying from his chin.

And then White's head blew apart. Scott shoved the corpse away and saw Danton at the door of the tent, clutching the M4.

Scott leaped to his feet, ready to stun Danton with lightning, but stopped when he remembered what Lilly had said. Still, he stayed wary. "Drop the gun, Danton."

Danton obeyed. "Relax, man. I just helped you out."

Scott paused long enough to turn his midsection to smoke and back again in case White had knocked something out of place. "Yeah, you did, which begs the question: Why?"

"I'm no longer with Rachel."

"The question still stands."

Danton shrugged. "I guess I realized I was acting for the wrong reasons."

"There's a lot of that going around," Scott said, thinking about his own behavior. He scooped up the M4. "Do you know where to find Leah?"

"This way."

Scott checked his watch. Little more than fifteen minutes remained before the air strike. "We don't have much time before this place goes up."

"That's not the only thing we have to worry about. Rachel is trying to bring someone back to life. Leah seems to think it's Andre."

"Great."

As they ran from the tent, Scott glanced back at White's headless body and felt a twinge of remorse.

"I know what you're thinking," Danton said as they crossed into darkness side by side. "But don't beat yourself up. It isn't worth it."

"White didn't deserve to be turned into a monster. Nobody deserves that."

"The guy would have killed us, Scott. In my book, we acted in self-defense. And since I'm a linguist, my book counts double."

Despite the lame joke, Scott realized Danton was right. The threat from White had been imminent and would have cost Leah her life, too. Still, he wished there had been another way. "You mentioned Andre. Do you know for sure that he's been brought back to life?"

"No, but I know Rachel is trying."

Scott gritted his teeth. They had precious little intel, and precious little time. It would be a miracle if they got out of this in one piece.

Chapter 34

"I killed him," Rachel told Leah.

Her voice sounded calm, but Leah could sense the warring feelings within the other woman. Rachel hadn't wanted to talk about it—that was clear—and now Leah knew why. Even a sociopath had a weakness, and it was obvious this Nazi scientist had been hers, no doubt the reason Rachel so desperately wanted to bring him back from the grave.

"You killed Josef, but obviously with regret," Leah said, trying to tap into those wrecked emotions and use them against Rachel—the reason she'd wanted to get the whole truth from the other woman.

"I swore I would never go back there, would never revisit that day. But, yes, I shot him because I had to." Rachel's eyes were an icy blue when she said, "Josef Neumann was the enemy. I did the right thing . . . the only thing I could do at the time. When I returned to the States, I was declared a war hero, you know."

Leah did know. She had read Rachel's records. She simply hadn't known the details of what had transpired, or the true nature of the mission, since so much of the information had been blacked out.

"But you failed your mission. You didn't bring back the formula. That's in your records."

"Only because Josef lied to me. He wasn't carrying

he formula on his person at all. I searched him before
he GIs found me. If he'd been carrying it, it was in-
ide his own head."

"So you never had it."

"Not then."

Which meant she'd somehow gotten it through
Andre, Leah realized. The bastard had delved into
Rachel's subconscious memories, had somehow "seen"
and memorized the formula. Then, as Josef, he'd made
er remember so she could in turn use it on his behalf.
As tough as Rachel might be, that weakness she'd had
or Josef Neumann made her susceptible to being
ooled into thinking she was going to get what she most
wanted out of the deal.

Andre had also manipulated Rachel to enlist Dan-
on's aid, Leah realized. He'd been a necessary pawn
o retrieve Andre's fingernail from Rebecca's body
and to figure out how to reverse the effects of the formula to make it grow. The revised formula would
ncrease age, thereby giving Andre renewed life, re-
urning to him the very same body that she and Scott
ad taken from him barely a week ago.

Leah suspected there was more in this for Rachel
Ackart than regaining a lost love. The secret agent
was brilliant if changed by her experience. Her mind
ad gone from sociopathic to something far scarier.
And now she had vampiric powers to boot.

Who knew how far she would take her need for
evenge? And for power?

Leah suspected she didn't have a prayer of surviv-
ng unless she was smarter and chose to be more ruth-
ess than Rachel—an admitted problem for her since
he tried to avoid violence at all costs.

Unless she figured out a way to stop Andre's regen eration from happening, Leah thought, wondering she could somehow undermine Rachel with the sim ple truth.

"Your Josef won't really be coming back to you," Leah said. "It will be Andre, the vampire whos blood you carry."

"This plan is Josef's," Rachel insisted.

"No, you've been fooled into thinking that he wa speaking to you."

"I am no one's fool."

"There is nothing redeeming about Andre Es pinoza de Madrid. We destroyed his body but not hi essence. His black soul. He's using you as a way to re gain a body by tricking you into thinking he's th man you once cared for. If he succeeds, it will be th end of us all. You will have failed your mission again Josef is gone, Rachel, forever."

"You're lying. All of this can't have been for noth ing."

"Not lies, Rachel. Truth is a weapon." One tha Leah was counting on, though she knew the chanc of Rachel accepting it was slim. "You can still use i to protect yourself, to protect us all from him. The you would be a hero again."

Drawing herself together, Rachel coldly said, "I'v never met this Andre. He couldn't know so muc about me."

"He has ways of getting into your mind, Rache All those months you were drugged made you suscep tible to his influence. To the voices . . ."

Obviously refusing to believe it, Rachel grew ver quiet, very centered. "Either you cast the spell or will rip Danton Dumas limb from limb before your eyes. And you know he will return to rescue you out of some misplaced sense of loyalty. You will do what I tell you or suffer the consequences."

Leah nodded.

The consequences—there were bound to be many, no matter the outcome. Leah had no idea of where Scott might be, of what he'd encountered. Considering how close their connection had grown through the sex magic, she was certain she would sense if he were dead. In her heart, she trusted that he was still alive and fighting and that if he knew where she was, he would find her. But nothing was certain in life. She hadn't wanted to accept that. She'd wanted guarantees where there were none. Now she knew she couldn't count on Scott being there for her when she needed him, no matter what *his* heart dictated.

How could *she* defeat Rachel's scientific knowledge and vampiric powers combined? That was the question.

Leah knew she had to rely on herself. On her own weapons, as different as they might be from those the military wielded. "I will do whatever is necessary."

Even use spells from *The Grand Grimoire* if she had to.

The thought of using black magic made her sick inside, but knowing she might have no choice, she paged through the book, quickly memorizing spells she would normally avoid. Then she fetched her bag and removed a dozen or more candles, began lighting and placing them on rocks that edged the water.

Rachel was deep into her own work with the formula, chopping the greenery she'd cut into shreds, placing it in a mortar, and crushing the juices from it with a pestle. Leah wondered if even now Andre was instructing her.

No time for a real altar—a makeshift one would have to do. Stopping just below the head of the waterfall, perched on rocks that set her above Rachel, Leah lit a white candle on the upper right and another on the upper left, then placed a cup of sea salt in the path of the water's stream, a lit incense cone on the shelf behind it.

Concentrating her energies, she drew white light into her mind and allowed it to hover over her. She softly murmured, "This black soul who destroys all life, you will destroy no more. Your evil is not welcome in me, around me, or anywhere on my plane of existence."

"What are you saying?" Rachel called, looking up from her work in measuring the ingredients for the alchemical portion of the process.

"Simply preparing the magic circle," Leah said.

After watching Leah suspiciously for a few minutes, Rachel went back to what she'd been doing, her attention now divided. Even from a distance, however, Leah could feel the other woman's roiling emotions—excitement and fear and a dark hatred that had no bounds.

In truth, Leah was preparing herself against this coming evil that Rachel would let loose on the world. She would have to allow the tissue's regeneration process to begin so that Rachel would think she was cooperating. All the while she hoped to find a way to turn the magic back on the other woman, hopefully before Danton returned.

Rachel was swept up in what she was doing, swirling the beaker gently, watching the fluids collide and coalesce, the green juices of the cycad flooding the glass. Then she dropped in the fingernail, which immediately began to shimmer and pulse.

Leah flinched as she sensed the nail begin to take on a life of its own.

The beat of victory already pulsing through her voice, Rachel asked, "Ready, Leah?"

"As I'll ever be."

"Then let the *real* war between powers begin."

"Yes," Leah said with regret. "Let it begin."

Rachel tilted the beaker and freed the chemicals and the already glowing organism into the lagoon.

Followed by the Philosopher's Stone.

Upon touching the water, the Stone took on an unearthly red glow, as if turning the very water to blood to feed Andre's cells.

Following the Speed Up Spell from the grimoire, Leah drew a pentacle on her left hand, covered her forehead—her third eye—and visualized grains of sand imploding one on another.

"Sands of time, speed up the way, turn night into day, day into night, speed up time now with supernatural might."

"It's happening," Rachel said. "Look."

Indeed, from her higher vantage on the rocks by the waterfall, Leah looked down into the lagoon, where the mixture of alchemy and magic was already at work. Her stomach churned as the fingernail pulsed and then changed shape and texture—to become a blob of indistinguishable pale flesh within the river of red light pouring from the Philosopher's Stone.

"Josef," Rachel said, her gaze intent on the waters as the flesh began to take a shape that was vaguely human in form—and then grew larger. "Come back to me, my love. I will make it up to you. We will share more power than you ever dreamed possible. You will have everything you ever imagined. I will make it so for you. . . ."

A chill shot through Leah. Just as she had thought, Rachel would not be content to bring her lover back from death's edge. She had plans—no doubt dark, unthinkable—her will guided by Andre's.

Leah pulled her hand through the waterfall behind her and eradicated the first pentacle, then drew another, this time on her right hand, once more covering her third eye. Now she visualized the sands falling slower and slower so they came to a virtual stop.

"Magic go round and round but power be bound by my very will. Interrupt nature's progress to slow time down to a standstill."

Flesh continued to grow but in slow motion. Even so, Leah could see the edges delineate themselves into a narrow and pale version of Andre Espinoza de Madrid, with long, stringy black hair dripping around a strong-featured colorless face. Knee-deep in the lagoon, the shell of a body remained frozen in time, as if it were no more than a statue.

Leah prayed she could use magic to keep Andre's black essence from filling the human shell and using it to scathe the Earth with his evil.

Suddenly, Rachel yelled, "You're not Josef. Who is this man?"

Leah stood her ground. "The voice in your head, Rachel. I told you you'd been tricked."

"Yes, by *you*. Stop this now, Leah, I warn you. Bring my Josef back to me."

"I've done what you asked. This is the result. I don't have the power to bring back someone who is truly gone."

But her spell was working, if not to bring back the Nazi scientist. The figure in the water continued to expand at an achingly slow pace. Fear that she couldn't stop what was happening consumed Leah. Before she could think of how to stop the flesh from turning into muscle and bone, Rachel screeched, and the next Leah knew, the blonde used telekinesis to tear cycads from the ground to pelt her with their poison.

Ducking out of the way through the waterfall to cleanse her flesh of the effect, Leah cleared her mind and drew on a Power Spell she'd memorized from *The Grand Grimoire*.

Even knowing it was wrong to use black magic— Leah believed in healing, not destroying—she was left with no choice.

She held her arms parallel, left hand open, right hand in a fist. She visualized the negative energies of the universe, summoned them to enter through her open hand to her fist until the power was so immense she could no longer hold on to it. She flung both arms toward Rachel, opening her closed hand to set the force free to counter anything the other woman could send her way.

Swirls of energy created an invisible barrier between her and Rachel. No matter that Rachel used her telekinesis to next hurl rocks and boulders at

Leah, her vampiric powers weren't strong enough to overcome the grimoire's black magic. The objects fell harmlessly into the pool.

"Stop, Rachel, now, and think of what you're doing."

"I know exactly what I'm doing, Leah. I've always known. I merely held myself back, but no more."

Leah countered, "All-powerful God, bring Rachel Ackart to justice for the evil she seeks to unleash on this human world. Make her feel the pain that she has caused others. Let the evil that she has generated punish her to fit her crimes—past, present, and future. Do this now with swift justice."

Leah aimed another bolt of energy at Rachel. Standing at the precipice of the lagoon, the blonde was already on uneasy footing. She swayed and screamed, her feet dancing over wet rock as she fought for balance, but in the end, she lost her battle and plunged into the water. Rising to her feet with an outraged gasp, Rachel shrieked as she faced the ghostlike Andre.

Her very presence in the water seemed to regenerate the shell's growth. It filled out all sharp planes and angles as Rachel grew thinner, grew older. In a matter of seconds, the blonde's face matured, aged, gave up its beauty. Her breasts sagged, and loose flesh hung from her arms against her wet blouse.

Looking down at herself in horror—her hands were already blue-veined, her fingers talonlike—Rachel screamed and screamed and screamed as the youth and beauty she had once stolen were torn from her in mere seconds by the formula she'd concocted to bring back her Josef. Her voice grew higher, lighter, and her hair began to molt.

The shell that looked like Andre seemed to vibrate, and Leah could feel Andre's black soul trying to escape the Astral Plane, trying to breathe life into the casing he wished to inhabit on Earth once again.

Leah called on her reserve of energy and, remembering another spell from the grimoire, shouted, "Obey these words of power, guardians of the threshold, guardians of the gate. Unbar the guarded door, obey this command of this servant of power, and bring forth spirits to waylay the dark one that seeks entrance here."

Frantically spinning swirls of air currents circled the body. Leah hoped they could disperse it or consume it, but Andre's essence easily swatted the magic spirits away as if they were nothing.

Trying not to panic, Leah knew what she had to do. Abandoning her body in the material world, she plunged her consciousness into the only place she might be able to stop Andre from taking over—backward into the eternal abyss of the Astral Plane.

The maw as bleak as the vampire's dark essence threatened to suffocate her. She was lost. Without a map. She fought panic and tried to keep her head. This time, she couldn't see him, but she could sense the evil that floated around her in the dark, caressing her . . . as if thanking her . . . waiting for an exit back to Earth.

She'd thought she could do this—overcome Andre by tricking Rachel—and she had failed. She couldn't leave the Astral Plane or let down the field of energy lest Andre kill her and anyone else who stood in his way.

She couldn't allow his dark evil to attain the light of the corporeal world.

She sent a silent, heartfelt message to Scott and only prayed he would somehow hear and hear in time.

Help me stop Andre, Scott.

In the meantime, her only option was to hold Andre's soul *here,* caught in the Astral Plane, in a realm where he had not yet the power to reinfect this world with his evil. She didn't know how long she could hold him back or to what end, but any choices she might have had were gone.

Knowing she could be damning herself by doing so, she reached into her mind for one of the darkest passages from the grimoire. *"Expugno Lumen, Nillus Lux, Vis Levis, Luciens Nux."* Even saying the words put her soul in danger. "I extinguish the light in you. . . . I render the death of light. . . ."

Andre's response in trying to free himself of her was a soul-cracking burst of energy, one that pitched a wail so high it reverberated along the ceiling panels of the greenhouse. The glass began to tinkle and crack. Once started, the quake continued and the cracks spread and spread until the top of the building severed and broke with an inhuman scream, raining shards of glass down on Leah's inert body.

Lancing pain threatened to thrust her from the Astral Plane, but she couldn't let go.

Wouldn't.

If she did, it would surely be the end of them all.

Chapter 35

The portal opened like a wound.

Oblong and seemingly infinite, it created its own horizon line and blazed with crimson energy from the Philosopher's Stone that streamed across the boundless white of the Space Between like fingers of blood through linen.

The sight filled Andre with terrified awe. Although he rejoiced in his victory over Rachel—his manipulation of her had been a success—nothing his father had taught him about alchemy or interdimensional portals could have prepared him for this.

He trembled as the massive portal continued to open, thundering across the dead white stillness of the Space Between like heavy cavalry across a battlefield.

But despite his fear, Andre knew that he must continue forward. This gateway was his only escape. The only way to reclaim his mortal body and soul.

Tentatively, he opened himself up to the portal. Almost immediately, he felt the terrible, rushing force of it latch onto his phantasmal body, and *pull*.

For a moment, his fear blossomed. He struggled against the sucking tide, but it was no use. Now that he was caught, he couldn't break free. Resigning himself to fate, he let go completely and allowed the current to take him. He fully expected to be over-whelmed by the force, prepared for the torture of being ripped apart, piece by piece, before being re-assembled on the other side.

But to his profound surprise, nothing like that hap-pened. In fact, he found the experience of being swept along to be a delicious one—a seductive pull that of-fered a prelude of the human sensations he had once lost as a vampire but would reacquire on the material plane thanks to the Philosopher's Stone.

Whispers of pleasure traced up and down his phan-tom limbs, as did shivers of craving and vibrations of pain. The sensations hummed through him separately at first and then in rapid, overlapping succession as he began to be drawn more quickly toward the crimson portal. He cried out in exquisite agony as his essence was consumed by the swirling vibrations, as he streaked faster and faster through the boundless white of the Space Between, leaving it behind forever and leaving brilliant, sparking colors in his wake.

Andre trembled in anticipation of his rebirth. He could practically feel the corporeal weight of his re-constituted body and rejoiced that he would become human again after existing as an undead creature for so long. Even better, he would become mortal with-out losing any of the vampiric and alchemical powers that he'd acquired. The ability to manipulate light-ning and magnetic metals, the ability to transform into mist, the ability to bend others to his suggestion and wield superhuman strength, would still be his. He would become the entity he craved after centuries of waiting.

And then the portal's umbilical snapped.

Andre howled as he tumbled end over end in white space, the sensations that had buffeted his body a moment before abruptly snuffed out by the unrelenting vacuum of *nothingness*. Before him, black clouds swelled in from every direction to cover the portal, eclipsing its brilliance. Sealing it like scar tissue.

Shaking with tactile withdrawal, Andre's mind reeled. Had Rachel interrupted the spell? If that were the case, he would strip the flesh from her bones once he managed to reinhabit his body. And then he felt a tremor in a far corner of the Space Between, like a spider feels a tremor in its web.

He felt *her*. Leah Maguire. She was the one who had blocked the portal.

Andre seethed. He would not let the bitch rob him of this. He would not. Knowing that distance and time had no meaning in the Space Between, he reached out with his mind and located her essence immediately.

He felt her growing weakness. Her humming fatigue. Clearly, she had expended considerable energy to cross the corporeal boundary into this plane of existence.

But, oddly, Andre felt *only* her. He could not sense the presence of anyone else—specifically, not Scott Boulder. Perhaps Rachel had killed the man, as she'd promised. Had Leah truly come alone? Didn't she realize her power would be no match for his in this place? What did she hope to accomplish?

Andre dismissed the concern. What Leah hoped was of no consequence. All that mattered was that he cast her out and reopen the portal.

Andre homed in on Leah like a hawk on a field mouse. Wherever or *when*ever she was, he would snare her essence. In the next instant, he did just that and drew it to him.

He then waved his hand, drawing forth flesh colored filaments from the white space around him like maggots from offal. The filaments adhered themselves to Leah's essence, taking a cue from her psychic imprint to create a duplicate of her nude body that mimicked her current movements.

Andre regarded Leah with loathing as she floated before him. The woman looked around plaintively, blindly, expression tight as she strained to maintain the integrity of her spell.

Foul witch . . .

He lunged for her, but his hands slapped up against an invisible barrier—something flat, hard, and cool. Grunting in surprise, Andre slammed his fist into the barrier but was thwarted a second time.

Leah jerked as she sensed the strike, features contorting in fear. Andre slammed his fist repeatedly into the barrier and felt it bow, but still hold. And then Leah's eyes met his. Although she couldn't see his essence, her eyes seemed to challenge him, and take strength from his failure.

Panting with frustration, Andre examined the barrier more closely and noticed that it had four slightly opaque sides that were squared at the edges, although she had encased herself in a box of tinted glass.

Andre took a moment to fine-tune his power according to what he had learned about her since their last encounter. Leah Maguire was a white witch who depended on white magic. In this place—in *his* region of the Space Between—white magic could never withstand a sustained, focused assault of dark alchemy.

Andre drifted back several feet and then cast multiple bolts of dark lightning from his fingertips. The bolts struck the barrier with thundering blue-black flashes and then skated and sparked along its surface until finally bouncing harmlessly away. Andre poured more dark energy into the bolts, turning them pure black—the shade of antimatter itself—as black smoke billowed into the pristine white around them.

Finally stopping, Andre saw that the barrier was still intact. There was no way white magic could repel such an assault in a place like this, he thought incredulously. It defied every law of enchantment, every tenet of alchemy and mysticism.

Rage washed through him, coupled with deep sadness. His goal for rebirth would be ruined. He glanced back at Leah. Again, her eyes met his, challenging him in blind fury from behind the opaque barrier.

Disgusted, he turned away, looking instead at the rolling black clouds that covered the crimson portal and diffused its terrible brilliance . . . much as Leah's defensive magic diffused the lines of her body. . . .

Andre sneered, suddenly realizing what had happened. Leah Maguire had employed black magic from *The Grand Grimoire.* Of *course* his dark alchemy had been ineffective. Whenever one type of magic was used against a similar type of magic, there was a chance that they would repel each other, like similar magnetic poles.

Now that he knew black magic had been employed, he could bypass it. But even better, the white witch had contaminated herself with the Dark Arts. A

malevolent seed would now grow within her. He wa
tempted to let her live once he reached the corporea
plane just to see the devastating results.

Andre drifted close to Leah. Her eyes remained
glued to his. "I am one with the darkness," he whis
pered, and reached out. This time, he was able to slip
his hands easily through the cold barrier.

He cradled Leah's face in his palms, drew circles or
her cheeks with his thumbs. She flinched at the con
tact, but he held her steady. Her eyes were the key
They were indeed a window to the soul and, as such
had been used as a portal into the Space Between. I
was now time to close that portal.

Andre tightened his grip and then drove his thumb
into Leah's eyes.

Leah shrieked as blood spurted from the sockets
and then she disappeared, blinking out like a shat
tered bulb, cast out of the Space Between. The black
clouds disappeared along with her.

Andre wasted no time. He dove back into the por
tal's slipstream and streaked toward the corporea
plane.

Chapter 36

"Hold it," Scott said after Danton pulled him through the northern wall of the greenhouse to emerge behind a tall cluster of rocks and prehistoric greenery. The sensation was different than when Danton had run through him in New Orleans. He'd felt heavy then, as though Danton's body weight had been added to his. This felt more *slick* somehow, like the molecules in his body had slipped around molecules in the glass.

"Let's go," Danton said. "I can do my part. I swear."

Scott empathized with Danton's urgency, but if they ran into the situation blind, they stood a higher chance of failure . . . this when their mission was difficult enough. They had to save Leah, retrieve the Philosopher's Stone, and keep Andre within range of the Predator strike if he'd been summoned. Scott was undecided about Rachel. Yes, she posed a threat, but she had been victimized by the military, too. Was she worth saving?

"I know you can do your part," Scott replied. "But we entered on this side so we could reconnoiter the situation, and that's what we're going to do. Are you sure Leah is in this wing?"

Danton nodded as he pointed at the dense foliage before them. "Through there."

Scott glanced at his watch. Little more than te
minutes remained before the Predator dropped it
twin payload of Hellfire missiles on their heads.

"Keep close," he said, and then quickly led the wa
through the sprawling prehistoric exhibit, careful t
avoid crackling patches of duff and the radiant yel
low glow of half-buried night lamps that might cast
shadow. The tropical surroundings and pungent
steaming humidity reminded him of special opera
tions he'd led in Central America. He prayed this mis
sion would result in less violence and loss of life tha
those had.

After a few steps, Scott noticed that Danton wasn'
making any noise behind him. A quick, over-the
shoulder glance told him why. Instead of trying t
mimic the silent maneuvers of a trained soldier, Dan
ton was using density control to pass through the fo
liage. *Smart*, Scott thought. He hoped the guy woul
be just as smart when executing his part of the plan.

Scott continued to lead them forward until the
reached a tall cluster of bushes at the edge of an ope
area. It was approximately twenty-five yards wid
and crisscrossed with cement paths from which visi
tors could enjoy the exhibits.

"Just like I told you," Danton whispered, indicat
ing the opposite side of the open area with a nod.

Scott's stomach tightened when he spotted Leah
She lay motionless on a rocky outcropping betwee
two blazing white candles and beside the head of
rushing waterfall. It looked as though her flesh ha
been sliced in several places by shards of glass tha
had dropped from the ceiling and now lay glittering

around her. Below Leah, an old woman screamed and thrashed in a shallow lagoon beside a nude, muscled man with chalky skin. Even though the man stood with his back to them, Scott could see it was Andre Espinoza. He stood frozen like a statue beside a lagoon that glowed eerie red, no doubt with light from the Philosopher's Stone.

"I thought Rachel was here," Scott whispered.

"She was," Danton said, confused. "Wait just a second. The woman in the lagoon *is* Rachel. She made me turn the water into a sort of reverse fountain of youth to grow a piece of Andre's body. She must have fallen in!"

"What are you talking about?"

"Look at the old woman, Scott. It's *her*."

Scott took another look. Despite the woman's papery flesh, worn features, and patchy white hair, her eyes held a familiar cold gaze. It was Rachel. Danton was right. Scott felt his dread grow. Whatever malignant forces were at play here had snared Rachel and might have taken down Leah as well.

"It doesn't change a thing," Scott said. "You do exactly as I described. Exactly. Here to there is due east about twenty-five yards."

"Twenty-five yards, got it."

Scott zeroed the back of Andre's head with the M4, switching the weapon from automatic to single-fire mode to improve accuracy. Still, Andre didn't move. "Danton, if it turns out you've lied to me, and you pull some underhanded shit that costs Leah her life, so help me—"

"Twenty-five yards, Scott," Danton said. "I'm ready."

"Then go."

From the corner of his eye, Scott saw Danton drop into the ground as easily as if he were dropping into a swimming pool. The guy would reach the lagoon in about fifteen seconds. Plenty of time to do what needed to be done. Normally, he'd have a problem with shooting an unarmed man in the back. But Andre Espinoza wasn't a man. He was a bloodsucking fiend with supernatural powers who'd returned from an alternate plane of reality to enslave humankind.

So fuck it.

Scott squeezed the trigger, and the gold-alloy round blew off the upper right corner of Andre's skull in a spray of pulp and bone. But the vampire didn't fall. Or move. Scott watched incredulously as Andre simply swayed on his feet—and then he noticed there wasn't any blood spurting from the wound either.

What the hell?

However ineffective the shot may have been, it attracted Rachel's attention, just as Scott had hoped. She stared at Andre in horror and cried, "Josef!"

A second later, Danton popped up in the lagoon behind Rachel, sputtering as the reddish water coated him in a thick, unnatural sheen. He clutched BB's frequency collar in his fist and was about to lock it around Rachel's neck when a tiny slide of rocks tumbled into the lagoon next to him.

When Scott saw the source, his heart nearly stopped. Leah had rolled from her back onto her side, nearly tumbling off the outcropping of rock.

Attracted by the noise, Danton whirled and held up

his hands instinctively to catch Leah in case she fell—giving Rachel the reprieve she needed.

Rachel turned and saw Danton trying to help her enemy. "Traitor!" she cried, then used her telekinetic power to whisk him from the water and brutally dash him once, twice against the rocks before tossing his limp body across the greenhouse, where he landed out of sight.

Scott immediately unloaded the M4 at Rachel, rounds thundering from the barrel. In a matter of seconds, their plan had gone to shit. Several shots would have struck Rachel, but she easily swatted them from the air with her mind. Others stitched across Andre's back, blowing free chunks of pale flesh, which went flying in every direction. Still, he did not fall.

Rachel clambered from the lagoon, her dripping blouse and black pants hanging grotesquely from her skeletal body.

Scott bolted for better cover. He had no intention of abandoning Leah but knew he had to hide from Rachel or risk getting tossed around.

He rushed into a grove of ginkgo trees and tall ferns, the branches whipping his face. For a moment, he thought he'd gotten away clean, when he heard an earsplitting series of cracks rush up behind him. He threw a glance over his shoulder to see ginkgo trees being torn up from the ground and go cartwheeling through the air. Rachel was parting the trees like the Red Sea in an attempt to reveal his position. The woman's body may have been frail, but her mind was still sharp. And powerful.

Scott ran faster through the dense foliage, vaulting over benches and night lamps, dodging around marble statues and fountains, but the mad, splintering rush that flung gouts of flora and soil high into the air soon caught him. He felt a brutal force snare him from behind like a gaffing hook and whip him back toward the lagoon.

As he pinwheeled through the air toward Rachel, he struggled to concentrate on his physical form, to visualize a galleon disappearing into deep fog. *My body is nothing. . . . My body is nothing. . . .* Still flipping end over end, he felt his corporeal weight slip away, and then Rachel's hold on him slipped away with it.

Now gray mist, Scott streaked up sixty feet to the metal structure of the greenhouse roof and rematerialized on a thick pane where the glass had been shattered. The lights of New Orleans glittered for miles around the darkness of City Park—residents and tourists blissfully unaware of the conflict that raged in the conservatory. The sight reminded Scott again of what he fought for and why he took extreme risks in the line of duty.

He looked down at Rachel. She hadn't yet spotted him as she stood on the stone lip of the lagoon, her body shrouded by tendrils of vapor that rose from the crimson water. She looked like some demonic sentry guarding Andre's inert body at the gates of hell.

Scott took a moment to catch his breath as he balanced precariously on the metal pane. Turning to mist was an effective defense against Rachel—his only defense, come to think of it—but he couldn't attack in that form. Couldn't remove Leah from harm's way in that form.

Leah . . .

Scott looked at her. She was still lying near the edge of the rocky outcropping. He prayed she wouldn't do anything to attract Rachel's attention.

He looked at his watch. Six minutes until the Predator arrived.

Scott scanned the verdant grounds, searching for Danton. The guy was tough, a fighter. He might be alive. If so, they could stage a counterattack. They could still pull this off.

And then Scott saw Danton at the foot of a distant greenhouse wall. The thick glass above him was spiderwebbed with cracks. He'd hit the wall hard. *Too* hard. Blood pooled around his head. Scott turned away, surprised at the grief he felt. Danton had turned out to be a noble man after all. He'd tried his best to do the right thing and had paid the ultimate price.

Gritting his teeth, Scott returned his attention to Rachel. The woman had given up her search for him and crept closer to Andre. She regarded his massive, nude body with clear incredulity, as though she didn't want to believe that everything she had worked for had fallen apart.

Rachel was distracted again. The perfect opportunity.

Summoning black lightning from his core, Scott cast a jagged, shimmering bolt at her—only to watch it pass harmlessly through her body.

Jesus! Like White, Rachel had acquired Danton's power of density control. Scott wondered ruefully if he was the only one in the entire city of New Orleans who *hadn't* acquired the ability.

He wasn't able to ponder the question for long. Position now compromised, he was an easy target.

Scott felt an invisible force seize his chest, then tear him from the metal pane. His head whiplashed as he streaked down through the air and then slammed into the outcropping of rock above the lagoon, where he collapsed next to Leah. Only his enhanced strength saved his life.

Trembling, he reached for Leah's bloodied hand. Her delicate fingers remained limp. "Leah?" he whispered. She said nothing, but her chest moved slowly, up and down. She was alive. Thank God. "Leah, I don't know if you can hear me," he continued, "but I want you to know how sorry I am about everything. I didn't mean to hurt you. God knows, I didn't. I was only trying to do what was best for both of us."

Before he could finish the sentiment, Scott jerked into the air, hovering several feet over the lagoon with his arms and legs pulled spread-eagle. He cried out in agony and struggled to keep Rachel from tearing him limb from limb.

"Rachel, listen to me," he rasped. Despite everything, she deserved a soldier's respect. A soldier's second chance. He wanted to save her from the air strike and offer her the opportunity to save herself with BB's antidote. He tried to continue, but molten pain cut him short as he felt the flesh at his shoulders and hips split like cheesecloth.

He caught a glimpse of Andre, who stood by impassively. The creature's wounds writhed as the flesh stitched itself closed. Scott now realized the body was merely a shell and would soon accept Andre's spirit. It was the only explanation that made sense. The vampire had dead eyes. A doll's eyes. And then those eyes suddenly sparked bright red with life.

Rachel noticed the awakening, too. With a cry, she released Scott, and he plunged forgotten into the lagoon.

The warm red water had the slimy viscosity of motor oil and closed over his head with a *slush!* All sound cut out except for the hiss of bubbles, and all he saw was the blinding crimson radiance of the Philosopher's Stone. He thrashed as the warm, acrid water flooded his mouth—and then the red glow disappeared, transforming the water into a deep, mottled green.

Thrusting his head above the surface, Scott saw that Andre now gripped the Stone.

Rachel glared at the creature. "What did you do with Josef?"

Andre ignored her and pressed the Stone against his left breast. Scott knew he planned to replace his own heart with it because he'd done the same thing during their last battle. With the Stone in place, he would possess all of his powers and none of his weaknesses. He would become immortal.

Scott tried to clamber to his feet, but his muscles betrayed him. He could only watch as the flesh on Andre's chest parted to accept the Stone—first creating a concave impression to seat it and then contracting to pull it in like a snake swallowing a rat. Once the Stone had disappeared, Andre's flesh darkened from pale to deep olive. He was now a hybrid of human *and* vampire.

It had taken a Voodoo spell to implant the Philoso-

pher's Stone before. Apparently, the lagoon gave
Andre the power to do it himself this time. . . .

The lagoon! Scott realized that the green water had
saturated his skin with its rancid warmth. He could
feel his cells transforming, breaking down. If he
stayed submerged as long as Rachel, he would become an old man.

He sat bolt upright—only to come face-to-face
with Andre.

"This is the last time you and I will meet," Andre
said, then gripped Scott by the shoulders and shoved
him back underwater.

Scott struggled against the hold, but Andre had enhanced strength of his own, and better leverage.
Worse, Scott knew from their first battle that contact
with Andre would negate his powers of transformation. He couldn't turn into smoke or lightning.

He was trapped. Aging in primordial soup. And
drowning.

His panic blossomed, not for himself but for what
Andre might do to Leah after he was dead.

Andre sneered down at him, features rippling with
the water of the lagoon.

Suddenly, Scott felt another pair of hands grope the
length of his back, hook onto the fabric of his jumpsuit, and *pull*. His vision went from watery green to
pitch-black. He felt a familiar sliding sensation as he
was pulled underground, and then, presently, he was
yanked headfirst back onto the surface.

Danton stood looking down at him. His scalp was
shellacked with blood.

"Your head," Scott said. They were back across the
open area, near their original position.

"Only a flesh wound."

Scott sat up. "I thought you were dead."

"For a second there, I did, too." Danton pointed to the hair at Scott's temples. "You're a little gray around the edges, man. Good thing you weren't in the water for very long."

Scott nodded dismissively. "We have to move. Rachel—"

"Already taken care of."

Scott looked back at the lagoon. Rachel was on her knees, holding her head in pain, with the black frequency collar around her neck. That would explain why she hadn't helped Andre earlier—Danton had taken her out before coming for him. Andre didn't notice Rachel's distress as he rooted through the water for him like a dog searching for a lost toy.

Scott looked at his watch. One minute, forty until the Predator strike. He told Danton, "Get Leah out of here. I'll take care of Andre."

"I can't let you stay here alone."

"We don't have time to argue. Get moving!"

Danton paused a moment longer but then nodded resignedly and bolted toward Leah. When he reached the lagoon, Rachel lunged at him, but her hand passed harmlessly through his shin. Danton then vaulted from the lagoon's stone lip into the air, extending his arms as far as he could, looking like a basketball player going for a dunk. For a moment, Scott thought Danton might come up short, but then his fingertips hooked Leah's right leg. All he needed. Both Danton and Leah slipped into the rocky outcropping, and disappeared.

Thank God. . . .

Scott summoned dark, crackling energy from his core and cast twin lightning bolts at Andre through his hands. The lightning struck the vampire between the shoulder blades and sent him headfirst into the rocks.

Andre whirled, clearly taken by surprise, but not the least bit fazed by the attack. He clambered out of the lagoon and then cast his own bolts. For a few long seconds, black streams of energy snaked between them, striking and flashing with arc-light intensity.

Scott's flesh steamed as he struggled to absorb what Andre threw at him, but he stood his ground. Little more than a minute remained before the Predator dropped its missiles. If he had to sacrifice his life to rid the world of Andre Espinoza once again, so be it. The people of New Orleans would be safe. Leah would be safe.

Suddenly, Andre clapped his hands. A huge swell of electricity arced from his palms and flashed forward to strike Scott with the force of a wrecking ball. With a grunt, Scott reeled back, fell on his ass. The lightning went dark between them as the conservatory reeked of ozone.

Andre appeared drained by the violent exchange of lightning. He stalked toward Rachel, who writhed in pain, and tore the frequency collar from her neck.

As Rachel struggled to her feet, Andre pointed at Scott. "Kill him, Rachel! Now!"

Scott prepared himself for the inevitable assault. But it never came.

Andre turned to Rachel, panting with exhaustion.

"I said, kill him!" Rachel shook her head. "Do as I say!" The creature raised his hand, intending to strike Rachel across the cheek, and then froze. He strained, muscles bulging, but was unable to move.

Rachel had him in her telekinetic grip.

Scott looked at his watch. Forty-five seconds. He struggled to his feet, but his body was spent. He sat back down.

"Where is Josef?" Rachel demanded.

"Release me before it's too late!" Andre spat.

Rachel exploded with rage. "What have you done with Josef? What have you done with my love?" She extended a clawed hand toward Andre's chest and whipped it back. Again and again.

Andre shrieked as Scott heard the wet, successive cracking of ribs. And then Andre's chest turned purple with massive subcutaneous bleeding as the flesh over his heart began to swell like a boil.

The Stone, Scott realized. Rachel was using her telekinesis to tear it from Andre's chest. Still frozen in place, Andre continued to scream as the area over his heart swelled to the exact size of the Philosopher's Stone before finally bursting. The Stone gushed free in a torrent of blood and plunked back into the lagoon, turning the water red once again.

Rachel released Andre, and he toppled into the lagoon with a resounding splash.

"Rachel, you have to get out of here!" Scott cried. She could still run from the building even if he couldn't. Maybe make it out alive.

But the woman was beyond hearing. She rushed into the lagoon, straddled Andre's chest, and pounded his face with her fists. "Where is Josef?" she cried. "Where is he? What have you done with him?"

Scott looked up into the night sky and saw two distant, glowing smudges that could have been falling stars. But he knew better. "Hey, Andre? Can you hear me, you rancid bloodsucker?" The vampire strained to glare at him, chin coated with blood. The creature would survive until he was decapitated or until his body was burned beyond recognition. The military was about to deliver the second option on a silver platter. "If you think that hurt, just wait."

Scott then used the last of his strength to transform his body into lightning.

As he flashed out of the conservatory, the Predator's twin Hellfire missiles struck the prehistoric wing with an earthshaking hiccup of flame and thunder.

Scott caught a glimpse of Andre and Rachel as a fireball rolled over them. Their bodies fused together for an endless, agonizing moment before blowing apart, the spiraling pieces immolating a split second after that.

God only knew what happened to the Philosopher's Stone. For the moment, Scott couldn't have cared less.

Scott landed as lightning among a distant group of oaks, then transformed into human form again. He slumped exhausted to his knees. Before him, a blazing mushroom cloud rose hundreds of feet into the starry sky, turning night into day.

Let Harriman try to come up with a cover story for that.

Scott looked around for Leah and Danton and then

heard a voice calling him in the distance. Hers. "Scott! Over here!"

She and Danton were rushing toward him. Clambering to his feet, Scott rushed toward them, too, as fast as he could, not about to let anything stop him.

Epilogue

The next day, Leah felt like she'd been used for a punching bag. She had multiple cuts, including a few deep ones that had needed stitches. On the way back to base in the Black Hawk, Scott had found a first aid kit and taped up anything still bleeding as best he could. After landing, she'd gone straight to the infirmary, where medical personnel poked, prodded, and stitched her back together. She'd spent the last several hours in a room equipped with monitors and other medical equipment.

Sleep, however, had eluded her.

That she had survived Rachel and Andre was a miracle, and she put that triumph to *The Grand Grimoire*. Using black magic had allowed her to hold Andre in the Astral Plane long enough for Danton to bring Scott to the conservatory.

The Grand Grimoire . . . Too bad it had been demolished in the explosion, its secrets buried.

Leah started. What was she thinking? It was good that the book of black magic had been destroyed. So why did she wish it hadn't been? Why did she want to know what other secrets it held? This didn't make sense. She believed in *healing* magic.

And yet . . .

She had to admit to being seduced by what she'd

felt in using the spells from the grimoire. She'd felt powerful, able to deal with trouble as well as anyone who used more conventional weapons. Employing black magic was wrong—she knew that—but there had been no other way.

What she didn't know was the price she would pay.

Magic *always* had its price—

A rap at the door startled her out of those thoughts. "Come in."

One of the military aides poked his head in. "Colonel Harriman wants to see you in the conference room."

"Fine. Tell him I'll be there as soon as I get myself together." Not wanting to go to a meeting in the scrubs she had on, she figured her only option was a military uniform.

"He, um, told me to wait, ma'am. I'm to escort you. Now."

Leah held on to her temper by a thread. Harriman hadn't blinked about her being collateral damage, and now that she'd survived, he thought it was okay to order her around.

"At least find me a jacket or something to throw over this."

He nodded and moved from the doorway. Leah went to the sink and splashed water on her face and finger-combed her hair in spikes. A moment later, the kid was back, offering her a lab coat. Leah slipped into it and followed him to the conference room.

Harriman wasn't there yet, but Scott and Danton were sitting at the conference table. Both looked the worse for wear with bruises and contusions taped or bandaged.

"What's going on?" she asked as the door closed behind her.

"I assume Harriman wants to debrief us," Scott said, his voice tense. "Again."

"Will I be able to leave after we're done?" Danton asked. Leah could feel his anxiety. No doubt he feared being detained like he had previously. Not if she had anything to say about it.

"This is it for me, too," Scott said. "Now that the threat is over, I'll soon be a free man."

Taking a seat across from him, Leah knew how he felt. She couldn't wait to get away from this horrid place. At least, part of her couldn't. Truth be told, she didn't want to leave Scott.

The door opened again, and Harriman walked in. Without so much as a friendly greeting, he said, "The team I sent out to find the Philosopher's Stone came back empty-handed." His craggy features tensed as he stared Scott down. "You know how important the Stone was to us."

Leah gaped at the colonel.

"I was a little busy." Scott didn't bother hiding his sarcasm. Only after a hesitation did he add, "sir."

Harriman glanced over at Danton, who looked as if he wanted to shrink down in his chair. "Good thing you brought him back here—"

"You *made* Danton into what you term a hostile by treating him like one, Colonel Harriman," Leah interrupted. With difficulty, she kept her temper in check. "If you had listened to me, allowed me to speak with him in the first place, he wouldn't have helped Rachel escape and things might have turned out differently."

"You don't know that."

"Nevertheless, Danton was a hero tonight. You can't jail him again."

"I don't plan to."

Surprised, she said, "I'm just glad this travesty is over and I can go back to Albuquerque and find some peace after the hell we've all been through."

Leah felt Scott's reaction—shock, mostly.

"What are you talking about, Leah?" he asked. "You want to leave? *Now?*"

"No one from Team Ultra is leaving," Harriman said. "The threat is not over."

Leah's chest tightened. "The threat was blown to a million pieces."

The last thing she wanted to do was stay. She didn't need to be psychic to know Scott and Danton were thinking the same thing.

"What about the creatures Ackart and White made?" Harriman looked to Danton. "That's right, isn't it? They fed and passed on the damn disease?"

"White did feed," Danton agreed. "Whether he killed or turned his prey . . . I wouldn't know for sure."

Harriman said, "We already have reports from New Orleans of several bodies drained of blood, one too fresh to have been White's victim. That means there are more vampires out there."

Scott shook his head. "You wanted me to take care of Andre and I did. I'm done here."

"And I could say differently," Harriman said. "Until you agree to cooperate, I could have you thrown in the brig."

The two locked gazes. Tension so thick she could

taste it filled Leah. So did fear for Scott. If he carried through with his threat, would Harriman try to have him killed?

Then Harriman said, "What is it you want, son?"

"An honorable discharge."

"You mean to tell me you can just walk away from the situation with what you know? Let the contagion spread through New Orleans? And boarding ships in the harbor there, vampires could spread to anywhere in the world. The three of you and BB are this country's best hope to stop the threat and recover the Philosopher's Stone. You know I'm right, son."

"Three of us?" Danton choked out, his face showing a sickly gray cast.

"I don't like it, but you have powers and a connection to the vampire, therefore a connection to anyone else turned. And Scott spoke up for you, said you were integral to what went down last night. I need all three of you." He swung his gaze back to Scott. "I know you can't desert the people who need you. What is it you really want?"

Scott didn't answer right away. Leah could feel the conflict in him. Anger at Harriman for what the man had already put them through, and for being cavalier with the lives of others in pursuit of his goals. But she could also sense his resignation. If he didn't take charge of this situation, then who would? A man like Harriman? Or worse?

"An honorable discharge," Scott said again, then added, "Team Ultra works as its own unit under my leadership with you as our connection within the military when we need weapons or backup."

Harriman shook his head. "That won't work."

"Make it work."

As the two men stared each other down, Leah felt her plans go to ashes. If there was still a threat, she *had* to stay long enough to be certain that it was contained. As would Scott. When he'd talked about finally being free of the military on the way back to base, for the first time she'd heard hope in his voice. Now his disappointment rushed over her like a tidal wave.

"I'm in." Color came back into Danton's face. "If you agree to Scott's terms. I want to help make sure this thing doesn't spread."

"Count me in." Leah stared at the colonel. "Only on Scott's terms."

She could tell Harriman didn't like giving up that much control. She could also tell he realized he had to give in to get what he wanted.

"All right," Harriman finally said. "I'll have the discharge papers made out immediately. Do what you have to and meet me and BB back here in an hour to make plans."

Scott nodded and then indicated to Leah and Danton that they should follow him. He led the way out of the conference room and didn't stop until they got to the lab. When BB saw them enter, the head scientist lit up like a Christmas tree.

"I was worried about you two!" BB impulsively hugged Leah and slapped Scott on the back. And then he looked to Danton, his expression nonjudgmental but curious. "Good that you made it, too."

"Danton's part of Team Ultra now," Scott said.

"So you bought into Harriman's plan."

"Not exactly." Scott quickly filled him in on his

terms and explained that they were all to meet back in the conference room in an hour. "Which means we all need to get in gear."

"Which means *I* need to find something to wear that fits me," Leah said. She didn't have time to go back to the motel.

"I can help you with that," BB told her.

A few minutes later, armed with fresh clothing, Leah went back to her room and changed. Her leather case carrying her tools was gone—blown up in the conservatory—so first thing when they got to New Orleans, she would have to buy new supplies that would allow her to cast her magic.

The case was gone . . . as were her photos of her father and brother . . . and the recordings she'd made of what memories she'd been able to access.

Having already lost the people she'd loved, Leah now realized holding on to what she couldn't remember no longer meant anything to her. It was time to put away the past. Perhaps someday she would find the key to recovering the memories, but for now there were more important issues to consider. Vamps roaming the streets of New Orleans—she shuddered. And was glad that Danton would be part of the team.

In some ways, Leah felt more connected to Danton Dumas than she did to Scott. Neither had any history of violence. They had common ground in their educational backgrounds. They'd both lost family because of Andre. They had similar psychologies. They would work well together.

"Hey, how are you doing?"

Leah turned to find Scott standing in the doorway staring at her, his expression filled with longing.

"Ready to get to work." She forced a smile.

"That's not what I meant. If anything had happened to you . . ."

Scott moved to her and took her in his arms. Leah sought the comfort she normally got from touching him, but for once she had mixed emotions. Something—the sense of excitement, of possibility—was diminished.

When Scott kissed her, Leah closed her eyes and clung to him, thought of the sex magic they had shared and wanted more. Her body certainly responded to his.

Then what was different about the way she was feeling? Did it have something to do with using the grimoire? She couldn't quite put her finger on it and so tried to put it out of mind.

"I couldn't believe you were thinking about leaving," Scott murmured into her hair.

"I thought the threat was over, that I wasn't needed anymore."

"I'll always need you, Leah. I was hoping this was it for us," Scott said, cradling her to him so she could feel his heart beat. "That we could start a new life. Together."

Suddenly uncomfortable, Leah pushed away from him. "Considering the circumstances, that isn't possible." If Scott had said all this to her the day before, Leah knew her heart would have soared with happiness. "We have more important things to think about now," she said. "Making sure the contagion doesn't spread."

She sensed the shift in Scott's emotions. He was disappointed, confused, uncertain.

What was wrong with her? Of course this was what she wanted. She was just being cautious to protect herself. Wasn't she?

She stepped back into his arms.

But as Scott kissed her again, she couldn't help but remember . . .

Magic *always* had its price.